HARM NONE

A DAVIES & WEST MYSTERY

WILL NORTH

Cover Design by Annie Brulé

This is a work of fiction. Names, characters, places, brands, media, and incidents are either the product of the author's imagination or are used fictitiously. Any resemblance to similarly named places or to persons living or deceased is unintentional.

PRINT ISBN 978-1-62015-213-3

EPUB ISBN 978-1-62015-309-3

Library of Congress Control Number: 2014906103

For Nancy, my most steadfast fan
and the best "kid sister" anyone could ask for.

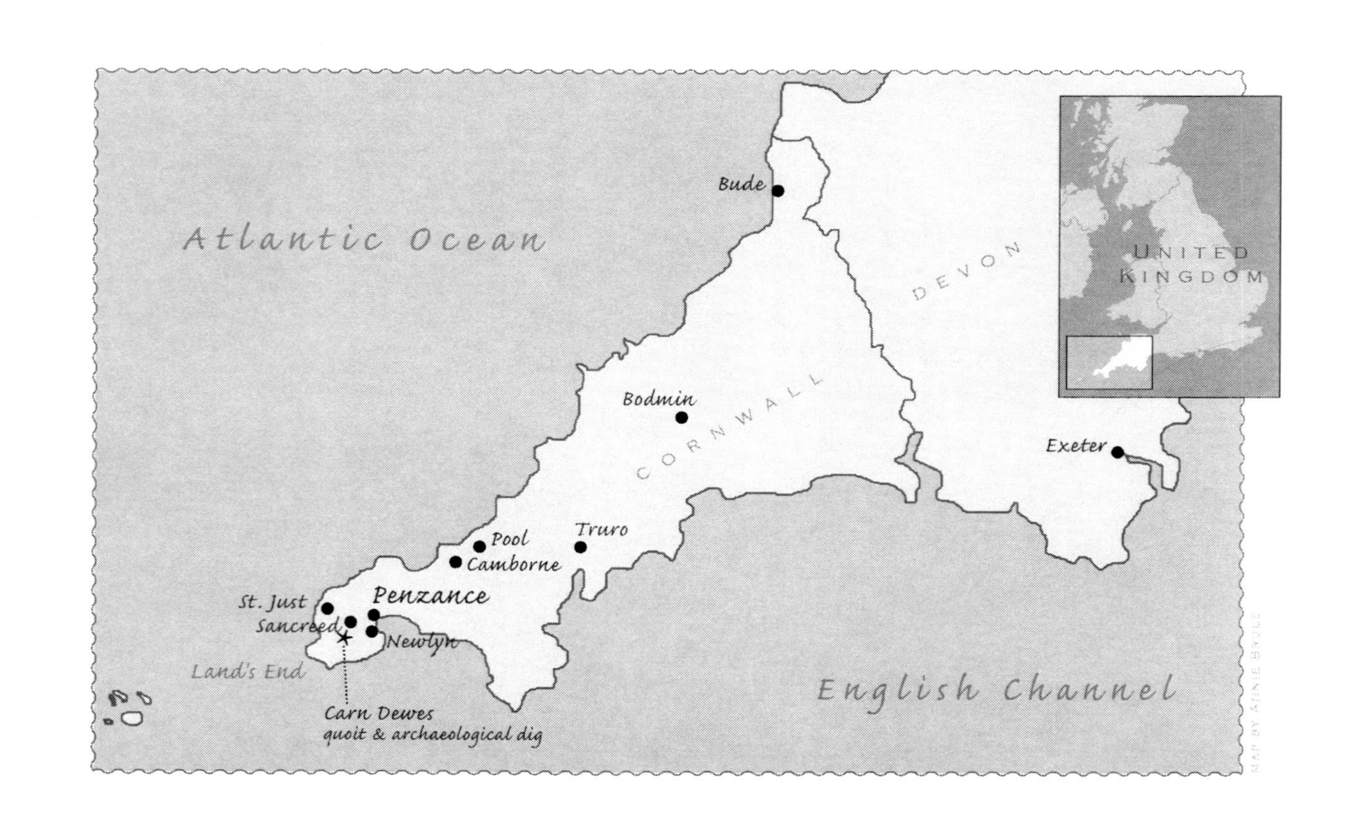

Atlantic Ocean
English Channel
UNITED
KINGDOM
DEVON
CORNWALL
Bude
Bodmin
Exeter
Truro
Pool
Camborne
Penzance
St. Just
Sancreed
Newlyn
Land's End
Carn Dewes
quoit & archaeological dig

An ye harm none,
Do what ye will

From the "Wiccan Rede"

Some There Are Who Know

Prologue

I KNEW BEFORE TAMSIN DID. I had one of my seeings. Gave me a shock, I can tell you. The problem with seeings is they fade fast, the way dreams do when you're just coming awake. Seeings aren't dreams, though. Uh-uh. In a dream, you sort of know you're asleep. Seeings happen when you are awake. Suddenly I can only see the normal world around the edges of my eyes, because there's like a video going on in the center, like suddenly I'm at the cinema on Causewayhead.

Clearness was the problem with my seeings of Becca those first few weeks after she'd gone off to...well, wherever she went. They were ever so dark and muzzy, like looking through a grimy window into one of those old miners' cottages up on the moor above Penzance. I knew she was trying to get through to me, but I couldn't see her true.

Tamsin says my seeings are a gift. I can tell something's gonna happen before it does, or sometimes after it has but I wasn't there. *Clairvoyance,* it's called. That's French and means "clear vision," she says. But mine aren't so clear. Tamsin tells me, "Don't worry, Tegan girl, they'll get clearer as you get older." That could be a long wait; I'm only ten.

I heard once that people who lose an arm or a leg can still feel it. That's Becca to me. I feel her so often, and I know she's still here, somewhere here in West Penwith. That much, at least, I can see. I just don't know where, you know?

Anyway, today I'm at Tamsin's cottage. Tamsin Bran's the village wise-woman in St. Euny. She never uses the word "witch," though other people do. Her cottage used to be a small mill for grinding grain, powered by the fast stream that gathers on the moors and races down through this narrow valley. Ages ago, someone built a long, level, stone-lined leat into the side of the valley to divert some of that stream water to a flume where it tumbled over the mill wheel. Tamsin says when she bought the place it was a ruin, but she's fixed it up nice and tight with the help of those she's done spells or healings for. One of the huge old grooved millstones now sits atop a granite pillar in the middle of her kitchen as a work surface.

That's where I'm standing today—Monday—measuring herbs for a powder. I love this room. It's a modern kitchen and all, but there are also shelves and shelves of labeled glass jars filled with all manner of herbs and stuff. There's a massive granite hearth in one wall with a big copper pot hanging from an iron arm set into the stone. It's for when she needs to cook up a spell. Beside the hearth is where she leans her tall staff, the one she always walks with. It's wood and it has two short branches at the top, like horns. Tamsin says the branches represent the duality of nature. I had to ask her about that; it means the two-ness, like day and night, good and bad, black and white, male and female. That's what she says anyways.

There are also two handmade brooms: one of skinny stiff hazel branches, the other—my favorite—made of snowy swan feathers bound to a stick with cord. And there's a short stick with a hook at the end, a "hook wand," which she says she uses to pull in good energies when she's doing a ritual. I never saw her do a ritual, so I don't really see how a stick could hook energies, but there's a lot I don't know.

There's also stuff I'm not to touch, ever. Like a sacred pottery bowl with the image of a hare inside, a cup made from animal horn she says is a chalice, and a knife she calls her *athame*. It has a carved black handle and cutting edges on both sides. She says it does good things, but honestly it scares the death out of me.

I'm here doing cleaning and tidying to earn pocket money. My teacher at school arranged that, as a summer job, like. She's friends with Tamsin. I live nearby, just a twenty minute bike ride over the moor-top. But Tamsin also lets me help her with her work, too. She writes the ingredient amounts for powders and potions on a slip of paper and I put them together for her. It's brill that she lets me do this now, like she used to let Becca. And she says I have "more promise."

Today, I'm putting together a Go-Away Powder for Brian Tregarren. He's the captain of the Lady B—that's for "Brenda," his wife—out of

Newlyn. It isn't to make him go away, of course, but to banish the fogs. Out on the cuttlefish grounds, he's been bedeviled by sea fogs and his catch is falling behind the other vessels in old man Stevenson's line, which isn't good as the Tregarren's have three kids to support. So he's asked for a spell.

Tamsin's cat, Desmond, who's black but for the one white paw, like he stepped in paint or something, is watching me from atop the herb shelves, as if my measuring is a test he's judging. Some cats, you know, they just seem to wander aimlessly in their own little dream world, or they're asleep in the sun somewhere. Not Desmond. He's a watcher. It would be creepy if he weren't such good company. He also has some kind of glitch in his brain that makes him twitchy, and sometimes he rockets around the cottage for no reason I can figure, howling as if he's possessed. But Tamsin says he's not really bewitched or bedeviled, just different. Desmond doesn't like most people, but he likes me, which is brill. When I ride up to Tamsin's cottage on my bicycle he races out through the cat flap to greet me, whirling around in circles and talking a blue streak, as if he needs to fill me in on everything that's happened since the day before.

But he's not worried today; we both know Go-Away is a simple powder to measure out, nothing like as complicated as some others. It's just three teaspoons of benzoin, one each of mullein and St. John's Wort, two of wormwood and salt, and two blackthorn tree thorns. I don't grind them, though. Tamsin does that bit: seven grinds clockwise, seven counterclockwise in her big black mortar and pestle, over and over till it's ready. I don't know how she knows when that is; I reckon that's part of the witchery, part of the Old Craft. That's what Tamsin calls her work: the "Old Craft."

Anyways, the tide will begin ebbing just after midnight, Tamsin says, and there's also a full moon which is a good thing. So tonight, after the grinding is done, she'll drive down to Newlyn in her funny little Morris 1000 estate wagon with the polished wood trim, which is way older than me, from the Fifties, she says. She'll scatter the powder onto the sea from the end of the ancient stone jetty that protects the anchorage, the tide will pull it out, and Captain Tregarren will be right as rain. Or at least not in fog.

I'm new at this, and I do wonder sometimes about these powders and such, but Tamsin's been the wise-woman in St. Euny for quite some years. Her mum was the wise-woman before her and I guess she passed the knowledge on. Folks come by all the time, and not just from the village, either; from all over. Maybe they have love trouble, or have a nagging pain somewhere, or a cow that's poorly. Sometimes they're under a spell from someone and they want it lifted. Or the other way 'round, though Tamsin's not much into the darker stuff, is what she says.

Except for Desmond, Tamsin's all alone, and I don't really get that, because she's really pretty. She's got these nearly black eyes flecked with golden speckles and when you look into them it's like looking up into the sky on a clear night, all sparkly and limitless, like you could see through them into the whole universe. She uses a lot of black mascara and liner, which really highlights those eyes in a way you can't look away from, and I've asked her to show me how she does that but she says I'm too young. She says that a lot. It frosts me, but then I think, well, at least she cares. More than Mum does, that's for sure.

So here I am, measuring under Desmond's glazy-eyed gaze, when out of nowhere, there's Becca. Well, not here in the kitchen, but somewhere, and this time she's clear as day. And naked as a babe. And she's screaming. I can't hear it, but I can see it in her face, in the twist of her mouth. Scares me senseless and I drop the bowl I'm filling. Desmond hisses, leaps to the stone floor, and speeds out of the room yowling. And then the phone rings.

"I've got it, Tegan girl," I hear Tamsin sing out from upstairs where she's sorting laundry.

And that's how it all starts.

One

DETECTIVE SERGEANT MORGAN DAVIES slid her white, unmarked Ford estate wagon to a stop in the yard of Trerane Farm, a few miles shy of the south-westernmost tip of Cornwall. She yanked up the emergency brake, shoved open the door, and made to get out but pulled her low-heeled navy blue pump back just before it reached the manure-splattered ground.

"Bloody hell," she muttered.

She looked at the mess in the farmyard and at the steep climb to the top of Dewes Tor, made a face, pulled off the heels, and reached into the rear seat for a pair of black rubber Wellies.

Several hundred feet above the farmyard, Bradley Hunter, professor of archaeology at The Pennsylvania State University, watched the new arrival beside his site manager, assistant professor Amanda Jeffers. Hunter was a slender but weathered forty-five-year-old with longish curling salt and pepper hair that danced in the wind off the Atlantic as if it had a life of its own. Amber-tinted aviator glasses hid his mahogany eyes. He wore heavy work boots, khaki shorts that revealed calves taut as knotted hawsers, a vented white safari shirt, and a multi-pocketed canvas vest more suited to fly-fishing than digging. It had belonged to his father, a digger of another sort: a Pennsylvania coal miner and avid fly-fisherman. Hunter would never admit to being superstitious, but he'd worn the vest on every successful expedition since his father had died of black lung disease a decade ago.

Behind Hunter and Jeffers, as if it had grown out of the ground, lay the stone foundations of Carn Dewes, a prehistoric walled settlement dating from the Iron Age, but which Hunter had just discovered could be far older, and far more important than a mere settlement.

THREE DAYS EARLIER, in a bell-shaped stone chamber several feet beneath the Carn Dewes settlement, Hunter stared at the screen of his ground-penetrating radar and felt the hairs on the back of his neck rise. The equipment was aimed at a ground-level granite niche roughly two feet wide and three feet high set into the wall of the chamber. Behind the slab at the back of the niche, the screen revealed a wavy anomaly; something that should not have been there.

Hunter scrambled through the tunnel to the surface and called out to the nearest graduate student, "Find Jeffers and get her down here!"

Amanda ducked into the chamber just as Hunter began prying out one of the short upright stone columns at the side of the niche.

"Jesus, Brad, what are you doing? English Heritage will have our heads!"

"Look at the scanner's screen," he ordered without pausing.

"Oh, wow."

"Give me a hand here—we need to get behind the back face of the niche without causing the chamber wall to collapse. I think the lintel above will hold."

Together, they loosened and removed the other vertical stone and, with a short steel pry bar, inched the rear slab outward as if opening a creaky door. Three-thousand-year-old dust drifted into their hair.

"I can't imagine why no previous researchers thought to take this niche apart," Hunter muttered. "It's been described as a hearth in the old literature, which is laughable…a hearth with no chimney?"

"Maybe originally there was a hole in the peak of the chamber through which the smoke escaped, like the cone-shaped roofs of the houses in the settlement above?"

"Think about that. This stone chamber is a dome, cruder but architecturally little different from St. Peter's in Rome. Its structural integrity depends entirely on the keystone at the very top which directs the compressive force of gravity outward along the curve to the base, rather than straight downward. Remove that keystone and the whole chamber collapses."

"Right; so no hole."

Hunter ran his hands over his scalp and twisted his neck until she heard a cervical vertebra pop; a habit he had when he was anxious.

"The niche is an altar is what it is, raised slightly from the floor of the chamber. It's not a hearth. And where is it situated?

"Directly opposite the chamber entrance."

"Precisely one hundred eighty degrees around the circumference of the chamber, the space between perfectly bisected. Why? Because before the late Iron Age tunnel outside the chamber was built, this chamber's entrance would have been set into the hillside and would have faced the very point on the horizon where the sun rises at the winter solstice, the moment of the rebirth of life, the return to the season of fertility after the season of death. At that moment, the altar would have blazed like a fire in the new light, at least for a few magical moments. That's why the altar looks like a hearth."

"But an altar to what?"

"I think we're about to find out."

Working together, they pulled aside the rear face of the niche, only to find another cavity, much smaller this time and, nestled within it, a figurine, obviously female, carved in white quartz that glittered, jewel-like, in the beam of Hunter's torch, its rough surface shooting shards of light around the shallow niche.

For a moment, neither of them said a word.

"Get me latex gloves and some bubble wrap from the operations tent, would you Amanda?" Hunter finally said. "And tell no one."

"On it," she said, backing out.

What Hunter could not tell her, what he did not understand himself, was that the moment the back wall of the niche had been opened a charged energy had vibrated within him like a tuning fork. She apparently hadn't experienced it. He'd read about Egyptologists experiencing something similar when opening a tomb, but this was a first for him and he tried to come to terms with it. He sensed no threat. If it was a message, he could not comprehend it.

But a part of him, a distant, primitive part of him, wished he'd never opened the niche.

DETECTIVE SERGEANT DAVIES was halfway across the farmyard and pulling on a rainproof jacket when she heard a second vehicle approaching at speed along the narrow country lane that led to the farm. Moments later, a Ford Fiesta hatchback, its side panels plastered with the neon blue and lemon yellow grid of squares emblematic of the Devon and Cornwall Police, pulled into the farmyard.

"How did she get here before us?" Special Constable Trevor Williams asked the woman behind the wheel.

"Always does, is what I hear," Police Constable Teresa Bates said. "We'd better get a move on."

Bates stepped out, ignored the muck, smoothed her black uniform, adjusted her equipment belt, tucked her short ginger hair beneath her regulation PC's black bowler hat with its checkered headband, and hurried to catch up with Davies. Everyone at the Penzance nick knew better than to keep DS Davies waiting. Williams followed, shrugging on his waterproof jacket which, like the Fiesta, was patched in reflective blue and yellow.

They met the detective at an iron stile set into a stone wall at the foot of a stony footpath that climbed up the eastern flank of the tor through thickets of gorse, bracken fern, and heather.

"You lot should have got here first," Davies snapped.

PC Bates came to attention and introduced herself and PC Williams. "We were on foot duty for the Golowan Festival parade, ma'am. It took us a while to get through the crowds to the Penzance Basic Command Unit and requisition a car."

"Bloody Golowan. Bunch of drunken pagans in fancy dress clogging up the streets just because it's the longest day of the year."

"Actually, ma'am, it's also the feast day of St. John," Williams volunteered.

Davies shot him a look that would have blistered paint and began climbing.

THANKS TO THE WEEKEND Golowan celebration, which drew hundreds of pagans, Davies had the CID office all to herself. Given Golowan, she might have been out on the streets managing crowds like the rest of the force, but DS Davies detested the Golowan revelries. The event, the dancers, the musicians, the fancifully-constructed giant paper and wire creatures, and the crowds that thronged the streets of Penzance on Golowan weekend were, as far as she was concerned, ardently to be avoided.

Instead, she'd been going over, yet again and just as fruitlessly, the case files on the murders of two very young prostitutes in nearby Newlyn, the fishing port immediately adjacent to Penzance along the broad sweep of Mount's Bay. Both had been strangled (apparently in the throes of sex, given the forensic evidence) and then dumped, two weeks apart, like so much rat bait in the maze of cobbled alleys that climbed the hill above the port. So far, and despite door-to-door inquiries, Morgan had got no closer to a perpetrator. And the other Toms catting around the port were keeping mum. So when the emergency call about the Carn Dewes find came in from Comms, Davies welcomed the distraction.

Minutes later she was blasting south along the A30 in her staff car. At Drift, she veered right onto the minor road through Sancreed and headed up into the high moors. The entire trip took twenty minutes, half of it extracting herself from the one-way traffic pattern in Penzance.

"THIS IS GOING TO shut us down, dammit," Brad Hunter mumbled as he watched the police ascend the tor.

If Penn State's highly-regarded archaeology department had a "star," Brad Hunter was it, though he would have rejected the label. He was known as a mesmerizing lecturer and a caring mentor. He was also uncommonly successful in his expeditions. His reputation pulled in streams of talented graduate students. But, in his field, that reputation was only as good as the latest find. Now he had a new one, a stone figurine that could rewrite the history of the Neolithic, Bronze, and Iron ages in Britain. But a second discovery now threatened to bring his dig to a halt.

The trouble had begun less than two hours earlier.

Hunter had been in the operations tent poring over data on Neolithic figurines on his laptop when he caught sight of his second in command pounding across the gently sloping ground within the settlement's inner ramparts. An athletic brunette just turned thirty, Amanda Jeffers had the honed frame of the distance runner she proved herself to be early each morning, arriving long before the rest of the crew and racing over the moorland paths. She ran effortlessly, her body fluid, like water flowing. Not for the first time did he consider what that athlete's body would be like unadorned by her usual uniform of Vibram-soled work boots, olive drab multi-pocket expedition trousers, khaki spaghetti-strap knit cotton shirt, and muddy gray rain jacket; a beauty in mufti, but one who signaled "Keep Your Distance" as if in blinking neon.

"Brad!" she yelled. "Something you need to look at. Now!"

Hunter had never quite got used to the curiously commanding nature of his assistant. Her clipped attitude ruffled feathers among his graduate students and the internal tension at the dig would have been lessened by her absence, but he respected Amanda's professionalism. She wasn't autocratic, just focused and precise. In that regard, at least, they were well-matched.

Jogging to keep up, he followed Jeffers across the settlement. To his surprise, she carried on right out through the only gap in the Iron Age walls. Beyond the entrance, a narrow path led through wind-stunted gorse and dense heather thickets across a finger ridge that ran southwest from the hilltop. Roughly two hundred yards along stood Dewes Quoit. A hulking Neolithic stone structure far older than the settlement, the quoit looked out toward the seething Atlantic a mile or so to the west and far below. Three massive, five-foot-high granite megaliths stood like the legs of an elephantine tripod, and atop them lay a two-foot-thick granite capstone crudely shaped in an elongated oval. Roughly twelve feet long and eight wide at its widest point, the almost unimaginable mass of this capstone was perfectly balanced across its uprights.

There were quoits like this one crowning hilltops elsewhere in West Cornwall, as well as Ireland, Wales, and Brittany in France. They were thought to have been tombs for revered Stone Age chieftains and would originally have been covered in earth after being erected. But thousands of years of weathering by Cornwall's relentless storms had eaten away at the soil and rubble cover and left the great support stones exposed. Obvious as the naked monuments were upon the skyline, all had long since been plundered for whatever artifacts or grave goods might have been interred with the chieftains. They remained today simply as engineering marvels, silently bearing witness to the skills of a primitive civilization in a mysterious, ancient time. No one fully understood how the great capstones, weighing tons, had been placed so precisely that, millennia later, they remained in place. Given the absence of sophisticated tools in the Neolithic, the quoits beggared explanation.

"I was just policing the quoit," Jeffers called over her shoulder as Hunter caught up. "Walkers like to picnic up here..."

They squeezed beneath the hulking mass of the quoit and in the dim light, Hunter saw it: the curled first two segments of a skeletal finger rising from the ground. Working with a bristle brush from Amanda's tool belt, it took him only a moment to conclude the bones could not possibly be ancient. The site had been excavated more than once at least a century earlier and the soil around the exposed finger wasn't compacted enough to be even that old. It was everything he could do to keep from unearthing more of the remains. Instead, he had Jeffers call the police from her mobile.

DS DAVIES ARRIVED ATOP the summit ridge flushed, sweating, and disgusted. She hadn't planned on mountain climbing this particular Saturday afternoon—or any afternoon, for that matter. On any other off-duty Saturday, she'd be at home watching some romantic old black and white movie and nursing a vodka tonic. Bodies, she grumbled to herself, showed up in the most inconvenient places—reservoirs, mountaintops. So inconvenient.

Handsome in a strong, Katherine Hepburn sort of way, albeit with a bit more heft, Davies was as fit as any largely desk-bound detective might be, but lately she had begun feeling her forty-five years. When PC Bates reached the summit ridge behind Davies she grabbed Williams's coat and waited while Davies, pretending to take in the view, caught her breath. The afternoon was waning and the western light had reached that burnished gold peculiar to higher latitudes in high summer.

After a moment, she turned, approached the archaeologists, and flashed her warrant card.

"What have you got?" Morgan Davies wasn't long on pleasantries.

Hunter pointed to the quoit. "You'd better have a look," he said, leading her there.

Holding on to one of the upright megaliths, Davies lowered herself to her knees and peered into the shadowy space beneath the capstone. Brad Hunter was beside her, his sunglasses removed. In her twenty-five years of service in the force, she'd seen her share of bodies, but this—this single skeletal finger, curled as if desperately clawing its way free of the earth—raised the hackles at the back of her neck. She shook the feeling away.

"Who's the fool's been digging under here?" she demanded.

"That would be me," Hunter said.

"SOCOs won't be pleased," she said as she backed out and stood. She steadied herself on one of the uprights. Davies hated confined spaces.

"SOCOs?"

"Scene of Crime Officers. You've mucked up their site."

Davies turned to Special PC Williams and barked, "Get Ms. Jeffers away from here, take a statement, and caution her about saying anything about this to anyone else."

Williams nodded sharply and marched the unwilling young professor across the ridge toward the settlement and the dig's operations tent.

"I'm issuing you the same caution," she said turning to Hunter, "and I want you to give the same instructions to anyone else who's working with you here. Got that?"

Hunter nodded.

Davies smiled. What she saw was a man accustomed to controlling events but for whom events had suddenly spun out of control, a man of certainty newly faced with uncertainty. He was also arrestingly handsome in a weathered sort of way. On another day, in a different situation, she would have fancied him. Any woman would.

"A word, then, if you don't mind..." She took his elbow and led him a short distance along the ridge from the quoit, leaving PC Bates at the quoit and out of hearing.

"You're in charge here, I gather?"

"Yes, it's my project, sanctioned by English Heritage and the Duchy of Cornwall."

"Means sod all to me, professor. Look, I'm a detective; you're an archaeologist. What I want to know is what do you make of this?"

"The bones can't be ancient; that's why I had my assistant call 999."

"Why not?"

"Okay, the bones are already skeletonized, but that's not surprising; the conditions up here are brutal. If I had to guess I'd say this body—if it is a body and not just a hand—has only been in the ground, shallowly buried, between one and two years. The soil is too loose for it to be much older. But I'm no forensic expert."

"You'll do in a pinch. And for what it's worth, since I am even less of an expert, I tend to agree with you, based on other cases. I appreciate your expertise."

As if clicking off a switch, she turned and left him, rummaged in her shoulder bag, pulled out her mobile, and clumped off along the ridge toward the settlement. He watched her go with a curious combination of awe and interest. He'd seldom met a more compelling woman; tough-minded, bordering on belligerent. Not his type at all. And yet…

Davies leaned against one of the granite megaliths flanking the entrance to the settlement and described the situation to the on-duty senior investigating officer at the Bodmin police hub, who turned out this day to be her former superior in Penzance, Detective Chief Inspector Arthur Penwarren.

"All right, Morgan. You know the drill. Get the response unit to cordon off the site until Calum West and his SOCO people arrive. Comms called West just after they called you. Knowing the way he drives, he'll only be minutes away by now. Wait for him, will you? I'll notify Penzance their constables will be there a while. We'll have a Major Crime Investigating Team meeting first thing tomorrow: eight o'clock, Camborne nick."

Davies rang off and found PC Bates at attention behind her. Discipline and intelligence radiated from the young woman's eyes. Her body language said, *I await your orders.* Davies liked that she'd said nothing yet.

"I'm guessing, Constable, that you're the one with brains here…"

"PC Williams is a novice Special, ma'am; a new volunteer. Just a bit green is all."

"Very charitable, but you're confirming that he doesn't know what he's doing, so I'm putting you in charge. The SIO's already on to Penzance.

Cordon off the scene; keep others out. After that, I'm afraid you and Williams will be here all night."

"Nature of the job, ma'am."

"Hours of boredom punctuated by moments of bloody terror, that's us," Davies said. Bates smiled and nodded in a way that said she relished the task.

Then, as if controlled by wires, the two women's heads suddenly pivoted east at the sound of another approaching car, this one's engine deep-throated and roaring. Almost immediately a big Volvo estate wagon executed a perfect four-wheel power slide and came to a halt in the farmyard at the base of the tor next to Morgan's car.

Davies shook her head, smiling. "West."

"Ma'am?" Bates asked.

"Calum West, SOCO crime scene manager and would-be race car driver. And, as he's also part of the national anti-terrorism unit, he gets issued that fire-breathing Volvo: top cruising speed one hundred forty. Thank god he's a brilliant driver is all I can say.

"While I wait for him here, tell the professor I'll want to take formal statements in Penzance as soon as possible from him, his assistant, and anyone else involved in this discovery. Have him dismiss the rest of his people."

"Ma'am."

Davies watched Bates stride across the summit toward the operations tent. It was like watching a shade of herself, twenty-five years earlier. But it was a bittersweet image. She had learned so much since then, been through so much. She remembered her optimism, her sense of mission, her passion to make the world, or at least a small part of it, safer, more secure. Yet it never would be; her own childhood taught her that. But when she joined the force she resolved to make it so. A quarter century later, she knew the best you could hope for was to continually beat back the forces of chaos to a stalemate.

CRIME SCENE MANAGER Calum West, lugging a pre-packed SOCO kit, took his time ascending. A balding, genial middle-aged chap, quick to smile, West was at the top of his game, but lately his heart had taken to fluttering like a very small bird trying to escape his ribcage. He'd told no one. But Davies noticed he was pacing himself.

"Ah, this is indeed my lucky day," he crowed as he reached the ridge-top and caught his breath. "Human remains *and* the ever-lovely and talented Morgan Davies!"

"You're lightheaded from the climb."

"And you're so gracious in accepting compliments. Where's the body?"

"Finger."

"One is ever hopeful."

They regarded each other for a moment and Davies finally smiled. She led West across the ridge to the quoit and filled him in en route. When they reached the site, West climbed into a white Tyvek jumpsuit he pulled from his kit bag and put paper booties over his shoes. Then, stepping only where others had, he entered the space beneath the giant capstone and examined the exposed finger. He took several digital record photos of it and the rest of the dim interior which he'd later download to the laptop in his car. Then, he slipped a clear plastic bag over the exposed bone and backed out.

"Have you spoken to Mister?" he asked as he shed the coverall. Davies nodded. "Mister" was what they all called DCI Penwarren, at least in private. The chief inspector was admired by everyone in the force except those who resented his complete disinterest in the politics of the Devon and Cornwall Police. He was a detective and he liked being one. He hadn't sought promotion; he'd been elevated to DCI for the simple reason that his accomplishments could no longer be ignored.

"Major Crime Investigation Team meeting tomorrow morning. Camborne," Davies said.

"Well then, much as I may wish to tarry with you in this scenic spot, Morgan, I'd better line up the experts."

"Jennifer Duncan's already been notified."

"Our best pathologist by far, but we'll also need a forensic anthropologist and a forensic archaeologist. I'll call them in from the Penzance BCU. Long night; even longer for those two PCs you've got up here, poor devils. Creepy place, you want my opinion."

"Mine, too; not fit for man nor beast."

Two

THAT SAME AFTERNOON, Kenwyn Chynoweth was in his office: a cramped, windowless room barely larger than a walk-in closet in the loft space above his Penzance shop, Penwith Gothica, when his sales manager and sole employee who called herself "Cassandra" but was actually Jane gave him a bell from downstairs.

"Visitor down here, Kenny."

"Who?"

"Dunno, do I? Says she knows you, okay? Needs to talk. Bit twitchy, she is, if you get my meanin'..."

Penwith Gothica was near the top of Causewayhead, a narrow street in the heart of the market town. Designed for the horse and buggy era, the lane now was restricted to pedestrians and delivery vans. It rose westward from the intersection called Greenmarket where commercial Market Jew Street curved to become the somewhat more official Alverton Road, along which lay various estate agents and the massive Victorian Guildhall. Greenmarket itself was anchored by the white-domed, gray granite neoclassical edifice that once was the town's bustling covered market hall but now housed a far less festive branch of the equally gray Lloyd's TSB Bank.

The shops at the bottom of Causewayhead, close to Greenmarket, tended to be far more up-market and well-managed than those at the top: designer shoe stores, fashionable clothing and furnishings shops, a trendy cafe, the town's premium greengrocer, a bakery, an organic food shop, and a bulk-sale spice emporium, among others. Beyond the Savoy Cinema, though, roughly at the street's midpoint, quality began to run downhill even as the street itself climbed. Penwith Gothica, a dimly-lit cave of a place, was near the top, wedged between the Market "Plaice" Fish Bar and the Modern Chinese Takeaway.

It was not the most salubrious shop location, perpetually perfumed as it was by the stench of deep fried fish and chips mixed with the pungency of hot garlic and Asian spice, but Chynoweth's clientele didn't seem to notice. Penwith Gothica catered to a black-clad, face-pierced, tattooed, hair-dyed, heavily made-up, chain-strung, occasionally dandy-dressed crowd of young discontents whose only common faith appeared to be loud, angry music. They existed to be seen, not particularly to be understood. He also carried a line of goods for would-be pagans.

Stocked with T-stands and rounders of black leather miniskirts and trousers, thick-soled black boots, artificially-torn, medieval-themed black lace blouses, mock-Elizabethan dresses, push-up black or red bustiers, black fishnet stockings with pre-set holes, and pentangle-printed black tee shirts, not to mention tiers of vaguely medieval or witchcraft-related jewelry, neck chains, studded collars, candleholders, altar pieces, and related knick-knacks, the shop pulled in a steady stream of nonconformist patrons.

Chynoweth, dressed in suitably sooty Goth gear, his eyes ringed with kohl, both ears and one nostril pierced, stomped down the back stairs and hesitated at the rear of the shop. Thanks to the Golowan Festival, the place was hopping. The combination of the tourist season and a pagan festival collected clients like, well, black flies. His eye caught one customer, a not-so-young, well-built woman with hair bleached nearly white who wore four inch "sheet-ripper" black patent boots and torn lace stockings held in place by elastic suspenders made visible by a leather skirt not much longer than a belt. She wore a see-through, frilled, black mesh blouse that made no secret that her nipple-pierced breasts were unencumbered by a bra. A belly corset plumped her breasts skyward.

"Good afternoon, my dear," Chynoweth oozed as he approached, trying to disguise his pigeon-toed waddle. "Something I might assist you with? We are all about *personal* service here. Every dark delight you discover in my shop is a product of my own twisted Gothic imagination..."

The woman lifted a black-dyed eyebrow, took in Chynoweth's slacker's paunch, puffy face, and fast-receding dyed hair and said, "Piss off."

He hitched up his trousers, adjusted his groin, and shrugged; she wasn't his type anyway.

"Kenny!"

He turned and saw Cassandra at the till with a line of fidgety customers.

"Give us a hand here, boss, eh?"

Chynoweth approached the scratched old section of a pub's oak bar that served as the sales desk. Cassandra, a six-foot Amazon with a helmet of short black spiked hair, was busy with a chap in a jet black Mohawk who seemed more inclined to peer down the canyon of her cleavage than complete his purchase: black ribbed condoms with a skull on the front of the packet.

"Feeling lucky tonight?" Cassandra cracked, a ring-pierced eyebrow raised as she scanned the purchase.

"Only if you tell me when you get off," the lad responded, his shoulders angling with attitude.

"I get off every night," she said without looking at her customer, "with my girlfriend and my electric Rabbit…"

"Bloody hell!" This was from Kenny as he stepped behind the counter.

A waifish woman was curled up on the floor behind the counter beside Cassandra's jack-boots. The woman was Judith Chynoweth, his sister. And she was clearly having a bad evening. A tiny, tightly knotted parcel of human being, she shuddered on and off with tremors and pawed at her face like a dog trying to clean.

When she heard his voice, she looked up into the pin-prick halogen shop lights.

"Kenny…"

He leaned to Cassandra's ear. "Finish with this bloke, then go out on the floor and announce a ten percent Golowan discount on everything in stock. Cover me."

While she did so, Chynoweth hauled his sister off the floor and up the stairs at the back of the shop. She was limp as a rag doll. He dropped the doll onto a leather couch that looked like it had been upholstered with the saddle-worn hide of a knackered horse.

"I told you never to come here, Jude! Jesus, look at you!"

Kenwyn Chynoweth's older sister, Judith, was only thirty-five, but at barely eight stone, her skin stretched over raw bone, her face already etched like a parchment map of fault lines barely concealed by her makeup, she looked every day of fifty, and fifty hard years at that. She sat on the edge of the couch clutching her trembling knees. Her head, with its greasy bleached platinum hair that looked chopped with a butcher's cleaver, jerked episodically to the right, as if the spasms were beyond her conscious control, which they were. There was a black collar tattooed around her neck, complete with stylized spikes. She was minimally dressed in her accustomed streetwalker outfit: vertiginous heels, skin-tight black leather skirt, spaghetti-strap pink jersey knit blouse with deeply scooped neckline, the better to display her best assets, presented as if on a platter by a scarlet pushup bra.

"I need it, Kenny. I di'n't know where else to go."

It wasn't a statement or even a confession; it was a plea. As she spoke he saw that a round steel stud pierced her tongue, the better, he guessed, to give thrilling blowjobs.

"Dunno what you're talkin' about."

"Fuck you don't!"

Her brother dodged. "Fixin' you up is what that wanker squat-mate of yours Brendan's for, innit?! Just the guy for a slag like you. Disgustin,' the both 'a you."

"Disappeared."

"Huh?"

"Gone. Hasn't been back to the squat for two days. Dunno where he's got to, but I'm that desperate, Kenny!"

"Not my business to help you. Go on, get out." He nodded toward the door.

His sister's laugh sounded like the caw of a crow and quickly became a cough so harsh and thick with phlegm it was like she was struggling to pull something up all the way from her feet instead of her lungs.

"Not your *business*?" she rasped when she caught her breath, "Who you jokin'? You think I don't know where them fuckers in the Treneere council flats get their smack?"

"Shuddup."

"You think I believe you got your posh car offa them black leather bras below? Beemer bought from bustiers? Go on, ya' paunchy perv; what do you make me? I could turn you in in a heartbeat."

"I make you to be a junkie hooker, Jude, like you been for years, 'specially since your girl Rebecca done a runner last year. And no wonder, with a mum like you. *If* she ran off."

"What'r you sayin'?" Jude Chynoweth's dead hazel eyes suddenly flared to life.

"I'm just thinkin' it'd be bloody brill in…what shall we call it?… 'your line of work?' for that inconvenient kid at home to, you know, just vanish? Unless, of course, you let her watch while you gave the lads your best turns…"

As if propelled by an out of body force, Jude Chynoweth was off the settee and lunging toward her brother. He knew his sister to be capable of violence in a flash. She'd beat him often enough when they were children. He stood abruptly and stepped back from the desk.

"You spread that 'round, I'll bloody kill you!" Jude spat before she fell to her knees, short of her objective, shuddering.

Kenny kicked her over on her back, placed a booted foot just below her breasts, leaned in, and smiled.

"Now, now; calm yourself," he said, pressing the boot a bit more firmly, "I think we have the makings of an understanding here, eh? You don't welsh on my little private enterprise here, and I don't let on what you maybe had to do to that girl to simplify your social life?"

His foot pressed against her ribs until his sister hissed, "Can't breathe..."

NOT MUCH LATER, shot up by Kenny, the shuddering and chills gone, Jude Chynoweth floated down Causewayhead and entered the human flood of Market Jew Street in mid-Golowan Festival. Market Jew was Penzance's main commercial thoroughfare—its apparently Semitic name actually a corruption of the old Cornish Marghas Yow, or "Thursday Market." The crowd pulsed like a longitudinal human heart, flushed and throbbing.

The parade's high point had long been the passage of "Penglaz," a larger than life, fearsomely pagan figure composed of a massive bleached horse's skull crowned with flowers and greens and mounted upon a tall pole held by a sturdy marcher hidden beneath colorful drapery. Penglaz was accompanied by "guisers"—an anarchic group of musicians and dancers disguised in masks and wearing hand-me-down gentlemen's formal dress. Ahead of the beast, a "teaser" capered about in a top hat to make the horse-headed demon twirl and snap its wired jaws menacingly at the crowds along the pavements, to delighted screams. Since the ancient pagan event's revival, local schools and volunteers swelled the parade with towering fanciful creatures made of wood, wire and paper which, like the 'Oss, snaked through the streets.

Jude's tenuous hold on the present was buffeted by the clangorous, strangely dressed musicians marching, dancers in masks whirling, otherworldly beasts of illuminated paper and flowing garb bobbing and weaving along the route, crowds screaming in feigned panic and surging along the route to stay with the mystical figures as they snaked downhill toward the port.

She bobbed along with them, a disassociated bit of flotsam on a human flood, dancing in spacey, ragged circles, her arms windmilling, until the full weight of the heroin leadened her limbs, jellied her legs, and finally dropped her like a bag of rubbish in a recessed doorway off a granite-staircased alley between the gay festivities of Market Jew Street and the blank-faced terrace houses flanking Bread Street, just above.

Three

PC TERRY BATES LOOKED at the organic peanut butter and mock-chocolate carob energy bars the archaeologists had been kind enough to offer them and decided, while grateful and still hungry, she couldn't stomach another. PC Williams had no such compunctions; he wolfed them down like a teenage athlete cramming carbs.

She and Williams sat in the Americans' operations tent. It was big, easily twelve feet by sixteen, with a debris-covered folding aluminum work table and buckets of rubble all around, racks of tools, and a generator. Between the noise and the fumes, though, they'd decided not to fire up the generator and do without light for the night. They had their torches. It was a reasonably mild evening for West Penwith, and the persistent wind off the Atlantic had dropped.

It had taken them less than half an hour to secure the crime scene—if crime scene it was. In the absence of trees, they'd used the neon-yellow traffic cones kept in the boot of their patrol car as stanchions and, looping what blue plastic police tape they had through higher gorse shrubs, had managed to create a small protected zone directly in front of the quoit, though its western flank was exposed. Bates knew the SOCO team would create a much larger "no-go" area in the morning, but for now this would have to do.

The tent was tucked into a sheltered depression behind the stone walls of the ancient settlement and, though they had a clear view of the approach from the farmyard below, they could not actually see the quoit off to the southwest. Ever since DS Davies had left, one or the other of them had set out to patrol the cordoned area every two hours. That gave each a chance for a bit of sleep between shifts. It also gave Bates some respite from Williams's incessant chatter. She put it down to anxiety; he'd never done this kind of duty before and he was a city boy, a Penzance local and out of his element in these lonely moorlands. A slight young man with thick spectacles, she wondered if he had volunteered to be a special constable because of a history of being bullied.

She'd taken the first shift. She welcomed the quiet of the high tors, not just because of PC Williams' prattle but because this open and, to some, austere landscape was home for her. She'd grown up on a dairy farm spread along a plateau above the ocean on the Atlantic side of the peninsula barely a mile away, near Zennor. Her father had been an avid rock climber and he'd fallen to his death from Sennen Crag when she was only twelve. The fall left him unconscious; the surf dragged him out to sea. The postmortem concluded death by drowning, not injury. Her mother had sold the farm and gone to work behind the bar at the Tinners Arms, Zennor's thirteenth century pub. Left to her own company much of the time, Terry had happily roamed these weather-thrashed hills for years as a girl.

When she reached the western slope of the summit ridge, the sun was moments from setting, igniting the prickly gorse, frilled bracken fronds, and electric magenta heather on the slopes below. In this all-too-often gray world, the lemony yellow blossoms of the gorse were like stand-ins for the sun. Up on the exposed summits that punctuated the skyline, the gust-carved granite bones of the Cornish peninsula poked through its green skin and smoldered gold.

From this height, the highest point in West Penwith, she could see England's south-westerly tip, spotlit by the dying sun. Beyond it lay only endless expanses of seething Atlantic Ocean. Out of sight and miles offshore lurked the jagged shoals that had brought ships and their sailors to untimely ends for centuries. Farther still were the Isles of Scilly which, according to Tennyson's version of the Arthurian legend, were the summits of the drowned kingdom of "Lyonesse."

Inland, the shadowy coastal plateau was a crazy quilt of almost impossibly emerald grazing meadows enclosed by a fractal network of stone walls. Stone, she imagined, must have been the first harvest of those who settled this rocky landscape and tried to make fields millennia ago. As she walked along the ridge she thought she caught the *chi-ow* of the rare Cornish chough from a valley somewhere to the west.

She returned to the tent at eleven and Williams took the next walkabout. He awakened her at one and she stepped outside to let the air chill her awake.

At some point while she'd been asleep the wind had risen and a full moon had hauled itself up from the English Channel to the east. It hung now above the moor tops, coating the slopes in silver-plate one minute, then in ink the next as clouds racing in off the sea obliterated the shining disk. The gorse and heather writhed in the wind as if tortured and the gusts lashing the shattered granite tors screamed like a wailing infant.

She was moving around the eastern flank of the tor in the lee of the wind when she heard a noise that was not the wind, a noise she thought came from the quoit above. She kept still, muscles tensed, until she heard it again during a lull. A scraping sound, like a bare branch at a window in a storm. But there were no trees on Dewes Tor. And no windows.

She began to move uphill, staying low and taking care to keep to the spongy, peaty areas that lined the creases of the ridge where her steps would not be heard. As she climbed she tried to think of other natural causes for such a sound but could come up with none. The landscape was barren: gorse, heather, bracken fern, rock, granite rubble. She was thankful for the occasional bursts of moonlight. She could not afford the noise of a stumble, nor risk using her torch.

As she approached the spine of the ridge, the quoit loomed above and flashed arc-light white each time the strobe of the moon struck it, an effect like lightning that magnified the already massive edifice and made it seem to pulse.

Exposed now at the ridge top, with the full force of the wind whistling in her ears, Bates knelt behind the gorse bushes at the edge of the clearing. She strained to hear more, as if by demanding it, she might. She heard nothing.

At the same time, though, her own history fought her. The deep knowledge she had of these tors, these weathered hills that were her home—their history, their legends—a knowledge which had been such a comfort only a couple of hours earlier, now crowded her mind with threat. She knew from the old stories that a full moon brought the spirits of the otherworld to the surface at ancient sites. And the most dangerous of these were the piskies, the spirits of the dead. They could be playful but also vicious; they hated to be seen by the living and, if seen, were said to subject the seer to brutal beatings. The archaeologists thought they'd found a skeleton; was its piskie haunting the site? Her rational mind and her policewoman's training struggled to shake off the dread and focus on facts. How had something or someone appeared? If someone had climbed up to the quoit this night, for whatever reason, either she or Williams would have seen the interloper's torch. The footpath from the car park below went right past the tent.

But if someone had not passed…had some*thing*?

Bates was suddenly aware that the only sound louder than the wind was her own heart pounding against her chest. And despite the wind, she was sweating; her armpits itched. The fine hairs at the nape of her neck tingled.

She should call Williams for backup but she'd unclipped her radio from her collar strap when she went to sleep and had forgotten to pick it up before she left the tent. She was on her own.

She had a talk with herself. She hadn't joined the force to cower in the shrubbery in the face of danger. She was certain of that much. She let a few more moments pass and, taking her fears in hand and making as much noise as possible, she strode across the stony ground to the east face of the quoit.

"Police! Come out at once!"

There was nothing but the hammering wind.

Bates, a petite five feet four, could see neither over the granite cap of the quoit nor around it.

"I repeat," she shouted again, struggling to disguise the tremor in her voice. "Come out at once!"

Then she heard it: scuffling over the granite rubble that surrounded the quoit.

Bates was essentially unarmed; she had only the torch in her hand and the regulation PR26 telescopic baton at her waist, her "nightstick." She unclipped the baton and realized to her everlasting disgust that it trembled in her hand.

She took a deep breath and held it. Crouching, she scrubbed her shoes on the ground as if running to the right, then wheeled and ran left, switching on the torch and pointing it upward at the very moment she collided with a horror and froze. The baton fell to the ground.

Looming above her was a great horned beast with the bearded head of a ram, its nostrils flared, its eyes burning like coals.

It was the last thing Teresa Bates saw before the pain and darkness.

Four

HERE'S THE THING ABOUT BECCA: We'd been friends since I don't even remember. A long time, anyway. From Pensans Primary School at least, which was where us Council housing kids went.

You know how sometimes you meet someone and you smile without even thinking and then—boom!—you're best mates? Like, forever? That was us, Becca and me, is what I thought. She was twelve and like the big sister I never had.

I kinda always knew what she was thinking—and not because of my "seeings." Not at all. And she knew me, too. It was like we had some invisible texting channel or something. We just recognized and understood each other. She knew me; I knew her. We could even, you know, look at each other and start laughing, 'cause we already like knew what was funny without saying.

In that same way, I could see when she was troubled. And she was troubled a lot. I mean, geez, would we be in Council housing if life wasn't totally naff? I don't think so, you know? But would she say anything about her troubles? Never. That frosted me, I can tell you. We're supposed to be girlfriends, right? I shared everything with her—boys I thought were cute, clothes I wished I could buy at Mount's Bay Trading, my Mum's boyfriends and how they carried on when they thought I was asleep, whatever. But Becca? Get too close and she'd snap shut like an oyster.

Her mum was single, like mine. That's one thing we shared. But hers, well, sometimes I couldn't figure who was the kid and who was the mum. Becca cooked for them half the time or more 'cause her mum was gone or sick. She seemed sick a lot. So Becca did for her. I knew what that was like! She had an uncle, too. I only ever met him once, but he was good to her, was the feeling I got, in ways her mother wasn't. It was like they had a special relationship she didn't even share with her mum, much less me.

After she vanished, after I got over the shock of it and the fact that she never told me she was running away, I finally twigged that she never leveled with me about anything that really mattered. It was all surface. Push her a little and your question would skate away like it hit an ice patch.

But she was mad for Tamsin and I get that. Tamsin's really cool, and a little mysterious, like she's always holding something in…a secret or something. She and Becca, they were the same in that way, I guess. Becca, she totally wanted to be the next Tamsin. She read everything she could understand about witchcraft. She wanted to become a Wiccan, which is kinda like being a witch except not like Tamsin, but they told her she was too young. I don't know about the "too young" part; Becca was twelve but somehow way more grown-up than me or any of the other girls at school, like she'd already lived more than the rest of us or something. Like she'd seen more, learned more, you know? Like she was way older.

Except she wasn't.

Five

WHEN SHE REGAINED FULL CONSCIOUSNESS just before dawn, Jude Chynoweth found herself in a bed on a ward at West Cornwall Hospital on St. Clare Street, only a few blocks west of where she'd begun her gentle slide into oblivion the night before.

"Oi!" she shouted, struggling to sit up. Her limbs felt numb as bricks. The room was large, with six beds, four of them empty. The walls were an inoffensive tan and the floor was tiled in wavy blue linoleum that looked like water in the tropics somewhere.

"You hear me out there?!" It was a struggle to form words and they sounded to her like talking under water.

"Stuff it, bitch" someone growled. The words seemed to come from the massive, inert, vaguely female shape in the bed next to hers.

Too weak to argue, Jude collapsed against her pillow.

In time—units of time which seemed oddly elastic to her, as if the present kept fading away from her and then snapping back again—a nurse with the bulk of a professional wrestler materialized in a royal blue tunic at the foot of her bed. Jude did not know how or exactly when this had happened.

"Well now, what d'you know," the nurse was saying, "it's our old friend Judith, back for a visit. How've you been keeping, Jude? Sleep well last night, did you? All comfy-cozy in those clean white sheets? Nice change, that, eh?"

Jude struggled to make her lips work to form words. "I'm leavin'," she said finally.

"Goodness, where are our manners? Treat you like a queen and we get this? Unkind, I call it."

"Got no reason to keep me here!" She was finding her voice.

"Except that you nearly died last night?"

"Bollocks."

"They found you in a doorway off Market Jew."

"I was only havin' a kip…"

"You weren't on the nod, dearie, you were nearly gone. We barely brought you back, for all the credit we'll get from you lot. What was it, China white?"

"Dunno what you're talkin' about."

"You tellin' me those tracks on your arms were laid down by Britrail? We lost two addicts in the last two days, you hear me? Whatever they shot up, they never came out of it. Three's the charm, they say, so you were the lucky one. Whatever they're using—whatever *you* used, it's bloody dangerous. It's killer smack, okay? So when The Bill comes around for a chat later, why not tell the officer where you got it so we'll have no more corpses layin' about here? Bad for business, it is, luv. Ruins our reputation as a healing institution..."

"Fuck your reputation; fetch my clothes or I'll start screamin' again.'"

"Scream all you like, but that beauty next to you? She likes her quiet."

Jude gave the woman next to her another look.

"Knifed her girlfriend, she did. Can't strap her down in this hospital; authorities won't let us. So we drug her, like we did you. But you might not want to rile her. No tellin' when her sedative will wear off, you know? I'm just sayin'…"

The whale-like woman in the next bed looked at Jude with arctic eyes, pressed her lips together, and blew Jude a kiss. Disgusted and frightened, Jude turned away. The nurse was gone.

POLICE CONSTABLE TERESA BATES struggled but the horned beast held her down in a darkness so complete that the only thing visible was its rheumy, burning eyes. One of its cloven hoofs pressed against her skull so firmly that however she twisted she couldn't escape. The pain from the sharp hoof sapped her strength and she was desperate in her helplessness. Even more terrifying, the beast made not a sound. Those eyes, cold despite the fire there, burned into hers and the pressure on her skull increased relentlessly until she was certain the fragile shell would shatter. She cried out, furious at the impotence of doing so. She mustered her remaining strength and once again tried to pull away, her limbs thrashing in the darkness. But then her arms were pinned, and the beast began growling her name, low and slow, as if from a dream.

"Miss Baaates…Terry…"

She thrashed again.

"Open your eyes."

Another voice cried "No!" and she realized it was her own. She struggled against the force restraining her and burst to the surface of consciousness at last, gasping for breath.

"Who are you? Where am I?"

"Welcome back, dear," the nurse said, releasing her arms.. "I'm your nurse and you're in hospital and safe. Let's have a look at your head, then, shall we?"

Bates blinked several times in an effort to clear her vision. "Hurts," she mumbled. "Diabolical, it is."

"We can fix that, constable. You've had a nasty crack on your head but you're going to be fine."

Reality came slowly into focus. "How long have I been here?"

The middle aged, graying nurse wore a name tag that said she was called Shirley. "You were admitted at about four a.m. It's just gone nine."

"I'm late for work," Bates said. She tried to climb out of the bed but her head throbbed sickeningly and she threw up on the polished linoleum.

Six

THE EAST-FACING SLOPE of Carn Dewes shone nearly incandescent from the sun high above Mount's Bay on Sunday morning as Calum West arrived at the farmyard. It had just gone ten. His team was close behind. The initial MCIT meeting at Camborne had been less a matter of discussion than of marshaling resources. DCI Penwarren had West lay out the site strategy. Procedure was West's catechism, continuity of evidence his religion, scene of crime his domain.

West looked at the climb ahead of him and sighed. It had been a short night. He'd managed a few hours of sleep before ringing Ruby, his mother-in-law. West's daughters, Meagan and Kaitlin, six and eight respectively, had spent the night with their grandmother and would now stay with her another day at least. He and Ruth were a right pair; she fiercely protective of the girls, he encouraging them to be adventurous and brave. But they were united in their love for the girls and for Catherine, Ruby's only daughter and West's late wife, lost to them all from uterine cancer three years past. He and Ruby had held each other together through the first year of grieving. Having helped each other across that chasm, they were now closer than West was with his own mother—not that Ruth didn't chivvy him about his irregular schedule.

"I won't tell them yet, but they'll be blue not seeing you again today."

"Don't be daft; another day with Gram? They'll be delirious."

Ruby laughed. "You're a terrible father, you are."

"Thankfully, they have a splendid grandmother. Thanks, Ruby."

"Off you go then, Calum, and come back safe."

WEST HAD JUST REACHED the quoit when he heard raised voices below at the cordon entrance. He could see a stranger arguing with a very tired Special Constable Williams, who was still on duty. Down at the farmyard the SOCO vans were unloading equipment. To his surprise, he saw that Morgan Davies was also climbing up to the cordon entrance. He walked back to the makeshift gate.

"I have an excavation to run and a permit from English Heritage to run it, dammit!"

"I'm sorry, Sir, but my orders are to protect the integrity of the site," Williams said.

"Then who the hell is *he*?" The man demanded, pointing at the descending figure above him.

Davies's voice behind him said, "That would be Detective Sergeant Calum West, the crime scene manager. Constable Williams is correct, Professor Hunter; this is now a crime scene."

"The whole tor?"

"Yes, for now."

"Look, detective, our permit's about to expire and we still have a lot of work to do."

The SOCO team had ascended and now crowded the cordon entrance where Williams was trying to log them in. Davies took Hunter's elbow and guided him away.

"I appreciate your passion for your work," Davies said, "and I understand your very real time constraints. But Sergeant West heads the Scene of Crimes team and he determines when a scene can be cleared. On the other hand, West has a scientist's heart. He'll understand. I'll try to get you back in business quickly. Our people need to do a thorough search of the entire hilltop, but when that is done and we are focused solely on the quoit, I will do my best to free up the rest."

Hunter stared at her for a moment, then his shoulders sagged. "I don't like it, but I'll take it."

Davies smiled. His intensity aside, there was something deeply likeable about Hunter, an inner honesty without pretension. A good chap. And handsome. Very. She shook off the thought.

"Right then, professor, why don't you fill me in about what you and your people are doing up here? I should have thought most of these prehistoric sites had been well-studied in the past."

"Well studied, but in this case not well understood. Our principal interest here is the fogou and, to lesser extent, evidence that a Bronze Age site may have preceded this Iron Age settlement. Based on something we found only yesterday, we think we can demonstrate that the fogou is far older than anyone has previously thought."

"Sorry…the what?"

"Fogou. Have you never visited Carn Dewes?"

She smiled. "Professor, I'm an avid indoorswoman. Hill climbing is not how I tend to spend my free time, what little of it there is."

Hunter led her to the settlement's entrance.

"Okay, Carn Dewes is a late Iron Age walled settlement. It's ringed by the ditch and stone bank ramparts you see here, though, after more than two thousand years, they, like the structures within, are much deteriorated."

They entered and she could see several walled enclosures.

"I should look so good after two millennia," Davies said, scanning the ground. "You can still see the building foundations!"

"Yes. There were six courtyard dwellings here. They're roughly oval, thickly-walled, and inside them you can still see a clear pattern: an entrance marked by two large standing stones, an inner courtyard, a few outbuildings, and a round, stone-walled residence built against the wall opposite the entrance, facing the courtyard and with its back against the prevailing Atlantic wind."

They entered one of the enclosures and Hunter pointed out a flat granite stone with a deep socket ground into its center.

"That hole would have held secure the wooden post which supported a conical thatched or turfed roof."

"And this was when?"

"What you see here today dates from between 50 BC through perhaps 400 AD, towards the end of the Roman occupation. Thanks probably to a colder, wetter climate, the last generation who lived here finally abandoned the site then. But we've proved that the site itself was occupied at least as far back as 500 BC, and—we now suspect—even earlier. Like Troy and Jerusalem and other ancient places around the globe, new civilizations and cultures simply built atop the foundations of older ones."

"Hard to credit that anything remains at all."

"Not really. There are several such settlements in this area. What distinguishes this settlement from the others is an underground tunnel some sixty feet long—a fogou. It's an old Celtic word for cave. They are unique to West Cornwall. There are others in the area, though none as extensive as this one. Come; I'll show you."

Halfway up the grassy, sloping site a short series of steps led down to a stone-lined tunnel roughly four feet high and the same wide. The walls were mossy and the ground muddy.

"What makes this fogou unique is this other passage at right angles to the main tunnel." He picked up a torch resting on a stone ledge and did not notice Davies's hesitation. Following him, Davies found herself in a domed subterranean stone chamber, its walls curving up and inward like a beehive to a height of perhaps eight feet.

"This chamber predates both the tunnel and the settlement above by centuries," Hunter explained.

Davies could feel sweat prickling her armpits. She despised this fear of being underground. She knew its source. But she could not control it. She turned and climbed out. Hunter followed.

"A storage chamber?" she asked when they reached the surface.

"It's been suggested, but the chronically damp conditions in here would have quickly spoiled grain or foodstuffs. Some have suggested the tunnel and this chamber could have been used for refuge, but it would have been a simple matter for invaders to smoke out those in hiding or simply wall them in."

He paused for a moment, looking out across the site, then added, "And there are those in the pagan community in Cornwall who believe this to be a place of holy ritual."

"Wait, now you mention it I remember reading an article in *The Cornishman* about demonstrations here months ago."

"Yes, the press covered it. The local pagan community fought for months to block our project, claiming that the site is sacred and that tampering with it is sacrilege. The protesters, complete with occupation tents and signs, were peaceful but persistent and led by a woman called Tamsin Bran, who claims to be the "village wise-woman" in St. Euny, just down the road toward Sancreed. All this preceded our arrival. The Duchy of Cornwall, which of course belongs to Prince Charles; the Cornwall County Council's chief archaeologist; and officials at English Heritage argued in our favor and eventually prevailed. Of course the Prince is a history buff and that didn't hurt. When I arrived in May, I met with Ms. Bran and her allies at her home and the issue was resolved."

"To everyone's satisfaction?"

Hunter smiled. "We still had a few die-hards, but they gave up after a week or so. Our agreement is to leave the site exactly as we found it when we're done."

She pointed back along the ridge. "And the quoit?"

"It's from an earlier period and not a part of our investigation, really. We came upon the skeletal finger by accident."

"Except that the finger is likely not there by accident."

Hunter looked toward the quoit. "No. No, I appreciate that, and that you have a job to do."

"JENNIFER!"

Davies had just returned to the cordon entrance to find West trotting over to his favorite forensic pathologist. She was inside the cordon and already pulling on her Tyvek coveralls.

"Come now, doc, you know the rules. Let's let my lads secure the approach before we go tramping around there." The SOCO team swarmed around the quoit in their white jumpsuits and booties like an army of rumpled snowmen. They had already erected a tent the size of a small barn which sheltered the entire quoit and were now laying squares of rigid aluminum grating atop the ground where others had previously walked. They had also taped off an area completely surrounding the quoit, leaving only a narrow, now-secured approach. While they worked, the constable who'd replaced Special PC Williams logged in a new arrival, Curtis Baker, a member of the police force in Plymouth but also a fully credentialed forensic anthropologist.

"Where's Bennie?" West asked him. Dr. Benjamin Wolfenden was a forensic archaeologist from Exeter University often called in to police investigations. "He was at the MCIT meeting this morning..."

"Called away. Family emergency."

"Bloody hell. We can't do this without an archaeologist."

Davies turned, saw Hunter descending the ridge, put two fingers between her lips, launched an ear-splitting whistle, and waved him back.

"Jesus, Morgan!" West exclaimed.

Davies grinned. "Crude, I know, but efficacious."

"LOOK, PROFESSOR," SHE SAID when Hunter rejoined them, "having banished you I find myself now in the embarrassing position of having to beg your help."

"I don't understand."

"We have strict protocols in a situation like this," West explained. "We have to have both an anthropologist and an archaeologist to disinter the remains. Our usual forensic archaeologist has just buggered off. Will you be willing to stand in? You and Baker here will be in charge of excavating."

Hunter laughed. "Fact is, I wanted to dig that skeleton out yesterday. So, yes. But I'll need tools."

"We have them. Climb into this," West said, handing him another Tyvek jumpsuit.

WEST AND HUNTER WERE the first to duck into the tent, bright now with lights the team had installed. Using string, the two men laid out a reference grid on the ground beneath the quoit's capstone, taking care not to disturb the bizarrely protruding finger.

As West took more reference photos, Hunter noticed him glance several times at the mass of granite above their heads. "Worried?" Hunter asked.

"That's a bloody big hunk of rock hanging there."

Hunter laughed. "That stone has been up there something between five and six thousand years. My guess is, the statistical probability of it crashing down on us this particular day is pretty close to nil. Of course, that's just my guess..."

"Very encouraging." West reckoned the roof above them had to weigh tons.

The grid now established, Dr. Duncan and Baker crawled in next to them. Davies, on her knees, watched from outside.

As Duncan looked on, Baker and Hunter began gently sweeping the area around the exposed finger with commercial paintbrushes. After a few moments, they began scraping with small metal mortar-pointing trowels.

"What does this site say to you?" West asked the archaeologist.

"This subsoil should be tight as hardpan, for one thing," Hunter said.

"Because...?" West's passions were forensics and cricket, not geology.

"Because workable topsoil in this part of Cornwall is wafer thin, where it exists at all. That's why the only thing you see down there in those walled fields is livestock, not crops; a plow is useless. The subsoil immediately beneath is normally tightly-packed decomposed granite and tough as ground concrete. Beneath that, only bedrock, mostly granite; the worn down nubs of volcanic intrusions that burst through the crust here millions of years ago."

"And this isn't."

"Right. It's been disturbed, and not long ago."

Working slowly, Baker and Hunter began to unearth the forearm attached to the desiccated hand. A few moments later, they stopped. Just above the wrist they discovered a sleeve of shiny reddish fabric with black fur trim.

West leaned in. "This is a costume of some kind. Synthetic—nylon or polyester. New. Fake fur at the sleeves. I don't like it."

"No, Sergeant, it wouldn't suit you at all," Jennifer Duncan cracked.

Hunter stretched his back and shook his head. "I don't envy the fellow who buried this chap. Had to be tough going."

"It's not a chap," Baker said, barely whispering as he crouched over the hand.

"It's a child."

Seven

WHAT HAPPENED AFTER BECCA done a runner was this: Her mum, who is mad as a bucket of frogs, if you ask me, said it was Tamsin's doing; said Tamsin had set some spell that made Becca disappear. Or maybe even did her in.

So the police, well, they were after Tamsin for ever so long; asking about this, nosing into that, even hauling her to the station in Penzance to fingerprint her. They spent a lot of time going through her tools and herbs, like the silly buggers thought that stuff could cause someone harm.

I got this all from her; she told me everything the first day I came to help with the cleaning. She thought I'd hear things about her and get afraid, and wanted me to hear it straight from her. But I could see how hard the telling of it all was for her. She stopped sometimes and just stared off into the distance, her lips pressed tight, before she started in again. And in the middle of this it comes to me that maybe this is the first time she's ever unloaded it all, you know, and I feel good she would do it with me. And anyways, I didn't have any fears about her. At least not then.

Of course it doesn't help any that Tamsin's a witch. Witches, well, they've been persecuted for ages and ages, she tells me—burned, quartered, drowned, hung, though that's mostly in the past. But I figured anyone Becca loved—and she did love Tamsin—had to be okay, witch or no. And since Becca was, you know, like my sister, I believed everything she said. Especially about Tamsin.

But Becca's mum, well, she kept on about how Becca had been bewitched by Tamsin, spirited away from her. I reckon this is because Tamsin looked after Becca and taught her things, the way her mum never did. The London newspapers were all over Tamsin: *Witch Questioned in Case of Missing Girl*. That one was from the *Daily Mail*. Tamsin showed me.

Tamsin tells me this detective bloke named Penwarren kept coming around. That's a local name, Penwarren is; you can tell from the first three letters. In school we learned this old rhyme: *By Tre, Pol and Pen* shall ye know all Cornishmen. Anyway this Penwarren keeps saying she is "a person of interest" and asking her to "help with their enquiries," which is code, I think, for, "We think you done it."

But she says she didn't. She tells him this, and she tells me. She had no idea where Becca'd gone, and no idea she'd planned to disappear. This detective's questions go on for a couple of months before one day, out of the blue, he comes by again and tells her it's over, she's in the clear. But not because they believe she's innocent. Uh-uh. "We have insufficient evidence to prosecute you further," is what he says.

When she's telling me this she shakes her head slowly and says, "How similar those two words are..."

"Which?"

"*Prosecute* and *persecute*."

Eight

BY NOON, Hunter and Baker had removed the rubble above the remains and West had used specialized adhesive tape to lift potential fibers or hairs from the shroud before they opened it. He'd just finished when one of the SOCO team members called to him and he backed out from under the quoit.

"Company, boss."

At the cordon entrance, West saw just under a dozen young uniformed constables waiting to be logged in. Davies was with them.

"Search team already?" he asked her.

Davies looked at him sharply. "I have two crimes to investigate: one possible old murder, and one new assault on PC Teresa Bates. These lot are here to search the tor for evidence of the latter."

West had been so focused on the excavation he hadn't noticed earlier that Davies hadn't changed clothes from the night before or that she was dancing at the edge of exhaustion like a drunken high wire artist. He reckoned she'd been at the hospital all night, keeping vigil over Bates.

"May I suggest that while your people get logged in you and I come up with a search plan that doesn't have us falling over each other?"

She nodded.

He lowered his voice. "When was the last time you slept?"

"What the hell do you care?"

"Right, then; that's my answer. Night before last, at best."

"I repeat…"

"Don't bother, Morgan. It wouldn't actually be lethal, you know, to accept that someone cares about your well-being."

Davies stared across the tor, avoiding his eyes.

"Actually, it usually is. Shall we get on with it?"

The two of them surveyed the search zone. It would be heavy going; the tor was choked with gorse and heather. And they had no idea what, if anything, they were looking for.

"My suggestion is," West said, "have your crew search the slopes for trace evidence first, and then perhaps you might zero in on the protected area immediately around the quoit?"

"Sounds like a plan," Davies said, smiling finally. Cranky as she was, West's affability calmed her, as if, like a hot spring, he radiated some kind of soothing warmth.

"So where are you with the remains?"

"We're about to unwrap the youngster's skeleton."

"Youngster?!"

"That's what our forensic anthropologist thinks. Not even a teen."

"Male or female?"

"No idea. Even the postmortem might not tell us. There's little skeletal difference at that age."

"Bloody hell."

"No shit, Morgan; I've got two daughters this age."

AT THE BACK OF his neck West could feel the wind rising. West Penwith, the farthest tip of Cornwall, had had a run of good June days but now the sky in the west was thickening and a curtain gray as old linen had been drawn across the far offshore horizon.

When Davies and her constables returned empty-handed a couple of hours later, she spent some minutes studying the faint prints in the rough gravelly ground beneath the aluminum plates near the approach to the quoit. They told her nothing. Her knees were sore and she hadn't a shred of physical evidence to help with the attack on Bates.

She cornered West while he was giving orders to the Tactical Aid Group chaps sifting the dirt that had been removed from the excavation under the new tent.

"How long?" she demanded.

"We're closing down. Weather's changing. Got to secure and protect the evidence area first."

"I hate this part…"

"I know you do, Morgan. Your job's conviction, but my job's collection. Hurried collection? Tainted evidence? No conviction. So we take our time. Slow and methodical, that's us. Plus, there's the obvious point…"

"I know, I know. Old body. Whoever's involved here is either long gone or so confident after all this time he or she feels at no risk. I heard about the satin; what do you make of it?"

"That's weird, that is."

"Fancy dress sex game gone all pear-shaped?"

West laughed. Gorse-prickly as she was, and no matter that she used her stodgy plainclothes suits like a carapace, her chopped hair like a shield, her dismissive sarcasm like a sword, she was a striking woman; tarnished, but underneath, sterling silver. And when she gave it a chance, funny as well.

"Got to get this lot of PCs home before their mums call them in for tea," Davies said, nodding at the youthful crowd loitering by the white police transport van far below.

She looked at West, index finger raised. "Tomorrow." It was like a warning.

He wondered if she would sleep.

DAVIES PULLED INTO in the car park behind the Penzance nick just as PC Terry Bates came out the back door.

"You're out of uniform, constable," Davies barked, but she was smiling as she walked away from the Ford.

Bates looked at the regulation black bowler hat in her hand.

"Hurts too much to wear."

"I shouldn't wonder; that was some coshing you got. Come inside and let me have a look at you."

"I was just…" she began. "But okay," she corrected and followed the detective to the CID office.

"Sit," Davies ordered. Then she pulled her own chair up to face the young woman and peered at her eyes.

"Concussion. You shouldn't be here."

"I was bored."

"Any nausea? Troubling staying awake?"

"Not any more. The nurse said you stayed with me till dawn. Thank you."

"Had to. You're my only witness."

"To what?"

"The assault, the demon. The nurses said you were screaming about it. Care to put me in the picture?"

Instinctively, Bates touched the bandage on the side of her head and winced, then closed her eyes.

"Horrible, it was, massive, with the horns of a ram but so big, and with a long beard and fiery eyes." She took a breath and opened her eyes. "I'm not delirious; I'm not making this up."

"How many legs?"

"What?"

"*Legs*, Bates. How many?!"

"I never saw!" Bates cried.

Davies grabbed her arms "Get hold of yourself, girl!" She had little patience for hysteria, nor much of anything else, come to that; twenty-five years on the force will do that to you. "This apparition: close to the ground or above you, short or tall?"

Bates hesitated, eyes closed again. "Above. Taller."

"What else?"

"My head hurts."

"What else?!"

"A cloak of some kind, maybe black. Or red. It was dark."

"Did you see what hit you?"

Bates started to shake her head and thought better of it.

"Focus," Davies ordered.

And then Terry could see the movie re-playing, the horror in her torch beam and, almost instantly, the blow, delivered by a hand. Human, wielding another torch.

"It was a somebody, not a something!"

Davies quietly admired the girl's poise. "Good. And left-handed as well, eh?"

Bates concentrated and then nodded. "How did you know?"

"You were facing it. The injury is to your right temple. Simple. And very helpful, Terry."

Bates made a face. "I should have figured that out."

Davies placed a warm hand on hers and gave the slightest squeeze. "You're doing just fine. When you're ready—tomorrow, the next day, you're seconded to me. You hear?"

Bates nodded. She hoped she wouldn't have to keep getting coshed to advance in the force.

IN THE CROW BLACK DARK OF NIGHT, Morgan Davies screamed herself awake. Her sheets were soaked with sweat.

"Bloody hell," she mumbled as she struggled to consciousness.

Always the same dream: the ground closing in above her. Trapped. Underground.

She flung back the sopping sheets, pulled on a cool cotton wrap, and went to the kitchen, where she poured herself a double vodka without benefit of vermouth. Then she padded back to her bedroom, ignored the bed, and sat at a desk in an alcove beside a dormer window that, at this hour, let in only inky darkness. Her computer told her it was three in the morning. She pulled up one file after another from a special folder: Aberfan disaster; Aberfan inquest; Aberfan victims; *Aberfan/National Coal Board testimony…*

The nightmare was always the same, with minor variations. And she knew that this time it had been triggered by just those few minutes with Hunter in the fogou.

She opened the first file and stared at the page she knew by heart: a computer facsimile of a yellowed newspaper story from the *Times of London*:

At 9:15 yesterday morning, 21 October, a mountain-high coal mine waste tip collapsed, sending an estimated 120,000 cubic metres of slurry hurtling down upon the Welsh mining village of Aberfan, 35 kilometers north of Cardiff. Due to dense fog, survivors say they could not see what was coming, but they could hear the roar of it. Some, with memories of the War, thought a low-flying bomber was descending. Then, the crushing black avalanche of mine tailings hit. Local officials report that as many as one hundred forty-four people have perished or are missing, one hundred sixteen of them children at a primary school buried by the massive slip. The National Coal Board announced it would immediately begin an inquiry…

One of the children at the school had been six year old Lewis Davies. He would have been Morgan's brother, but Morgan was still weeks from being born. While many of the children's bodies were eventually recovered, their mouths and noses choked with slurry, their limbs crushed, Lewis was never identified; forensic experts said he would have been among the many children for whom only body parts were found, torn apart by the furious rock and mud flow.

The chairman of the National Coal Board, Lord Robens of Woldingham, was busy that day being invested as chancellor of the University of Surrey and did not feel the disaster required his immediate attention; the Secretary of State for Wales lied to reporters that Lord Robens was personally directing relief work. When he finally did show up, a day later, he claimed nothing could have been done because this particular tip sat upon "natural unknown springs."

The formal inquiry for the disaster lasted seventy-six days, the longest in British history. Morgan had all the transcripts, and now she pulled up that file as she had so often before. The inquiry revealed the springs were well-known and clearly marked on Ordnance Survey maps. The director of the investigation called the disaster, "a terrifying tale of bungling ineptitude" and said blame rested solely with the NCB. But because there were no rules governing mine tailings, the NCB was found to be innocent of violation. Not a single NCB official was demoted, sacked, or prosecuted.

Morgan pulled up another file, this one digital photocopies of fuzzy carbon copies of letters typed on an old typewriter by someone who clearly was not accustomed to typing. They were written by her father. Colliery engineer James Davies was the chargehand for the coal mine waste tips at the time of the disaster.

He had written repeatedly to the National Coal Board warning about the safety dangers of the tips. He specifically warned that one of the tips was saturated and unstable. They paid him no heed.

At the back of her father's file was a copy of his death certificate. Morgan's father committed suicide the day after the inquiry ended. Her mother, pregnant with Morgan and unhinged by her losses, spent the rest of her life in a mental institution in Cardiff. Morgan was raised by her father's alcoholic mother.

Quietly, privately, Morgan had been searching for legal redress for the victims' families ever since. A miscarriage of justice had occurred, but the documentary evidence had been cleansed; she could find nothing in the official record by which to fix blame and secure appropriate compensation for the victims. Her father's letters were not revealed at the inquiry; NCB authorities alleged the carbon copies were suspect. A court eventually had awarded the families of those who lost relatives a settlement of only five hundred pounds sterling, a travesty. The years passed and most people—most people outside of Aberfan, at least—had long since forgotten about the disaster.

But not Morgan. She was convinced the NCB had concealed evidence of the dangers and, whenever she had time, she kept digging for proof—proof which would exonerate her father and help the families in Aberfan—no matter how much time had passed.

Her reward was these nightmares.

Some There Are Who Know Not

Nine

JUST AFTER DAWN THE NEXT DAY, Calum pulled his Volvo estate into the farmyard at Trerane and performed his usual morning ritual: brewing Douwe Egbert filter coffee in the coffee-making kit he kept in the car. Years of serving in police stations where the communal tea had been stewed to tannic lye had put him right off that most commonplace of British beverages. Well-made, carefully filtered fresh coffee was his drug of choice.

The wind had dropped and shards of sunlight knifed through a mother-of-pearl sky. West looked around the nearly derelict farm at the foot of the tor: granite house circa God-only-knew how long ago, stone walls scabbed over with orange and grey lichen, windows with their graying lace curtains staring out at the world blank-eyed as a cadaver, sagging stone outbuildings yielding to gravity as if from exhaustion. He'd seen places like this in West Cornwall many times before. It was the kind of farmstead where a wife had long since died of some wasting illness and the aged widower scraped by on his niggardly state pension and the scant income from fields he once worked but now leased to some younger chap trying to make his way in the heartbreaking business of grazing thin-soiled moorland with sheep and cattle. Any day now, the old man would end up in a care home somewhere and the farm would be sold to some rich investor who'd turn the whole complex into posh holiday cottages, the units let out at a weekly rate that probably exceeded what the farmer earned over six months in a good year.

The widower, West knew from his on-board laptop, was called Jakes. They had tried to raise him the day before, to no avail. Jakes did not greet his dawn visitor this day either, though West thought he saw an upstairs curtain move slightly. The name "Jakes" had no doubt had been "Jacques" generations back. This part of Cornwall was more closely related, by both language and culture, to Brittany, just across the Channel in France, than it was to the rest of England. The same prehistoric stone megaliths, quoits, and circles existed in Brittany as they did here in Cornwall.

But Jakes wasn't his priority just now. If there was anything to be learned from the old man, Davies's suspect team would question him later.

Above him, West watched the morning light shine on the naked granite outcrops atop the tor, the stone weathered by wind and frost into layers like stacks of honeyed pancakes.

The SOCO and TAG teams arrived in two vans just twenty minutes behind him and he ascended the tor while the others gathered gear below.

Anthropologist Baker, pathologist Duncan, and Brad Hunter, this day accompanied by his assistant Amanda, were right behind him. Beneath the quoit, Baker and Hunter laid plastic sheeting over the bones to protect them and began excavating a trench around the remains.

At roughly two feet, Hunter said, "I've hit hardpan."

"Yeah," Baker said from the other side, "I'm there, too. Let's go all the way around and see how much we can remove beneath the shroud."

From time to time they shifted overburden to buckets and passed them to the Tactical Aid boys to be sieved. All of the removed rubble was legally the property of the Coroner and would be stored at the mortuary as evidence. The process was painstaking, a matter of slice, scrape, brush and shift, specifically designed to preserve whatever possible evidence lay in the soil directly about the buried body: hair, fragments of fabric, personal effects, even pollen and insect larvae. As for the skeleton itself, they took pains not to touch or disturb it. Remains belonged to the pathologist, and Dr. Duncan kneeled opposite her colleagues, silently overseeing their work.

As West watched, it occurred to him that their job was not unlike Michelangelo's: remove the excess marble to reveal the David within. And to West, these remains, now revealed, were no less precious.

IT WAS NEARLY NOON when West realized that Davies was standing behind him. She looked rejuvenated: the puffiness gone from her eyes, the blond highlights in her hair sparkling, her dark blue pants-suit sleek over a crisp white blouse.

Hunter, on his knees beneath the capstone, was leading the forensic team through ancient burial arcana.

"The position of the body is significant. The head is oriented to the point where the sun rises at the winter solstice, the moment of seasonal rebirth. I don't think this is accidental. The bones of the arms—you see how oddly crossed they are? Hands and elbows are aligned to the four points of the compass, or, in some belief systems, the four sacred elements: fire, earth, water, air."

From outside, Davies interrupted. "What kinds of belief systems?"

"Almost any pagan culture, detective."

"So you're suggesting…"

"That this is some kind of ritual burial, yes, and deliberate in its positioning. But it's also slipshod. Common elements of ritual burial are missing: a decent depth, a proper shroud, and grave goods; symbolic items meant to accompany the soul on its journey. It's amateurish and, I suspect, hurried."

"So, from your point of view, a suspicious death?" Davies pressed.

"Yes. And recent. But understand; I'm not a forensic archeologist."

"You'll do."

"Are we ready then, people?" West asked.

"Yes," Dr. Duncan replied. "But if we simply lift by the cloak the skeleton will probably break up, even if the cloak remains intact, which it may not. Let's get a body board underneath and lift all at once."

West backed out, returning with a rigid white plastic board with built-in handholds. As Duncan supervised, four TAG officers inserted it beneath the remains and, using the red cape, eased the skeleton up until it rested on the slanted board. The spine remained attached all the way to the skull, but Duncan had to reposition dislodged parts of the ribs and limbs in their rightful places within the shroud. The specialists withdrew from the chamber and the four TAG boys maneuvered the board out from beneath the quoit and laid it atop a sterile white plastic sheet West had prepared. Then, they wrapped the sheet around both the board and the remains and taped it tightly before slipping the entire package into a heavy black vinyl body bag. West zipped and labeled the bag, locking it with a plastic ratchet seal.

As the men began their trek downhill toward the undertaker's van already waiting below, West caught Davies staring after them, blank-eyed, as if she were miles away.

"Morgan?" he said, touching her elbow.

But Davies was deep in her own personal hell of untimely deaths and anonymous lost souls. Now this: a ritualized burial. But she was remembering something; sometime in the past year or more, a child had gone missing when Penwarren was still head of CID at Penzance. He'd never solved the case. She knew it ate away at him and she owed her position to him.

"I have to go," she said.

Ten

THE LADY AT THE DOOR of Tamsin's place says she's police and shows me a black leather wallet with her picture and a badge. But I know that already, don't I? Knew before she came down the lane in her car, even though it didn't have those blue and yellow patches on the side like Panda cars usually do. Besides which, she'd phoned Tamsin a few minutes earlier to say she would be paying us a visit. But like I said, I knew that, too.

The lady has an aura that is full of death. I don't know why I see that, but I do. I can't see anything else about her, but then I'm not a reader. I don't get much time to think about this because Tamsin comes through the hall to the front door. She doesn't say anything, like, you know, "May I help you?" because she's reading the woman. That's Tamsin's gift. It's called *Claircog*-something. She can read people, what's on their mind and such. The policewoman, who's called Detective Sergeant Davies has eyes like the blue after a storm clears the sky and she seems bigger than she really is. She shows her identification again and still Tamsin studies her. Finally, her face darker now, Tamsin says, "Won't you please come in?" and the three of us go through to the big kitchen.

Tamsin has four old overstuffed chairs arranged in a curve facing the hearth, each with different, printed slipcovers. They're old and saggy but comfy, too, and the mix of patterns shouldn't go together, but somehow Tamsin makes them work. I don't think Tamsin makes a lot of money as a wise-woman; she does a lot of work by barter, which is how many folks hereabouts get by. She also gets a lot of her things from Sunday rummage sales around the area. She loves to tell me about her latest bargain. I reckon that's where the chairs came from.

She and the detective sit. The detective lady perches at the edge of her chair straight-backed and alert like a bird on a branch. I'm standing behind Tamsin.

"Morgan Davies," Tamsin says, drawing the name out like she's tasting it or something. "Welsh that is. I have known some talented Welsh wise-women. But I see you lack that knowledge. Someone in your family had it, though; that much I can tell."

The woman says only, "Yes, I was born in Wales."

"And suffered there a very great loss..."

"Ms. Bran," the woman says, ignoring this, "I am here because…"

"I know why you are here. You've found her."

"Found her?"

"Rebecca."

The policewoman lets a few seconds pass and says, "Why would you say that, Ms. Bran?"

Tamsin smiles, though sadly. I know she has so many ways of knowing things.

"Why else would you be here?" is what she says next.

The lady doesn't flinch. "Could be simply a visit from your community liaison officer," she says, and then she slants a look at me, "or the social services…"

"Except that your warrant card says detective sergeant, doesn't it? And the last time a detective visited me it was about Rebecca. And the plain fact is that I can read you, Detective Sergeant Davies. It is my gift, or curse, however you wish: Claircognizance. You've found Rebecca. That much I know.

"I also know," Tamsin says next, "that you did not find her alive. You are full of sorrow and anger about this. I can see that, too."

"No!" I shout. "I saw her just today!"

Now the lady detective looks confused and Tamsin takes over.

"Tegan saw her, you see," Tamsin says in a calm voice while she takes my hand and pulls me down to sit with her.

"That's not possible," the detective says.

Tamsin smiles. "Not literally, in this case, detective, not in this world, but in the Annown. Tegan saw Becca, saw her anguish at being disturbed."

"Excuse me? Annown?"

"The Annown, the otherworld, the realm of the spirits, the home of the departed. Tegan here has a gift, too, you see, different from mine; she can see things before they happen, or when they happen, even though she's not there. And you saw Becca, didn't you, Tegan girl?" Tamsin says to me. "You saw her spirit when they moved her?"

I should have known she'd read me, of course, but I'd not thought myself someone she'd bother with, given how busy she is with all her potions and healings.

"Can you tell the detective anything more that might help, Tegan?"

"The seeing wasn't so clear, Tamsin," I lie.

She pats my hand. "Don't you worry, luv. Just say what you saw and don't be afraid." Then, to the detective: "She hasn't yet grown into her gift, you see...."

"She was someplace high," I say, "and near an old stone cottage; miner's or hill farmer's, is what I saw. And Becca—Oh God, Tamsin—she was screaming!"

Then, for the first time since the seeing, I start bawling and I can't stop and it's because I can't help her, wherever she is. I can see her but I can't reach her and she is so frightened, Becca is. Tamsin pulls me close.

The detective lady, she watches this like she's watching, I don't know, maybe a program on the telly and isn't really here with us. She blinks finally and looks at some papers in a folder and says, "You were Rebecca's friend, is that right, Tegan? Tegan St. Claire, isn't it?"

I nod and scrub away the tears.

"If you can see things before they happen, as you say, did you see danger coming to Rebecca before she disappeared?"

"Tegan was only..." Tamsin starts.

"Let's let the girl answer."

And I don't know what to say because I didn't understand back then what I know now, thanks to Tamsin: that I see things before they happen or far away from me. You tell someone you saw something that hasn't happened and they think you're 'round the twist, you know? So you keep it to yourself, unless you find someone, like Tamsin, who understands. Back then—it seems like years now, but isn't—I always felt Becca had a secret; it was exciting for her, but also scary. And I never could make it out. I just couldn't. There was something coming for her, or someone, and soon, is what I thought then. But I'm not like Tamsin; I can't read people.

"I don't remember," is what I say.

"Detective Davies," Tamsin is saying, "you did come to tell me you'd found her, didn't you? Found Rebecca?"

"Not exactly, Ms. Bran."

"Then?"

"I came to ask you where you were at midnight, night before last."

"I don't understand," Tamsin says, and I see her fear.

"I think you do, Ms. Bran."

Eleven

THAT EVENING, Morgan Davies was well into her third vodka tonic at the bar of the Fisherman's Arms on Fore Street, opposite the quay in Newlyn, the commercial fishing center bordering Penzance. Morgan owned a small but airy home: an oak-beamed, two-story former net-drying loft just around the corner and up a steep cobbled alley. She'd had the nineteenth century stone building renovated "with all mod cons;" conveniences like high-end kitchen appliances and cupboards, black granite counters speckled with shiny silica chips, a new loo, whitewashed interior stone walls, halogen overhead lighting, stripped and polished floorboards upstairs, scrubbed and sealed old slate flagstones down.

She was a regular at the Fisherman's not for its atmosphere which, if nothing else, demonstrated just how hard a crowd of drunken deckhands can be on the closest bar to the quay, but because the rowdy crews were her friends and neighbors. Weather-beaten and rough around the edges, yes, but they'd welcomed her as one of their own. They were the closest thing she had to family and she'd locked up enough of them overnight that she had their respect. Oh sure, one of the single blokes, fresh off a boat, might hit on her now and then, but the older men would straighten that out before the poor chap could make a second move...and get hurt.

But the boats were late returning this week and the pub was nearly empty, so she lingered over her drink thinking again about the two murders she was supposed to be investigating: two young women, barely teens, prossies according to locals, but apparently nameless and invisible. Dental records had given them names, if not identities:

Jackie Stark and Holly Johns, not that their names were necessarily those they'd used on the docks along Newlyn harbor, or even their real names, since the dental work was recent, expensive, and no doubt paid for by their handlers to make them more presentable to their clientele.

Dental work or no, they'd both ended up as limp piles of limbs and fancy tart's clothing, found within shouting distance of the Fisherman's. No one, including Jerry, the former long-liner who limped around behind the bar at the Fisherman's and whom she trusted completely, admitted they'd known either of the girls.

And now there was this Tamsin Bran. There was a raw, bitchy part of Davies that hated the detestably slender and graceful "witch": skin smooth as silk charmeuse; skull carved as if by a master sculptor; raven hair with its thin shock of white at the temple that shone as if spot-lit. Not to mention that the woman radiated a calmness and air of mystery Davies struggled to keep from calling otherworldly. She was accustomed to her warrant card intimidating witnesses and suspects. It had no such effect on Bran. A part of Davies wanted to possess that same kind of mystery and knew she never would. Instead, the dark protective moat she'd built around herself, thrashed about as it was with sarcastic alligators, kept her secrets safe. Like hostages. The only "mystery" about her, she knew, was what she never shared. With anyone.

Davies had checked the HOLMES II system immediately upon returning from Carn Dewes. The Home Office Large Major Evidence System—redundantly named so it could spell out the fictional detective's name—was the force's data management system, through which every item of evidence taken, every interview, every report by witnesses, friends, family, every forensic result, was assiduously recorded by members of the major crime investigation teams. It was designed not only to manage data but also to provide instant cross-referencing that would point up discrepancies in reports.

Davies found the missing girl's file, but the record was scant: Rebecca Chynoweth had essentially been on her own with a single mother, a prostitute who did turns to fund a heroin habit. A kid could go two ways in that situation: anger and rebellion, or caretaking and unnatural maturity.

Davies looked out across Fore Street, to the quay and the harbor beyond and wondered which course the girl might have taken.

Initially, the witch, or "village wise woman," as Bran preferred to be known, had been the principal person of interest when Rebecca disappeared, not simply because the girl had worked for the witch doing odd jobs, but because the girl's mother swore the witch had placed a disappearing spell upon her daughter. Anywhere else in the United Kingdom, such a claim would have been written off as delusional at best, but not here in southwest Cornwall, where pagans were thick upon the land and such assertions were never dismissed out of hand by the locals.

The Cornish were a wary and superstitious lot; Davies believed it was to do with the peninsula's isolation, a place on the way to nowhere, the end of the road. These stubbornly-held beliefs had neither died nor been quashed over the centuries, though from time to time they went into hiding. Conquerors of Britain had come and gone, monarchs had risen and fallen, witch purges had flared briefly and burned out, wars had been waged, but in West Penwith, as far south and west in England as one could go without a boat, there were stubborn pockets of the old ways, places where belief in both the spirits of the seasons and the spirits of the dead persisted. Those spirits lived, it was claimed, in the sacred places that dotted the barren landscape: the ancient wells, the stone circles, the towering burial quoits, and the lonely megaliths that punctuated the sky throughout the county's wind-whipped tip. Prehistory existed in the present tense in West Penwith.

It was all codswallop as far as Davies was concerned. She had no patience for what she called, "the woo-woo stuff." Still, there was something about Tamsin Bran that Davies could not easily dismiss; not just the unnerving revelation that the woman knew they'd found the missing child—was that an indirect admission of guilt?—but also the queer feeling that Bran had access to levels of knowledge deeper and more profound than Morgan would ever experience, no matter how hard she searched. Davies had built a career upon the belief that there was an answer behind every question and if you hadn't discovered it yet you weren't trying hard enough. Fate hadn't annihilated her family; the incompetence of the Coal Board had. Murders happened because someone wanted something they couldn't get by other means. Accidental deaths? Someone being stupid or irresponsible. Was Bran a charlatan, a nutter, a murderer, or something else outside Davies's experience and beyond the reach of her rational analysis? She wasn't sure. And the spooky girl, Tegan, almost a Rebecca clone, didn't help matters.

According to HOLMES II, Rebecca Chynoweth had last been seen on Causewayhead the evening she disappeared, as had the witch. But witnesses put the witch at a monthly "pagan moot," a gathering of like-minded people held in a community meeting room behind a shop at the top of that same pedestrian street. The girl had been seen at eight that night; the moot had not adjourned until nine. Where had the girl been between eight and nine? No one knew. She'd vanished at some point after eight but there was no telling how long after. Had she waited for the moot to be over to join her mentor? Had she accompanied the witch afterward? Where? Was it something the girl planned or the woman suggested?

Ms. Bran lived alone; the police had no choice but to accept her word that she'd returned home to St. Euny directly after the moot. There was nothing to suggest she hadn't, but no one to confirm she had. Tucked away in her narrow valley, she had no near neighbors who could account for her comings and goings. Every line of evidence, and these were scant, led nowhere.

Davies slugged back the rest of her drink and waved goodbye to Jerry. She glanced at the packets of fags on a shelf behind the bar and longed for a cigarette. She'd managed to live without one for more than a year, but cursed the extra weight she'd gained. Of course, maybe that was the drinking, which had accelerated as the smoking stopped. Dueling vices.

Out on Fore Street there was a heaviness in the air and, just as Calum had predicted, the sky to the west was shrouded in angry black clouds and the wind was up. On her way home she stopped at Billy Stanfield's little wharfside kiosk and ordered batter-fried cod and chips.

"Evening, Sarge!" Billy called out from behind the fryer. "Not much action waterside tonight, eh?"

"Bored to death is what I am, Billy. No one to arrest. Terrible waste of police talent."

Billy laughed. "This'll fix you, this cod will. Fresh off the first boat returning."

"Who's that then?"

"Brian Tregarren! That old boat of his, he's usually the last in, but this time he had help."

"Hire someone? I didn't think he had the ready."

"Hired someone all right, some witch over St. Euny way. Cast a spell for him is what I hear."

Bran.

"You believe that, Billy?"

Billy shrugged. "All's I know is he's first in tonight, hold full of cuttlefish and a good by-catch of Ling cod I nabbed just a few hours ago."

Morgan paid Billy and took the package, the whole of it wrapped in newsprint in the old manner to absorb grease and keep everything hot, and trudged up the hill to her cottage. Bran indeed…

Her kitchen opened to a stone-flagged sitting room. In it, a shiny black leather settee that opened to a bed for guests and a matching easy chair faced a new gas fireplace above which was a large flat screen telly, black as a Gorgon's eye. A chrome and glass coffee table set upon a hairy white wool rug from Greece was scattered with mystery novels she read for amusement because they were so often wrong.

Glancing around as she went to the kitchen, she wondered why she'd gone to the expense. She seldom cooked; seldom entertained. Maybe it was an investment in a kind of fantasy of tasteful living she could afford but would never actually live. Spotlit on the wall behind the settee was a Tate museum poster of Turner's masterpiece, *Snow Storm—Steamboat Off a Harbour's Mouth.* She loved the swirling power of it, the tiny vessel struggling through a miasma of storm. She could relate.

She pulled out a chair at the stripped pine table in the kitchen, uncorked a bottle of expensive Australian chardonnay from Tescos to go with the fish and chips and thought, *talk about gilding the lily!* She squeezed a dollop of Heinz salad cream on the newsprint for dipping. Another night off the diet she'd promised herself she'd follow.

Morgan drank, off duty and typically alone, to slow her constantly revving mental engine. She'd never been drunk in her life, control being far too important to her. And "relaxed" she would never be. But calmed—at least on her own terms—well, that condition was possible after a few drinks. She could feel the wine slowly lifting her foot off the accelerator, her tachometer needle backing off ever so slowly, as if her brain were finally idling or coasting.

She supposed she was what was known as a "solitary." She wasn't sure if that was a choice or a habit. She'd been alone almost from birth. She'd lost her father and older brother before she was even born. She'd lost her mother to the mental institution before she learned to walk. Raised by her father's mother, a hard drinker who was either abusive or unconscious, Morgan had been alone farther back than she had memory. Solitude was like a skin that fit her perfectly, one she'd never shed.

She punched the power button on the Bose CD player sitting in a stone niche by the table and the whole house filled with Miles Davis's "Kind of Blue." Perfect. It reminded her, as it always did, of Max. She hadn't always lived alone. Morgan and her ex-husband, Max, another detective in the force, had loved jazz. They'd travel to gigs in London clubs when they both were free. They'd been divorced now for nearly a decade and yet whenever she sat down to eat—even in this, her new home—she felt his presence. Maybe it was the music. Their best times together had been intense talks over supper, sharing their day, comparing notes, commenting on each other's cases, with the jazz in the background. Neither of them could put a finger on why they'd parted after only four years. But they'd remained friends for reasons that seemed simple to each of them but incomprehensible to others: they loved each other but agreed they were a poor match. They'd acknowledged it was for the best they'd had no children; they respected each other's talents. Tonight she wanted to call him, talk over this new case as they always had in the past, but she knew he'd be otherwise occupied. He'd recently remarried. His pregnant new and younger wife, Celia, was polite and patient, but only to a point.

Morgan liked strong men and had had several short, steamy flings since Max but, like ships caught in storms off Land's End, they eventually foundered on the rocks of her own inability to trust. Knowing what she knew about the world now, knowing what she'd experienced as a child, how could she ever surrender her heart to another's safekeeping? How could she even recognize who would cherish it, protect it, even—yet more unlikely—strengthen it? No. Too dangerous.

So yes, she was a solitary. Some years back, a female colleague asked her why she wasn't in a relationship. "I want a dominant man," she'd said, "but I'd never put up with one…." It was a lie. She knew she chose solitude because she feared intimacy more than loneliness. So much to lose.

So steep was the slope upon which her cottage perched that the view from her kitchen table stretched out over the shiny black slate rooftops of Newlyn, past the lights of Penzance, all the way across Mount's Bay to the castle atop St. Michael's Mount, the island outcrop for which the bay was named. She stood at the French doors that led to her tiny bricked patio, almost as high as the roof of the house below her, and watched the choppy water turn leaden in the shadow of the approaching clouds.

Much as she wanted to enjoy the grand sweep of a view she never tired of, she could not; all she could think about was how badly she wanted the pathologist's report on that child's skeleton.

Twelve

AFTER THE DETECTIVE LEFT, after she'd discharged Tegan, after night had fallen and the mist had rolled in, snaking through the valley, wraithlike, Tamsin Bran went outside and swept an area of bare ground in her garden free of leaves with her handmade broom of thin hazel-wood twigs bound to a long wooden handle.

As she did, she called out, *"Hekas Hekas Este Bebeloi: Be ye far from here, all ye profane."*

She worked anticlockwise, circling three times. When the space was cleared, she set aflame a small whisk made from a bundle of thirteen dried blackberry bramble branches bound with twine and waved it across and around the cleared area to ward off evil influences. This task completed, she used its embers to ignite a small fire of herbs in a brazier at the circle's center. Next, she drew her athame from her belt and pointed the knife's blade toward the center and the flame.

"Be this fire hood by knife and will and breath,
A beacon to alight the paths of spirit,
Illumin my craft, ablaze my calls.
For the hidden to draw with me.
I conjure thee oh serpent red, coiled in the land.
Give unto my blood the breath,
And let my Cunning Burn!
I conjure thee. I conjure thee. I conjure thee."

After a moment, she pointed her athame to the six poles—east, south, west, north, and above and below, and then drew into herself the spirit of the earth serpent, the spirit of the Annown, the otherworld. Next, she divided the circle into quarters marking, respectively, the East Road, the South Road, the West Road, and finally the North, placing a lit tea candle in each. At the intersection of the four quadrants, she inserted her forked staff in a hole in the center. The staff would now become the channel, the "world tree," the organic route between the spirits below and the world above.

At the center, Tamsin placed the troyl—a small bowl of bread and a cup made of horn filled with a measure of wine—offerings to the spirits. Then, taking up her staff and walking this time clockwise three times, she called as she walked:

"I conjure thee Compass Round,
Be ye cast and be ye bound.
By road above and road below,
By snake and hare and toad and crow,
By red spirits, white spirits, gray spirits, and black,
I conjure ye by threefold track.
Be ye cast and be ye bound,
Hollowed be O Compass Round."

Coming back to the center, Tamsin raised her staff aloft then set it firmly in the ground again. Crossing her arms at her chest, she said,

"As above...
So below...
And by the quarter ways,
So mote it be."

Another moment passed and she sank to the ground within the circle and began stringing forty-five Rowan berries on a red thread, tying a knot between each berry and with each knot muttering, "Rowan berries and red thread, put all evil to its speed!"

Nearly an hour later—though she could not herself have said how long—she tied together the ends of the string of berries to form a loop, passed it three times over the smoke of the dying herb fire and, after quenching the embers, hung the loop of berries beside her front door.

The wind had risen steadily while she worked and the dark sky hunched with the weight of rain. She stood at the threshold as the protective spirit armor settled around the mill and, at last, as the first heavy raindrops pocked the path to her door, she withdrew for the night.

Thirteen

THERE ARE MORE THAN two hundred bones in the human skeleton. It had taken hours for Curtis Baker, the forensic anthropologist, to piece them all together and still more hours for him and Jennifer Duncan, the pathologist, to search them for a possible cause of death: fractures, nicks, fragments from an attack. Then, sometime after midnight Tuesday morning, beneath the glaring lights of the postmortem room at Treliske, Baker, his body bent close over the autopsy table, smiled.

"Ah."

Duncan left the area she was examining and joined him at the upper end of the table. She was an arrestingly attractive blond who looked far younger than her thirty-five years, so much younger, not to mention female, that she was forever dealing with the question, "When's the pathologist coming?"

She peered at the small bone at the base of the throat to which Baker pointed.

"I'll be damned," she whispered. "The child has a hyoid bone."

"It hadn't fully ossified, but there is a definite fracture of one of the structure's horns."

"Could we have done that during the excavation?"

"Uh-uh. There would be a contrast in color and texture."

AN HOUR LATER, the examining team left the sterile zone and

slumped in the worn easy chairs in the staff room.

"Well done, you two," West said. He'd only observed and yet he, too, was exhausted.

"We got lucky tonight," Baker said. "The hyoid bone generally hasn't fully developed at this age, which I reckon is pre-teen. Only one in ten advances this far by then."

"I just wish I could say for certain whether the child was male or female," Duncan added. "Pelvis not yet distinctive."

She cast a glance at her colleague. "I don't know how you do it, Baker, searching through all those little bones. Give me a real body anytime. Flesh. Blood. Organs. Sometimes this job does me in, you know? My brief from the Coroner is simple: determine cause of death."

"Which in this case is definitely strangulation," West said.

"Right. Fine. But what about that actual former person in there," she said, nodding toward the postmortem room. "How could that happen to someone so young?"

"Does the age really matter?" Baker said. "Someone was killed. We found out how. Problem solved. Christ, I could use a whisky." His arms hung over the arms of his chair like dead eels.

"Maybe you're right. Maybe I haven't been at this long enough to be inured. But our little person in there had barely got started. I can't relate to it—to him or her—as simply a collection of desiccated bones."

"We'll know more soon enough, Jennifer; Oleg's on it," West said.

Oleg Kaminski was a dentist in nearby Wadebridge who also served as a forensic odontologist for the county. Since the National Health Service gave every child in Britain free dental exams at school, it would only be a matter of hours before Kaminski had the records. But since the Coroner would want more than one item of evidence, he'd also taken a tooth and had it sent to the hospital's path lab. With luck, and some pressure from higher up, they'd have the DNA results from the root in twenty-four hours.

West looked at his watch. He wanted to call Davies with the cause of death but couldn't bear to wake her at this hour. He realized he wanted to hear her voice, crabby as it most certainly would be. He decided to wait.

UP ON THE MOOR TOPS later Tuesday morning, the sky was still ragged and stormy and daylight seemed to have stalled in mid-development, as if uncertain about its prospects. Short, vicious squalls raced in off the Atlantic, erasing the horizon as if a shabby wet blanket had suddenly been flung across the seascape. The ragged clouds gave the high tors a short, furious drenching, then flew east. With each squall's approach, the wind would rise quickly, lash the heather-topped summit ridge, rip at the guy-lines of the archaeologists' operations tent, then drop off just as suddenly. There would be shy intervals, as if the heavens were gathering strength, and then the whole process would repeat. In the dark coombes below, ectoplasmic fingers of sea-fog curled through the clefts in the granite coast and wreathed among the stunted trees that huddled for shelter in the narrow valleys, a snaking white miasma that obscured every feature. On a good summer day, the fog, created at the intersection between the cold surface of the sea and the warmer, humid air above, would have burned off by now. Today, it only thickened and rose, as if a fire were bubbling it up from below.

The police had found nothing in the way of evidence among the courtyard houses within the perimeter wall of the Iron Age settlement. At Davies' insistence, and because of Hunter's assistance in the exhumation, they'd reduced their security zone to the immediate area around Dewes Quoit and permitted his team to return to Carn Dewes. So careful were the searchers that Hunter was hard-pressed to discover any obvious damage or disturbance, for which he was grateful. He and Amanda had left the rest of the expedition team behind in the flats he'd leased for them at "Bosun's," a handsomely restored seventeenth century stone maritime warehouse next to the shipyard in Penzance.

He was in the operations tent when heard Amanda shout and came running through yet another downpour. She'd gone to check out the fogou, the tunnel of which tended to flood in heavy rain. He dove down through the narrow entrance and sloshed, bent double, along the stone passage to the dry beehive chamber. Amanda stood rigid just inside the opening and shone her torch across the arched darkness toward the disassembled niche behind which they'd found the stone figurine. Today, however, on the ledge at the base of the niche, there were the guttered stubs of two beeswax candles and a crudely fashioned little doll, smaller than a hand, covered in burlap. Its tiny legs were spread and a two inch hawthorn needle pierced the triangle between them.

Hunter turned to his assistant. "Are you all right?"

"Of course I'm all right," she snapped. "What the fuck's going on here?!"

Hunter looked again at the weirdly threatening scene before them. "I don't think we know."

"Don't be an idiot; of course we do."

"Amanda, listen..."

"No, you listen. The searchers—what did the police call them, 'the fingertip lads'? Why didn't they find this? If they searched the fogou—and they must have—they'd have found this. If they didn't search here, we need to know. Because otherwise this happened just last night, or this morning, after the cordon was lifted and the police left.

"But how could…"

"Call the cops, Brad."

Fourteen

"WHAT I'M SAYING IS that she knew!" Morgan Davies insisted. "She already knew the skeleton was Rebecca Chynoweth's. Give me a reasonable explanation for that, other than guilt or complicity!"

DCI Penwarren rose from the conference table around which the Major Crime Investigation Team had gathered early Tuesday morning and stared out across the rumpled rural landscape beyond the brand new Operational Policing Hub at the edge of the mid-Cornwall market town of Bodmin. Pelting rain blurred the hills and hedgerows and attacked the wall of windows as if by sheer persistence it might wear away the panes and finally gain entry. Penwarren used its rattle on the glass to calm himself.

It was unconscionable that Davies should interview someone potentially associated with their case before they'd even identified the victim's remains. He tried to balance the fact that she had undertaken an unauthorized interview with the near certainty that she did it out of loyalty to him. She knew the case of the missing child plagued him. And he knew she was trying to help him. Still, the infraction demanded a response and, for now, before her colleagues, he resolved to caution, rather than reprimand. That would come later. He turned from the window.

"Be that as it may, detective sergeant, in future you will refrain from interviewing citizens until they have been identified formally as persons of interest, until the postmortem results in a clear victim identification, until the HOLMES II file has been established or, in this case, reactivated, and until this committee has met to determine its investigative strategy and make assignments. This is CID, detective, not some DVD on your telly. Am I clear?"

Morgan, ankles locked beneath the table, arms clasped beneath her formidable breasts, vibrated with anger.

"Sir," she said, the word squeezed through clenched teeth.

Feet shuffled uncomfortably. West was the first to speak.

"With respect, guv, it's hard not to agree with Morgan's logic. As I mentioned at the top, Oleg's dental record search identified the remains as those of the missing Chynoweth girl. We hope to have tooth root DNA results tomorrow morning as well. This so-called 'village wise-woman,' Tamsin Bran, organized and led the protests against the Americans' excavation of Carn Dewes. Why that passionate opposition? Because she was hiding something, specifically, the body of the girl with whose disappearance she's been connected? I would suggest, Sir, in support of Sergeant Davies, that Bran is certainly our most likely suspect at this point."

Davies uncrossed her ankles and one eyebrow rose a fraction, in some combination of surprise and gratitude.

Penwarren ran his left thumb and forefinger down the bridge of his long, narrow nose and said nothing. He was mildly amused at West's burst of chivalry.

"The difference," Penwarren said finally, his voice level, "is that we did not have the dental report at that time. We did not know who the victim was, much less have a suspect. Evidence is what makes a suspect, not guesswork. We still have no evidence. Bran is simply a person of interest. Am I clear?"

Silence.

"Let's move on, then. What have we got on the victim?"

"Girl of twelve, no prior history of doing a runner," Davies said. "We tagged her as a miss-per, initially, but the mother, Judith Chynoweth, claimed the alleged witch, Tamsin Bran, 'disappeared' the girl. Search of the girl's home yielded nothing."

"Yes; her 'home,'" Penwarren said quietly, his eyes focused on the middle distance, remembering. "Such as it was…"

"Yes, Sir," Davies said.

"Makes you hope she'd done a runner after all," Penwarren whispered to himself.

No one around the table said a thing. They all knew their boss had long hoped the girl would turn up.

Now she had.

Penwarren took charge again. "Calum, let's put the TAG boys out to pay visits to witnesses last interviewed when the girl disappeared. Also, I want someone interviewing residents at farms or cottages in the immediate neighborhood of Carn Dewes, in case they've seen something."

Switching subjects, he turned again to Davies. "Where are we on the Newlyn girls?"

"Women, Sir. Though barely, I agree. Victim number one's a cipher. No ID on her person, no dental work and so no records to help us."

"No mis per reports?"

"Thousands of them in this country, yes, and many answering to descriptions similar to our victim: young woman, bottle blond, runaway. But no connection yet. We know the ID of the second victim from dental records. Glasgow lass. Her family want nothing to do with her."

Penwarren ran the fingers of his right hand through his slowly thinning hair, looked away from the group, and said nothing for several long moments. No one interrupted.

"Morgan, I'm short of MCIT detectives here this week," he said when he turned back. "One's on a training course, another on medical leave. Can you lead the suspect team on the Chynoweth case?"

As if automated, all heads pivoted her way in amazement.

"Yes, Sir. Thank you, Sir."

"Good. By the way, I've checked on PC Bates. She discharged herself from hospital yesterday."

"Yes, Sir. I've spoken with her."

"How is she?"

"Not ready for work, but don't tell her that."

Penwarren smiled. "I've asked Penzance if they'll be willing to put her on this case, if she's up to it. I have in mind the young constable's emotional recovery. I reckon the best way to get her back on her feet is to put her to work on this case. I know it's not your usual remit, Morgan, but I want the two of you to work together. You have some confidence in Bates?"

"Yes, Sir. Tough one, she is. And smart."

"Sounds familiar."

There were stifled chuckles.

"Also, she's a trained Family Liaison Officer and we need to track down the dead girl's mother," Davies added.

Penwarren stretched his lanky limbs and rose. "All right, you all know your jobs, let's get to it. By the way, I want the Americans sworn to silence; they've got their work to do, we've got ours. Off you go, then."

He paused. "Detective Sergeant Davies."

"Sir?"

"You will remain for a moment."

Davies flushed. Smirks from some of the other team members. A worried look from West. They filed out.

Penwarren was at the rain-swept window again. Davies stood beside her chair.

"Morgan," he began, still not facing her. "I have great respect for your professional skills or I would not have recommended you for the position you now hold; nor would I have asked you to help lead a part of this latest investigation. I admire your persistence and your intuition. But I will not tolerate loose cannons on my ship. When you go off half-cocked as you did with this Bran woman you not only make a fool of yourself, you place the entire case before us in jeopardy. If Ms. Bran does indeed turn out to be our prime suspect, any solicitor with half a nut in his noggin will ferret out your procedural violation and demand dismissal. By rights, I should put you on suspension. The only reason you're heading the suspect team is that I have no one else available."

He wheeled to face her. "Pull this sort of stunt again and I'll send you down. Are we clear?"

Had there been a lit match in the room, Davies would have ignited, fueled by equal quantities of indignation and humiliation.

"Sir," she said with a quick nod before stalking from the room.

Penwarren shook his head after Davies left. He had a fleeting sense that he would always be defending Davies to his superiors. But he would not report this particular infraction. She was often impossible. She was also relentless and effective. He needed her.

Fifteen

"**YOU CAN ALL GO FUCK** your bloody selves!" Jude Chynoweth shouted as a uniformed police constable pulled her through the reception area toward the exit at West Cornwall Hospital. "Every last one of you!"

It was just after ten on Tuesday morning, two and a half cold, hot, freezing, clammy, shudderingly miserable days after she'd been admitted. She wasn't discharged as recovered; she was ejected for disorderly behavior. The hospital wanted to extend her detox, but they had no authority to do so. Outside the hospital door, she slapped away the PC's arm and stalked off toward St. Clare Street and upper Causewayhead.

She wanted a word with her brother.

Entering Penwith Gothica, she didn't bother to pause at the cashier's counter. She strutted straight to the back and up the stairs to the office… and found it empty. She clattered back down and marched to the register, where Cassandra sat, pointedly ignoring her, sipping a coffee, and reading a battered paperback.

"Where's 'e?!"

Cassandra looked up, telegraphing disinterest. "'Dunno, do I? Hasn't been in last couple of days. Figure he's up to London on a 'buying trip.' Maybe more leather push-up bustiers or pre-torn black lace stockings. Maybe stuff I'm not meant to know about. None of my business, if you get my drift. Me? I open in the morning, ring up the customers, and close out the register at night. That's all I know, okay?"

Jude laid a look on the young woman that would have turned a normal human to stone. "You know a damned sight more, you do. You're just not telling."

Cassandra snapped her book shut and stood. "Look, lady—and I use the term loosely—your brother runs the business upstairs, I run the one downstairs. Got that? He's got his customers, I got mine. Mine are mostly kids trying to find a way of expressin' themselves by lookin' exactly like all their phony Goth or Steampunk mates. His Nibs up there?" she said jerking her head to the stairs at the back, "Pays me well to run the business down here, more'n he ought, but who's complaining, eh? What goes on up there? Nuthin' to do with me. Except you probably know all about that, seein's you're family and all..."

Jude wanted to throttle the woman but the manager towered over her. What's more, the edginess was gaining on her; she needed the stuff again. She clattered out of the shop in her stilettos without another word to the fancy-dress bitch and headed for the squat that she and Brendan and a revolving host of other junkies shared just uphill from the railway station. She walked up Taroveor Road and turned into Belle Vue Terrace, a narrow dead end alley pocked with squat, moldering, two-story Victorian-era terrace houses—two up, two down—many of which had been long since abandoned and, while nominally for sale, would never find buyers. The few residents left on the street, most of them elderly with nowhere else to go, pretended the squatters didn't exist. It was mutual. That was fine with Jude.

She went round the back by way of a rear alley and slipped through the cellar window of one of the empty houses. A radio played above. She recognized the voice of BBC Radio One DJ Fearne Cotton. They listened to radio because Brendan said they couldn't afford a CD player—or the CDs, for that matter, unless they'd stolen them. She liked Fearne's tough East London accent.

She was about to call out to Brendan when she saw a woman's strappy heel on the dusty stair to the floor above. She removed her own heels and, with the music as cover, ascended. In the back bedroom she found Brendan busy shagging some skinny slut she didn't recognize, at least from this angle. The girl was frantic and Jude saw another scene, from long ago, in her mind's eye, and shook it off. Watching this new girl thrash, she knew it wasn't about the sex. Brendan simply wasn't that good. It was the drugs. Cocaine, of course. That's how she'd started with Brendan, too, for the drug-driven sexual rush, for the sense of being so screamingly sensitive and erotically alive.

Now it was this new slag doing the screaming. He hadn't even bothered to completely undress her; a short faded denim skirt was flipped up over her bony hips, a neon pink thong yanked to one side. Jude watched and waited. It wouldn't be long; it never was with Brendan. She waited for him to groan and the girl to collapse beneath him when he popped. She waited, her nerve endings flashing like lightening, as if her touch alone could kill. She waited for him to roll off the girl and onto his back, the way he always did.

And then she pounced. She flew across the room, grabbed the girl's hair, which was dyed with a slash of neon blue on one side, dragged her out of the room, gave her a brutal kick in the ribs, and left her a howling tangle of hopped-up limbs in the hall before she skittered away like a crab.

Brendan Rice-Johnson, former Eton College boy genius long since gone to seed, watched the action as if taking in a play, his arms behind his head, a bemused smile on his swollen lips. When Jude flung herself at him, he didn't even bother to turn away.

"You bloody bastard! You shit!" she yelled as she flailed at him with both fists.

He let her have at him for a few moments, because he always found this sort of scene arousing. Finally, he seized her wrists with the strength of the former crew captain he'd once been, and forced them upward until she cried out. Instantly, he was on top of her chest yanking her blouse and bra to her chin.

"Now look'it what you've gone and done, my tart," he laughed, nodding toward the new erection which throbbed in the hollow between her breasts. "You do know how to set a chap afire, don't you, girl?"

"Fuck off!" Jude yelled, arching her back to buck him from her, to no avail. "RJ," as he was known on the street, was a full sixteen stone of muscle and sinew. He laughed at her writhing and kept her pinned.

"What'r you gonna do about this big problem between us, eh?"

"Get away, you perv!"

"Now, now; two days in the clink…"

"Hospital!"

"Wherever. Don't you tell me you're not hot for me, Jude. I know your needs, luv, and you know I do. Two days and you're…well, let's just say, squirmy, yeah? Unless…oh, wait!...unless there's something else you need even more than me this day? Is there? Is there, Judie?!" He leaned close and grinned.

The woman beneath him spat but hadn't enough breath in her lungs to reach him. Instead, the spittle dribbled from her chin. He could see the desperate hunger in her wide eyes, and it wasn't for air. Or for sex.

"A little jab of something, perhaps, to calm the nerves? But it'll cost you, won't it, luv? What'll you do for me if I play doctor for you, eh? What form of payment? Can you think of anything in that kinky little brain of yours?"

Jude stopped fighting.

She'd do anything.

Sixteen

TAMSIN BRAN DID NOT EXPECT the gentleman at her door. Tegan was not around to warn her.

"Professor Hunter."

"Hello, Ms. Bran."

Desmond appeared and, to her surprise, began peacefully weaving figure eights around the visitor's feet, his purr rumbling like smooth stones rolled in a wooden bowl. The only human she'd seen the cat greet this way was Tegan and she listened to what Desmond was telling her.

"Do come in, professor. Tea?"

She turned without waiting for an answer and he followed her into the big, herb-festooned kitchen. Beyond it, Hunter could see a small study lined with books.

She filled and switched on an electric kettle, then gestured with her head toward the chairs before the hearth. A Persian carpet lay on the flagstone floor, the intricate Islamic pattern of burgundy red, royal blue, ivory, rose, and robin's egg blue worn thin in places but still noble in its beauty.

"The pot will be along in a moment. Will Earl Grey do for you? I prefer it in the afternoon."

Hunter nodded and sat.

"I have...," he began.

"Yes, I know. You have a problem at Carn Dewes. We tried to tell you, tried to warn you. It is a sacred place. But you did not listen."

"Ms. Bran..."

"Tamsin will do, thank you."

Hunter tried to ignore the witch's arresting beauty; her nearly black hair was asymmetrically cut so that it curved close along a knife-sharp jawline on one side while, on the other, it swept downward toward her collarbone, a lightning flash of white accentuating the part of the longer side. Her eyes, deeply kohled, were dark brown flecked with gold. A sharply pointed chin, with just the hint of a cleft, marked the tip of an inverted triangle the other two points of which were the corners of her lips, which curved upwards, catlike, at the outer edges. On this warm summer afternoon, she wore a long, black, thigh length sleeveless tee-shirt with a gold pentangle printed across her modest breasts and jet black Capri-length leggings. Her delicate feet were bare, the toenails, like her carefully manicured fingernails, painted a dark purple. He wondered if witches had any wardrobe alternative to black.

"You opposed my exploration of Carn Dewes," he began. "I couldn't imagine why. It is simply an Iron Age settlement. There are others scattered across these hills. It is historic. It reflects layers of cultures…"

"And is far older than anyone previously suspected, as you have recently discovered."

Hunter hesitated. He could not imagine how she knew. "Nonetheless, I have never seen a reason to also call it 'sacred.'"

Tamsin Bran smiled, faint crow's feet crinkling in the outer corners of her almost iridescent eyes. "Ah, yes; Reason. That is the problem, isn't it, professor?"

"Excuse me?"

The witch returned to the kitchen, poured steaming water from the kettle into a tannin-stained white porcelain teapot, and brought the tray to the sitting area. She said nothing at first, pouring a measure of milk in their respective mugs and then adding the bergamot-fragranced tea.

"You are a scientist and a historian, are you not, professor?"

Hunter lifted his hands as if in surrender. "I am an archaeologist, which is to say, I suppose, that I am both. I plead guilty."

She smiled as she sat. "That's two strokes against you, you see."

"I don't, actually."

"You are, by training and, I suspect, by nature, a creature of reason, a product of the so-called Enlightenment—which I prefer to call 'The Great Blindness'—and of the Scientific Revolution."

Hunter bristled. "What's that got to do with…?"

"Yours is a world in which reality is limited to that which can be observed and replicated by experiment, a world devoid of spirits, even though they are all around us. That is the blindness. The Enlightenment philosophers emerged only a few centuries ago, yes? How long have human societies flourished? For millennia. How did those societies get by without your Enlightenment rationalism? Were there no earlier great thinkers? No Roman or Greek philosophers, no Egyptian scientists and mathematicians, no Sumerian, Babylonian, or Assyrian astronomers or scribes?

"Yet all of them acknowledged a spirit world parallel to experienced reality and had no difficulty integrating the two. Think of your Greek and Roman mythology. Think of Ishtar, the fertility goddess of the Mesopotamian cultures."

"And your point is…?"

"Do you know what a *meme* is?" she asked, avoiding his question. "It's like a gene, but cultural, not biological."

"I know that, in some circles, it is believed to be the mechanism by which ideas and beliefs are passed on from generation to generation…"

"You needn't limit it to 'some circles,' professor. There has been quite a bit of research on the subject. Cultures pass on their understanding of the universe through writing, art, speech, and practices and not only do these beliefs reproduce, they also mutate, like genes. It keeps them current. Of course, like genes, memes can die out, become extinct. Don't you think it curious that true witchcraft—which is to say, reverence and respect for the endless cycle of earth, sun, moon, and the seasons and for our place in those cycles, and the application of substances in the natural world to solve ills of all sorts—have survived for centuries, indeed millennia, with only the slightest mutation?"

"I think you confuse memes with myths."

Tamsin's face hardened. Finally, she said, "The fact is, professor, that you have come here because your spirit is troubled. That is clear. There is power at Carn Dewes. You have experienced it. We tried to warn you."

Hunter rose and stood at the window set deep in the mill's thick stone kitchen wall. Beyond, a stretch of lawn dotted by constellations of the pinkish-white blossoms of English daisies scrolled away to the banks of the mill stream where the flaming orange blossoms of montbretia arced on stiff stems above their knife-blade fronds. There was something almost other-worldly about this hidden, narrow valley. The word "magical" rose in his subconscious. He turned back to the witch.

"There are things happening at Carn Dewes I can't explain, yes. And my work is at risk. But to attribute that to magic? I'm sorry..."

The witch shook her head. "There is a vast difference between witchcraft and magic, professor. Witchcraft, the Old Craft tradition from which I am descended and, more recently, Wicca, both aim to heal and cure, to liberate and protect. We use natural materials of known potency to create powders, suffusions, and the like. We may create charms and amulets. We may cast a circle and call upon the spirits of the Annown to serve someone's need."

"Annown?"

"The otherworld, the world of spirits long departed."

"That's not magic? Aren't you just splitting hairs?"

"Look here, professor. You came here because you are afraid. I can read that, even if you will not acknowledge it. You have reason to be afraid. You've found something important, something which unnerves you. Thus, you come to me as you did many weeks ago, at the beginning of your project. You were not listening then. Are you listening now?"

"This is nonsense."

"Is it? Your spirit tells me otherwise. I am not so much a mind-reader as a spirit reader. You spirit speaks, even if your voice is mute."

"And it says...?"

Tamsin Bran paused. Her eyes had gone pitch-black, as if some light suddenly had switched off behind them. It was some moments before the light returned and she spoke.

"It says that you have found a woman, long hidden, who threatens your work."

"Yes. A girl, apparently."

"Actually, an ancient goddess, I believe."

"No. A girl, I'm told. A skeleton in a shallow grave beneath Dewes Quoit. But that is not why..."

Tamsin Bran leapt to her feet, a hand pressed to her chest. She could read, yes, but she could not see, not like Tegan. Yet now she began to see and suddenly she could barely breathe.

"I thought you were here about the figurine," she whispered. She sank back into her chair.

"How did you know about it...?"

"*You* found her! It was you who found Rebecca!

"Who's Rebecca?!"

Just for a moment, Hunter saw a blue aura flare around Tamsin's head, like the flames of a gas range turned high. He froze. Then the woman across from him slumped into unconsciousness.

The moment passed and when she struggled back into the present she heard Hunter calling her, as if from another room.

"Ms. Bran? *Tamsin*?"

She shuddered and then blinked and found him on his knees before her. "Don't do that again," she snapped.

"Do what?"

"Bewitch me. Don't play stupid; it doesn't suit you."

"Bewitch? Are you sure you're okay?"

Tamsin watched him carefully for a moment, her fingers pressed against her temples, and it came to her. He was a channeler. Professor Bradley Hunter was a conduit for the Annown. He did not know it yet for the simple reason that, until he'd met her, he'd never had a receiver, no one at the other end of the line. Now he did, but whomever, or whatever, was trying to reach her through him had a terrible power. Perhaps it was Rebecca herself.

"I knew the girl had been found. A detective visited me and I read it in her, though she did not admit it. I didn't know you were the one who found her."

Tamsin watched Hunter's face, trying to read deeper.

"I'm glad it was you who found Becca," she said after a few moments. "But you have opened a door to the otherworld now. You may wish you hadn't. Becca may be trying to reach us through you. You are the first chance she has had. There will be messages you will not understand."

"Messages?"

"Signs. Events."

"In that case, there is something I need to share with you, something I came here to ask you about."

Hunter pulled out his mobile and showed her a picture of the tiny pierced doll and the candles. The witch shook her head in confusion.

"The doll is what is known here as a 'poppet.' It is used in certain rites. Have you examined it? Does it contain things? Nail clippings? Hair?"

"I don't know, Tamsin; the police have it."

"The threat of violation is clear. But whose? And by whom?"

"Has Rebecca sent it?"

"No. Though they have great power, the dead can't create dimensional objects. Someone in the here and now is sending this message."

Hunter paused. "And it wasn't you?"

He immediately regretted it. Tamsin looked as if she'd been struck.

"I'm sorry. That was out of line."

The witch recovered, tilted her head to one side and smiled. A gentle smile. Of forgiveness.

"It was a fair question. But no; it was not me. There is something far more dangerous involved here. I wish Tegan were here with us. She has great power, the poor girl. She does not know this yet, but my job is to be her guide and protector. I failed with Rebecca—not that she had Tegan's power—but I failed to protect her. I shall not fail Tegan. She might be able to see who did this. But I can tell you this: this poppet did not come from the Annown."

Seventeen

ON TUESDAY EVENING, Hunter and Jeffers sat at a table at the Admiral Benbow Inn in Penzance.

"Did you know this pub features in Robert Louis Stevenson's *Treasure Island*?" Jeffers asked, reading from the glossy menu.

"What?"

"It's seventeenth century, this pub."

"Looks like a Disney amusement park to me," Hunter grumped, lifting his pint of Sharp's "Doom Bar" ale, its head creamy as a Starbuck's latte. "I'll believe you when Old Blind Pew comes limping through that door and slips me the black spot; that's the only thing missing in this joint." There was a brass-shaded lamp dangling above their table on an old pitch-stained braided rope threaded through an antique wood and brass ship's pulley hooked to a ceiling beam blackened by time. It was meant to add to the overall maritime theme, he guessed, but to Hunter the lamp looked like something that had been hanged.

Amanda looked around the room's softly-lit interior. The pub, midway along Penzance's Chapel Street and just uphill from their lodgings, was like a museum of seafaring history and piracy that also, almost as an afterthought, served food and drinks. She liked it for its warm light and cozy atmosphere but the fact was her boss was right; everywhere you looked, on the walls, in the corners, hanging from the low-beamed ceiling, the place was crammed with a hotchpotch of maritime clutter—everything from genuine antiques, like busty figureheads from schooners wrecked off the peninsula's coast, to phony ship's brasses, ship models, even a small polished brass canon. In Stevenson's tale, the Benbow was the inn young Jim Hawkins's parents managed, but its latest incarnation was like a florid seafaring yarn in desperate need of an editor. Hunter was right; the place was an orgy of maritime kitsch.

"That doll you found this morning," Hunter said into his pint. "It's called a 'poppet.' I visited Tamsin. She says it's used in certain spells or ceremonies."

"*Tamsin* is it? What, you're on first name terms now? May I remind you that this is the woman who led the protest against our dig? If it's a warning, it's from her!"

"She says not."

"And you believe her? What the hell's happened to you, Brad? For all we know she buried the body there, too. Why else fight us so hard?"

"She doesn't look like a murderer to me."

"Murderers never do."

"Look, Amanda, forget about the witch for a moment. I'm much more concerned about what we have uncovered. I don't think we understand it yet."

To his surprise, Amanda smiled and placed her hand on his. "Yes, we do, Brad, and it is priceless. The quartz goddess figurine, the white lady, is a triumph for you. You believed the site was much older and you found the proof."

He pulled his hand away and waved it as if fending off flies. "Yes, yes, we have the figurine, or at least the Royal Cornwall Museum does now. When I say I don't think we understand, I'm talking about the underground complex in its entirety and what it's trying to tell us. For example, why is the corbelled chamber so big when the original entry from the surface—not the Iron Age fogou, but the much earlier creepway we've discovered—was so narrow it barely accommodated a human being? For the simple reason, I suspect, that each individual had to crawl through the creepway as if in supplication before they could finally stand beneath the dome and together summon the birth of spring."

"That's something I don't get."

"What is?"

"If spring always comes, why create a ritual ceremony to ensure its return?"

Hunter smiled for the first time. "Because if you don't, perhaps it won't."

"That's illogical."

"Only to us. For the people who lived here in the Bronze or Iron Age, or pagans like Tamsin, the world consists of repeating cycles: the seasons, the phases of the moon, the changing arc of the sun, birth and death and rebirth. People like you and me, we see time as linear: yesterday, today, tomorrow. We name our defining eras along that same long line—Paleolithic, Mesolithic, Neolithic, Bronze Age, Iron Age and so on—an ordered and labeled march to the future.

"But not the people who lived at Carn Dewes. In their world, everything they comprehended had the shape of infinitely repeating circles, like...like..." He searched for an image. "Like a Slinky toy coiling through time, you know?"

Jeffers nodded, but one skeptical eyebrow rose.

"They saw their welfare as being as dependent upon these cycles as children are upon their mothers. And the Goddess, the mother of all creation, was their deity.

"For what it's worth, though I don't think we can prove it, I think the people who crawled into that chamber, the supplicants, were women. I believe the people who lived here before the Iron Age, and who worshipped the figurine, were matricentric, if not actually matriarchal. They had their warrior chieftains, certainly, the ones they buried beneath the quoits. But women were so obviously the source of new life, not just as mothers within the tribal unit but as tenders of the fields, too, that they were revered. They were the source of all things fertile."

"Which means the figurine--wide hips, saggy breasts—is the earth mother?"

"I think so. Or something like her. And I think the answer lies in the place in which we found it: a carefully-crafted mini-chamber in the shape of...well, what did it look like to you?"

"I don't follow."

"A hollow composed of two inward curving walls, smaller than two cupped hands, pointed at the top, carved in the shape of...?"

And suddenly Amanda saw it. "Oh my God: a vulva," she whispered.

Hunter nodded in assent. "I think the beehive chamber is meant to represent a womb. I suspect at some point the creepway was created to represent the birth canal. And though we know the surface dwellings on this site, in the form of the ruins we now see, were constructed in the late Iron Age and abandoned sometime after the Romans left, I don't think the Iron Age people had any knowledge of the figurine's existence. How could they? We only found it with our scanner."

Amanda's mind raced. "Let's say everything you've proposed here is correct. That's superb intuitive thinking. But where's the poppet come in?"

"It doesn't. That's what makes it so disturbing."

Eighteen

DAVIES AND BATES ARRIVED at Penwith Gothica on Wednesday morning just as a woman opened the shop door for the day. They identified themselves, and the shop manager, who identified herself as "Cassandra," told them "Mr. Chynoweth" would be along straightaway, as deliveries were due this morning. Davies told Bates to chat up the manager.

Meanwhile, Davies prowled the floor and pawed through the sexed-up clothing on the T-stands and rounders that jammed the narrow display space, marveling at the tartiness of it all. She smiled at the brand names: Black Raven, XXXess Punk, Dark Star, Hell Bunny. Had she found such items in a suspect's wardrobe, she'd have begun developing theories about their private predilections. But this was actually street wear; bloody bizarre.

As Cassandra promised, in short order a black BMW 325i with tinted windows pulled up in front of the shop and Kenny Chynoweth, clad to match the car and looking like some lesser undertaker's wayward son, waddled in, coffee in hand. He blinked several times at the unusual morning clientele. Davies presented her warrant card and he managed an unctuous, "How may I be of assistance, officer?"

Davies suggested they find somewhere to chat.

Kenny flashed a Cheshire cat smile, transparently false, and said, "Shall we adjourn to my upstairs office?"

When they reached the bare-floored windowless room, Chynoweth gestured to a cracked leather settee and settled into his vinyl office chair, gripping his desk's laminate edge as if to keep it from levitating. Bates sat; Davies stood.

"I was wondering, Mr. Chynoweth," Davies began, "if you might have some idea of the whereabouts of your sister, Judith? We need to have a word."

Davies watched as Chynoweth released the death grip on his desk and leaned back on his chair, obviously relieved, even amused. What had he been anticipating, she wondered; questions about tax evasion? Something more serious?

"Well, now, Judith and I are not much in touch, you see. Happens in many families, I believe. She chose her course, I chose mine. I started this business," he said gesturing importantly to the floor below, "and she…how shall I put this...chose hers."

"Which is?" Davies asked, knowing full well the answer but interested in his.

A moue of distaste played across the man's puffy lips. Saliva shone in one corner of his mouth, which he erased with a lizard flick of his tongue.

"She…ah…entertains gentlemen, as it were. Or so I'm told. In Newlyn, I believe. As I say, we are not close. Indeed I have not seen her these several months."

"I wonder, then, Mr. Chynoweth, whether you might be able to provide her address. And perhaps her mobile number? Surely she has a mobile for her…entertainment business?"

He took a sip from his coffee. "To be honest, I cannot." His eyes regarded her piteously. "I get word she is still in this area but as to her permanent residence or phone…," he shook his head, bulbous as a cabbage, and shrugged, hands palm upward in a show of helplessness and heartbreak.

"Has she a husband, or a partner, do you know?"

Again, the helpless shrug.

Davies stood. They were wasting their time with this wanker. "I think we shall trouble you no longer, Mr. Chynoweth; you have been very helpful." She let the sarcasm hang in the air. Chynoweth rose and offered his hand, which Davies ignored. She turned to the door, then turned back again.

"By the way, Mr. Chynoweth, where were you four nights ago?"

Chynoweth considered. "Let's see, then. That's Mazey Day Eve, innit? Golowan is a big weekend for us. Huge. Hammered we were, here in the shop. Then, after I closed up, I joined the rest of the city in the parade, to be honest."

Davies smiled at the "honest."

"Any witnesses?" Bates asked.

He grinned and she noticed his teeth were bad. "Hundreds, I should think, wouldn't you? Lord, the streets were packed."

"And after the festivities?"

"Went straight home, didn't I?"

"And that would be where?"

"Morab Road, just opposite the council library."

"Convenient, that," Davies said.

"Ma'am?"

"You and the library. Great books and all that."

"Why I took the flat, innit?"

"No doubt."

Davies held him in her gaze and let him squirm.

"Unless you are making deliveries to your shop, Mr. Chynoweth, let me remind you this is a pedestrian-only street and that Beemer of yours outside may well be ticketed and towed at any moment."

"BLOODY OLEAGINOUS WASTE OF HUMANITY," Davies mumbled as she and Bates walked back to the police station. "Makes me want to get my clothes laundered straightaway."

"He's a liar, too," Bates said.

"Oh?"

"That shop manager, Cassandra? Told me our lad's big sister'd been in just a couple of days ago, and in a bad way as well. Drugs, she figures."

"Why'd she mention that, I wonder?"

"I get the feeling she's frightened."

"Well done, Terry."

"You didn't tell Chynoweth about the dead girl," Bates observed.

"No. I didn't."

Davies said nothing more for a few minutes and Bates didn't press. They crossed Clarence Terrace and headed down Penalvern Drive toward the police station.

"Can you take a stroll with me along the Newlyn quays tonight?" Davies asked finally. "Trawlers will be unloading. I figure our Judith will be trolling for turns…"

"Just say when. It's usually not this hard to track down next of kin..."

"How long you been an FLO?"

"Trained a year ago. To be truthful, family liaison isn't my fave. It takes a toll. But it's something to move me up in the force."

Davies admired her ambition but didn't envy Bates's assignment. FLO's almost always brought bad news—someone dead, someone arrested. It suggested the woman's core was tough, despite her gentle affect. She liked Bates and had come to respect her. Her questioning of Chynoweth had been spot on.

"Meet me at the south quay at ten. Light will be fading then. The girls will be out, if the rain lets up."

Nineteen

IT WAS JUST AFTER NOON on Wednesday when, having done for now with Kenny Chynoweth, Davies pulled into the farmyard at Trerane.

She'd returned because something was nagging her about the attack on PC Bates. Why hadn't Bates and Williams noticed the arrival of the attacker?

She logged in with the latest poor sod assigned to guard the quoit and began circumnavigating the slopes. She found what she was looking for on the west side, overlooking the Atlantic—a faint path barely wide enough to accommodate a sheep, twisting through the thickets of gorse and heather. The ground was composed of bone-pale granite rubble weathered to the consistency of stale breadcrumbs. She followed it downhill and found that it eventually joined a tractor path leading north to the little cluster of stone farm buildings at Higher Grumbla, on the minor road between St. Just and Sancreed. It was in the soft verge above a drainage ditch, where the nearly invisible path met the farm track, that she found the faint partial print of a lugged boot, not completely obliterated by the previous day's rain. She stuck a few gorse branches in the earth around it, laid her jacket atop them like a tent, flipped open her mobile, and called in a SOCO team to take an impression.

Then, cursing her former years as a smoker, she huffed back up and over Carn Dewes again and descended to the Trerane farmyard. She was about to open her car door when she caught the flash of a ghostlike face at the front window of the farmhouse. Instantly, the face disappeared. She shut the car door and approached the house.

It took a while to flush the gent out. A sharp rap on the weathered door of the old stone cottage produced nothing.

"Hello, Sir?!" Davies called. "Police! Just a word, please!"

She waited almost a minute until, with a crack like a limb being broken, the gray oak door opened just wide enough to reveal a cloudy blue eye.

A wispy voice said, "What you be wantin' with all this clatter? Leave us'n be!"

She approached the door slowly and held up her warrant card. "Good day, Sir, detective sergeant Morgan Davies from Penzance. I know you must be busy, what with the farm an' all, but I wondered if I might have a word?"

"Paid my taxes, I have. Get away!"

"I'm sure you did, Sir, but that's not the purpose of my visit."

"What is it, then?!"

"A word with you about anything you've seen above, on Dewes Tor."

"Seen plenty there, I have."

"Perhaps we might have a bit of a chin wag about all that?"

He pushed the reluctant door open a bit wider. "Haven't used this door in ages," he said, looking at it as if it, too, were a stranger. "Not since the missus passed, y'see." The diminutive old man, with bent back and wispy silver hair circling his head like a halo in a windstorm, must have been nearly ninety. Leaning on a walking stick, he led the way through a dark hallway to a kitchen which, to Davies's astonishment, sparkled like the Truro postmortem room on a slow day.

His name, he told Davies, was Jakes. He looked back at the ancient front door as if it had appeared only this day. "No visitors anymore is why we don't use tha' door," the old man continued. "You be the first in, well, I reckon I dunno. We come and go through the back, we do."

"We?"

"Shadow'n me."

Near the back door, the gray muzzled head of an ancient Border collie lifted slowly over the lip of a woven willow basket and rested there, as if after great effort. Considering for a moment whether this unexpected alteration in the normal pattern of things required its attention, the dog finally hauled itself to its feet, stepped out as if in slow motion, and shuffled uncertainly toward the visitor. It sniffed around Davies's shoes for a moment, uttered a soft, "Woof," and collapsed to the lino kitchen floor, rolling onto its bony back.

"Wants a bit of a cuddle, Shadow does," Jakes said, smiling. "Guess you're okay, then."

Davies scratched the old dog's tummy a bit, rewarded with much tail wagging. After a moment the dog sighed and promptly fell asleep.

"Mr. Jakes," she began.

"Merlin."

"Pardon?"

"Merlin. Merlin Jakes."

"You're joking."

"What everyone says," he said, shaking his head slowly as he lowered himself into a simple oaken armchair. It was nearly black with age but had a well-preserved reed seat, upon which lay a thin, faded, needlepoint cushion. The chair was easily eighteenth century, she guessed, possibly older. Its match stood on the other side of a small, round, pine kitchen table, its surface scrubbed so assiduously over the years that its hardest grain lines were raised and rippled across the surface like the veins on the old man's hands. Against one wall, an ancient Welsh kitchen dresser with tiers of plate racks and a pot board base displayed china platters and serving pieces in blue Delft porcelain. The dresser was dusted and polished to what Davies suddenly realized was the highest point the slight old man could reach. Above that, cobwebs.

"Well, sit down, sit down; no standin' on ceremony in this house. What about the bloody tor, eh?" The old man did not offer tea, as if he'd lost the habit, and Davies said nothing.

Davies approached the subject slantwise. "You said you've seen things..."

"Aye, no doubt, over the years."

"What sorts of things, Sir, if I may ask?"

Jakes said nothing. Davies let the silence grow.

Finally, the old man nodded and giggled. "High jinks up high is what I think."

"Sir?" She wondered if Jakes was up to this.

He looked up. "Lights at night."

"Fires?"

"Nah, flickered, they did. Came and went. Candles, I reckon. Maybe torches. Moving' about. Disappearin'. Then showin' up again. 'Specially full moons."

"What do you reckon, Merlin?"

"Reckon witches, I do."

"Witches! Ever have a look-see?"

"Anger the spirits? Not a chance, girl, not a chance. They dance up there; usn's stay down here. Right, Shadow?"

The dog did not stir. Davies let more time pass.

"Reckon it's that witch, over St. Euny way, callin' up the spirits."

"Tamsin?"

"*Tamsin?* Never heard 'a that one. No, Melwyn. Melwyn Bran, she's called, though she must be gettin' on now. Proper witch she is, all right. We all turn to her, we do, whatever the problem. Bloody brilliant, she is. Why, I remember once…"

"Did she visit Carn Dewes?" Davies interrupted.

"Oh aye. 'Specially yon fogou. Sometimes with others, mostly on her own. Often stopped in to say hello."

"Has she been up on the tor recently, Merlin?"

"She has, by God, just after the missus passed."

"Was that recently?"

The old man looked momentarily confused. "Nah. Some time back. Few months? Hard to remember, really. Things changed after that."

"I'm sure they did…"

Jakes peered off into a cloudy past.

"There was screamin,' " he said suddenly. "Never heard that before."

"You could hear down here?"

"Still night, it was, new moon. Not like usual for tha' witch. Pitch black, nuthin' stirrin'. Noise didn't last, though. Maybe 'twas a chant or suchlike. Never know with witches, see what I mean?"

What Jakes meant, Davies realized, was that he'd been too frightened by the sound to ascend the few hundred meters or so to the top of Carn Dewes on the darkest night of the month. She changed the subject. "Have you seen lights since then?"

"There was you folk…."

"But before that?"

Jakes seemed to struggle to recall. Finally, he said, "Someone's up there summat' regular. At night. Comes from the west, I reckon, not through the yard like Melwyn done. Rough footpath up from the Sancreed-St. Just road, there is. Takes that, I reckon.

"I know the path."

"Do you, now? Clever girl."

"Any idea who it might be, Sir?

The old man shook his head. "Can't climb up there anymore. Heart, you see. Figure it's that Melwyn. Maybe she don't want to trouble me anymore, now the missus is gone. Fine with me, that is. Thoughtful, like."

"What was your wife's name?"

"Millie. A beauty, she was, and they cows loved her, they did…"

Jakes seemed now to wilt, as if talking with another human was so novel that it had drained him dry. Or perhaps he was remembering his late wife. Shadow noticed, too, and rose and nudged Jake's leg.

"Nap time, is it Shadow?" he mumbled to the dog. "All right then..."

The man and the dog shuffled off to a ground floor room that held a neatly-made single bed. Jakes seemed to have forgotten his guest and Davies didn't remind him.

Twenty

LIKE SALTED PILCHARDS layered in a barrel, Newlyn's quays were packed tight with returned fishing vessels on Wednesday night. They were rafted together three or four deep along the length of the docks. In addition to the cuttlefish boats, there were beam trawlers with articulated masts mounted amidships both starboard and port, side trawlers that dragged trawl doors on either side of a yawning net, and smaller gill netters and long liners. In the spotlights along the quay, their brightly painted, snub-nosed hulls shone like a maritime rainbow: turquoise blue, royal blue, fire engine red, English mustard yellow, rusty orange, emerald green. Most of them were tied up to the Mary Williams Quay, the newer of the two docks and the best equipped.

By ten, the high summer sun had slipped behind the steep hill at the back of the harbor but the overhead lights blazed. Pallet loaders scurried around like wharf rats, carrying red plastic tubs stuffed with iced fish for the predawn commercial auction only a few hours away. The air was thick with the stench of diesel and the tang of fresh fish.

DS Davies and PC Bates picked their way among the longline tubs and gill net rolls and found Judith Chynoweth with two other Toms in the shadows of the ice house, smoking and looking simultaneously bored and avid. Davies found the notion of hookers on a fishing dock blackly funny. Even if it were not the fact that the people swarming the quay were universally male, the women here would have stood out, hook ready. For one thing, they were wearing stiletto sandals, not rubber boots. For another, the rest of their raiment was skimpy at best. Davies thought it was lucky the evening was warm. These women were older than the two dead girls resting on refrigerated stainless trays in the Treliske mortuary. She wondered if they even knew about their deaths.

Seeing them approach, two of the women melted into the crush of men and moving equipment. Chynoweth remained, though, her pinched face defiant. Davies recognized her from the photos of her former arrests for soliciting.

"Got rozzer writ all over you, you do," she called out. "What you after here, anyway, a payoff?" Her voice was raw from years of smoking. "Got the wrong girl for that, I can tell you!"

Bates said nothing. Davies stood at a right angle to Chynoweth, effectively creating a box, and crossed her arms beneath her breasts. Judith had one leg bent, her high heel pressed against the ice house wall to show off a bit of leg. The skirt was miniscule, the leg so emaciated Davies thought it would have been better covered. Now she set the foot down and faced them. Davies watched as the woman's shiny eyes danced in their sockets. She was already high. It was drugs that drove most them into the life, but maybe it was also a necessity in this line of work. Davies showed her warrant card, which the woman ignored.

"Would I be correct in thinking you are Judith Chynoweth?" Davies began.

"What if I was?" Chynoweth spat, flicking her cigarette to the slick, fish scale-sequined pavement.

"We'd like to have a word, then. At the station."

"Bugger off," she hissed, straightening and thrusting out her chest. "I ain't done nuffin' wrong here; I'm just takin' in the local sights. Big night, you see, when the boats come in."

Davies said, "I'm sure it is."

Bates stepped forward, her approach calculated, closing the box. She spoke in a voice warm as an embrace. "Ms. Chynoweth, ma'am; we believe we may have news about your missing daughter, Rebecca."

Judith Chynoweth stiffened and pressed herself against the wall of the ice house as if trying to become one with it. It was not the reaction Davies or Bates had expected. Nor had either of them thought the woman to bolt, which was exactly what she did next. Davies tried to throw a block, but Chynoweth danced away. It was the high heels that did her in. Only yards away, one foot slid on the slick pavement and she was down, but crawling, crablike, away from them. Bates moved to lift her but the woman lunged, teeth bared, arms flailing. Davies whipped the woman's right arm behind her, marched her back to the ice house, introduced her face to its wall, and cuffed her.

"Call in a section five public order offence," she barked, but Bates was already on it.

JUDITH CHYNOWETH'S BEHAVIOR at the Newlyn quay had been so bizarre and violent that Davies, with Penwarren's assent, had her placed in protective custody at Camborne, where there was a police nurse available to monitor her for the night. It had just gone eight Thursday morning when Davies and Bates entered her cell.

Chynoweth leapt to her feet. "You got no right keepin' me here!"

"Good morning," Davies said, ignoring the outburst. "I trust you had an uneventful night and a good breakfast?"

"Piss off!"

Bates, in her role as FLO, stepped in, for which Davies was grateful. She wanted to throttle the woman.

"Ms. Chynoweth, I wonder if you recall why we stopped to chat with you on the quay in Newlyn last night?"

"Harassment, it was, plain 'n simple. Same as always. Just trying to get by, we girls are…boats'd just come in and you all buggered it."

"That's not why we came to see you. You don't remember?"

Jude looked confused, then reverted to aggression. "Remember you draggin' me offa the quay and haulin' me up to this rathole, is what I remember. Like anyone's gonna sleep with that fuckin' light always on above."

"For your protection, that is, actually." Davies said. "That and the camera."

Jude jerked her head upward, birdlike, and scanned the ceiling before she saw the tiny camera eye, beside the bright light.

"No bloody privacy, either! I know my rights and you can't hold me. I'm leavin'."

"Ms. Chynoweth," Bates said with a sudden firmness that got the woman's attention, "we looked for you in Newlyn because we have news about your missing daughter, Rebecca. We thought you'd want to know."

Judith Chynoweth thought she could hear an echo of this same story from the recent past but she couldn't place it. She was getting too twitchy.

Bates soldiered on. "We have found your daughter, but I am afraid the news is not good."

Chynoweth stared.

"Which is to say that police have found her remains, up on the moor tops," Davies announced. "Which is to say: she's dead."

Bates shot her sergeant a black look, but Davies had chosen her words to break the woman's shell and get a reaction. She got it.

Chynoweth unfroze. "Way back then," she began, jerking her head to the left as if to illustrate the passage of time, her voice rising like a storm, "I bloody well *told* you lot it was all that *witch's* doin'!"

"Sit down, Ms. Chynoweth," Davies ordered.

To her surprise, the woman obeyed. "Your daughter was not bewitched, as you claimed at the time. Our preliminary investigation suggests she was strangled."

"By that witch, I'm tellin' you!" Her face was livid.

Davies thought she'd seen everything, but this was a new one. The news that the woman's daughter had been murdered had sped by her like an engaged cab in the night. Any other mother would have hoped her girl was just a runaway. Any other mother would have prayed for her eventual return. But this daughter wasn't returning. The woman's—the *mother's*—only response was anger with the police. Was she so genuinely in shock she could not react emotionally and was simply reverting to the story she'd repeated to herself all these months? Or had she known all along?

Bates asked Chynoweth whether there was someone who could look after her while she came to terms with this news. The woman snorted.

"Your brother, perhaps? Kenwyn Chynoweth?"

Her head snapped around but she said nothing.

"May we have a car take you home, then?"

Suddenly, Chynoweth was wary. "Don't need you lot sniffin' around my 'ome," she snapped. "I'll take the bloody train." She rose again. "I'm leavin' unless you got some reason to keep me. And gimme back my purse."

"We will be in touch as we learn more, Ms. Chynoweth," Davies finally said. "Is there somewhere we can reach you when we do?"

The woman paused at the door of the cell.

"No."

Twenty-One

JUST BEFORE TEN, Cassandra found Kenny's sister pacing in front of Penwith Gothica, trailing cigarette smoke like a locomotive. Jude still wore her "evening wear," as she liked to call it.

"When's 'e comin'?" Jude snapped as Cassandra approached.

Cassandra, in her usual black work garb, stepped around Jude, unlocked the shop door, entered, and moved to shut it behind her, but not quickly enough.

"Hey!" she yelled, grabbing a skinny arm as Jude slithered through the gap, "We ain't open yet."

As Cassandra tried to eject her, Jude pulled her forward and rammed a bony knee into the younger woman's belly. Winded, but her hand still clenched around Judith's arm, Cassandra twisted and flipped the older woman to the floor. She'd taken training.

"Make one more move, bitch, and I'll rip your fuckin' head off, you hear?! 'Cause I bloody well know how and I can hardly wait!"

"Call him," Jude pleaded, her voice almost childlike as she scrabbled for safety.

"Call him yourself; he's your fuckin' brother!"

"My daughter. His niece. She's dead."

KENNY CHYNOWETH FOUND his sister stretched out on the settee in his office, smoking and staring at the peeling ceiling. She'd ground her used butts into the bare wood floorboards.

"Found our Becca, they did, finally," his sister said to the ceiling. She blew smoke and flicked cigarette ash. "Or what's left of her I guess."

"What?"

"Dead. Up on the moors, rozzers say."

"I'm so sorry," Kenny said. As he sat, the groan of his office chair sounded more genuine.

Jude swung her legs from the settee and nailed her stilettos to the floor. "I don't want your fuckin' 'sorry,' you bloody useless excuse for a brother; I want your help!"

Kenny shrugged, palms raised. "What do you expect me to do?"

"What I expect is for you to get me something on that murdering witch. This is your bloody niece were talkin' about here, the one you looked after when I was…unavailable."

Kenny shook his head, as if already exhausted before the day had even truly begun. *Unavailable.* He liked that. And did Jude think the police didn't already have her in their sights?

"What could I possibly do?" he said. "It's been a year or more."

"Search her place! Find proof!"

"Of what, Jude? Police said they'd nothing on her."

"Becca worked for her for months. There's gotta be some sign of her there, some clue the idiot rozzers wouldn't understand."

Kenny looked away and heaved a sigh. "Look, Jude; Becca's gone. We know that now. What do you get out of this? What are you after?"

"You don't get it, do you? I'll lose my child benefit, I will!"

"You're still claiming it?!" Kenny shook his head in amazement.

"'Course I am. Bloody Social Services never made the connection and I wasn't about to correct them. Eighty quid a month, it is. Now they've found her it'll be gone. I want compensation!"

Kenny leaned back in his chair, scratched his belly, and did the math. "So you got, what, a thousand quid this last year offa Becca by keepin' your mouth shut about her being missing and now you want more?"

"Loss of income is what it is!"

"And tell me, Jude. Let's say I do go snooping around the witch's place. What's in it for me, eh? Seems like I'm takin' all the risk…"

"I'll tell you what's in it for you," Jude snarled. She was perched on the edge of the leather settee and pointing a shaky finger at him, thin and sharp as a shiv. "I know enough about your little business enterprise up here to get you put away for a long time. You'll go search for me or you're done for."

She rose and walked out, her heels like gunshots on the old wood stairs.

Kenny came down a little while later just as a striking brunette in what looked like safari clothes walked out the front door.

"Hey, Kenny!" Cassandra called from the counter. "Need to ask you something."

With other things on his mind, he drifted toward the till. Cassandra was still looking toward the door.

"Who was that?" he said, following her gaze.

"American lady; archaeologist working up at someplace called Carn Dewes, which I never heard of. Tight little body. Figure her for a runner."

"Fancied her, did you, you twisted dyke?" Kenny leered. "Tight little body an' all?"

"Oh, piss off—too mannish for me and terrible chipped nails."

"Tragic flaws."

"Anyway, she shows me this picture on her mobile: it's a little doll covered in brown burlap. Female. Says it's a 'poppet' and wants to know if we carry them in our pagan line. I told her we didn't. You ever seen anything like that in your catalogues—a little burlap doll?"

He turned toward the door again. "Nah. I'd have remembered," he said finally. "Burlap? It'd never sell anyway, even to the pagan folks. Too primitive."

"It was primitive, all right; big thorn stuck right up the doll's you-know-what!"

"You do get coarse, Cassie."

"I'm just sayin'. Nasty is what it was."

Twenty-Two

SHORTLY AFTER IT OPENED for business, Morgan Davies sat at a table at the Cornwall Council's registration office, just off Alverton Road in Penzance, and pawed through two boxes of death certificates from the previous year. The files were a disgrace. They should have been available online, but the government's austerity measures had so savaged the budgets of local authorities that many services—routine record-keeping being one of them—had fallen by the wayside, especially death certificates. The subjects, after all, no longer voted.

In a way that she sensed was an indicator of her own advancing age, Davies much preferred working through the physical documents anyway. It gave them a tangible reality. Death certificates you could hold in your hands said to her: this person existed, lived, and finally died and this is the proof of that history. There was a certain justice in that, in a paper certificate, almost like an honor given postmortem. And she understood at some level that this was the same reason she had become a detective—to give validity to victims, to honor them by her investigations. It was not enough for her to get perpetrators convicted; she wanted to vindicate the victims: do it long and often enough and maybe it absolved some of your own sins, maybe even avenged past injustices.

She was a bit stunned by the sheer number of people who died every day in the little precinct. The boxes were crammed with records, none of them precisely chronological. It took nearly an hour, but she finally found the certificate for Mildred Jakes: cause of death, pneumonia, the commonest killer of old people whose multiple ailments pushed them over mortality's edge. The date was June nineteenth of the previous year, barely a week before Golowan.

DAVIES WAS BACK at the Bodmin headquarters just before noon.

DCI Penwarren was on the phone while the Major Crime Incident Team gathered in the incident room.

"Yes, Sir; of course I understand the urgency. Our best people are on it. Yes, Sir, as soon as we have something..." Penwarren looked at his phone. The caller had rung off.

"The Chief?" Davies asked, smiling.

"Seems obsessed with the notion that we hold back critical information. We should be so lucky. Have we any information, Morgan? About *anything*?"

"Early days yet, boss. The dead girl's mother is so bent she hasn't even asked about her daughter's remains, not that we'd release them yet. She's totally focused on police incompetence as the reason the girl wasn't rescued from whatever or whoever caused her death."

"Splendid." Penwarren turned to West. "What do we have from forensics?"

"Oleg's confirmed that the DNA from the victim's tooth is consistent with the dental ID. We have two points of proof that it's Rebecca Chynoweth, which should satisfy the Coroner. Meanwhile, forensics are also examining the cloak the girl was wrapped in. And I've got my pollen and etymology specialist testing it as well to see if perhaps the body was moved from elsewhere before burial. Results as soon as possible. Meanwhile, the knuckle-draggers found nothing despite hours of sifting."

Penwarren's eyes narrowed. "I assume you're referring to our Tactical Aid Group?"

West grinned. "SOCO's nickname for the big boys..."

"Lose it, Calum."

The grin vanished.

Morgan thought she saw a blush on Calum's cheeks.

Penwarren swiveled back to Davies. "And you've nothing yet on the Newlyn murders?"

"Beyond my previous report, no, Sir. The first victim is as yet unidentified, the second identified, but rejected by family, about to be cremated, and returned to them nonetheless.

"That poor lass..."

"Both of them, Sir. Like they were dispensable..."

"Yes. Yes. I know. I'll fill in the Chief."

Constable Bates, who'd thus far been silent, said, "Excuse me, Sir, but I keep thinking about the mother, Judith Chynoweth. Maybe she's just deflecting attention from herself with this blame game about her missing daughter. Isn't it possible she's the killer?"

"A good thought, Terry, but unless you and Morgan have information to the contrary, I gather Judith Chynoweth has no known connection to ancient sites or pagan rites."

"Sorry, Sir."

"No apology needed. It was a good question. At this point, every question is a good one. What else have we got, people?"

"There is one thing, boss," Davies said. "I met the old widower at Trerane farm below the tor. Not the most reliable witness, but he says witches have used Dewes Tor for years, or at least one has: Melwyn Bran—our Tamsin's own mother, according to county records. She's long since passed but these nighttime rites, which he notices because of flickering lights on the tor, continue. The daughter, I'm thinking."

"Easily ascertained. Visit her."

"Full search?" she asked.

"No probable cause yet for a magistrate to issue a warrant. Just keep your eyes open. And take Terry here with you."

"There's more, Sir," Davies continued. "Seems old Jakes heard a scream one night; remembers it because it was shortly after his missus died. Wasn't sleeping well is how he heard it. Her certificate shows she died just a few days before Rebecca Chynoweth disappeared."

There was silence for a moment and Penwarren stared out the window. *It all keeps gathering around Bran...just like before...*

"Anything else, Sir?" Davies asked.

The DCI tore himself away from his thoughts. "What? No. Carry on, people. Well done."

After they filed out he was still thinking about the buried girl.

And the witch.

Some There Are Who Doubt

Twenty-Three

DAVIES BLASTED HER FORD ESTATE along the minor road from St. Euny back to Penzance. She and Bates had just spent an unsettling half hour with Tamsin Bran.

It was Tamsin herself, not the girl, Tegan, who'd answered the door. Tamsin glanced briefly at Davies, but her attention was drawn to Bates. She asked them both to follow her to the kitchen and, as was her habit, offered tea. The other two women declined.

"If you don't mind, then, I'll make some for myself."

Davies figured she was buying time.

While Bran busied herself with the kettle, Davies prowled around the mill.

Cup finally in hand, Bran gestured to the upholstered chairs that faced the massive hearth and the two women sat.

"So, inspector, you return..."

"Sergeant, Ms. Bran."

"Not for long, I promise you...and you've bought someone else this time," she said nodding to PC Bates. "Someone injured in body and spirit." She smiled at Bates.

Bates blinked.

Davies shifted the subject. "We're here, Ms. Bran, because the remains found a few days ago are indeed, as you guessed, those of Rebecca Chynoweth, your former trainee—is that the right term?"

"It is not. And I did not guess."

"Then what would be the right term for your relationship with Rebecca Chynoweth, Ms. Bran?" Davies asked, ignoring the other correction.

"She did for me, same as Tegan does; cleaned, swept, ran a few errands. Good, capable girls, the both of them, and ignored or abused at home."

"Abused, Ms. Bran?"

"I could read it in them. Their pain. I meant to provide safety and work that would give them confidence in themselves."

"And is that all you gave them, Ms. Bran?"

"Pardon?"

"Did you not also initiate them into the secrets and practices of your occult arts as—what do you call yourself?—'village wise woman?' Were they not your understudies, as you were once for your own mother, Melwyn?"

The witch absorbed the challenge and studied Davies for a few moments. "You have no children, do you detective?" she asked.

Morgan felt her color rise. "I do not, and that is not an answer."

"Actually, it is part of one, if you will permit me to continue."

Davies flicked a wrist. If the woman wanted to talk, she'd let her.

"For the record, I have no children, either. But here is what I ask you to consider: If you did, you might have your little girl measure out the ingredients for a cake, yes? You might even let her help mix them. But you would not let her near the oven, because there is danger there. Rebecca loved to help, as does Tegan, who is far more innately talented. But I have never involved either of them in any of the spells or rites I am asked to perform for my clients. They are not permitted near my oven, as it were."

Davies considered the more desperate ways this woman might have "helped" these abused children but Bates spoke first, breaking her line of thought. "Do you frequent Dewes Tor, Ms. Bran?"

"I do," the witch answered immediately.

"How often, may I ask?"

"At the equinoxes and solstices, and often at the full moon. It is a spiritually powerful place at those times."

"What does that mean?"

"It means, simply, that the spirits of the Annown will come to you, speak to you, help you, if you know how to ask."

"And is one of those spirits," Bates pressed, "a giant, robed in red, with the bearded head of a horned ram?"

It was as if Tamsin had been slapped. She shook off the blow and focused on the young uniformed constable. Davies cleared her throat. The witch ignored her.

"You have seen it?"

"I was attacked by it," Bates said as calmly as if she were describing meeting a bus at a scheduled stop.

Bran was silent. Bates waited. Davies vibrated with impatience.

Finally, the witch looked at them each in turn. "There are things you need to know."

Davies was immediately suspicious but she shrugged. "As you wish. Bates, notes please." The PC opened a notebook.

"The Old Craft," Tamsin began, "at least as practiced by my mother and me and those before us, as well as others here in West Penwith, has existed for centuries, if not millennia. Times change, but the day-to-day needs of common folk do not, whether it is trouble in the body, trouble in the soul, or trouble in their work. They come to wise women like me much as you might to a doctor, or a therapist, or a solicitor. We try to help, as we have for as long as anyone hereabouts can remember. It has always been thus. But in the years after the Second World War, a charismatic pagan called Gerald Gardner founded what is today known as Wicca. Gardner spent years gathering spiritual traditions from Persia, ancient Egypt, the Middle Ages, and up into to the recent past in Italy and France. He sorted and systematized them into something like a religion which has become quite popular. You may have heard of it. The Old Craft is not directly related to Wicca, but we hold quite a few basic beliefs in common.

"Like the Old Craft, Wicca celebrates the cycles of the seasons and of the sun and moon. But it has its own practices and rites, many created or adapted anew by Gardner and his associates. For example, in Wicca the highest spirits of the natural world are the Goddess and her consort, the Horned God, the latter typically represented as having a bearded ram's head."

Davies saw Bates's eyes widen.

"To Wiccans, the two represent the duality of nature: male and female, sun and moon, light and dark, black and white, good and evil, and so on. In the Old Craft, we also recognize this duality, but we see male and female as two component parts of the singularity of life, almost like the Asian yin and yang. The two are in us all."

"What about the Horned God?" Bates demanded.

"As I said, he is the male half of the duality in Wicca, an obvious figure of sexual potency, as the Goddess is the symbol of fertility and rebirth. The new craft, Wicca, has its initiates pass through three degrees of study and practice. It is rigorous and takes some years. The final ritual, part of the third degree, is the so-called 'Great Rite,' which consists of either the literal or symbolic sexual union of the Horned God and the Goddess of the coven of local believers. Since those of us from the Old Craft already accept this unity as a given in all of us, we have no need to ritualize it."

She reached out and touched Bates's right temple, just below her hatband, then withdrew her hand. "You were not attacked by the Horned God, constable. The Goddess and her consort are but symbols of natural forces. They do not and cannot act against individuals. They exist to represent, not to be. And they do not cause harm; indeed they are expressions of harmony, of balance."

"Then this demon?" Bates said.

"An impostor."

"But that head!"

"A ceremonial replica, readily obtained from any number of online pagan websites."

Bates struggled to take this in.

Davies interrupted, "And have you such a replica, Ms. Bran…for ceremonial purposes?"

Tamsin was unruffled. "I do not, detective, though you are free to continue searching my home, as you did earlier. I am not a Wiccan. As I've just explained, in my spiritual world the god and the goddess are combined; as they are in each of us, both the male and the female."

Tamsin Bran leaned back into her chair. "For example, you, detective, have suffered terrible losses in your life, and at a very young age. Deaths, I believe. As you matured you have relied on the male strength of the Horned God within you. You have not accepted your Goddess half, for you feel to do so is to risk danger and be seen as weak. You have chosen aggression over conciliation, attack over surrender. It has served you well, this way of being, at least in your police work. But not, I believe, in your life beyond work."

Bates watched Davies. It seemed to her that the detective was struggling, almost physically, with Bran's reading of her.

"My private life is not under discussion here, Ms. Bran," Davies said finally, uncrossing her legs, planting her feet, and leaning toward the witch. Her eyes flared but her voice was wintry. "What is under discussion is the death of a young girl who was in your employ at the time of her disappearance just over a year ago, and the discovery of her remains in a place you frequent. What is under discussion here, is whether you deliberately or accidentally killed Rebecca Chynoweth and buried her beneath Dewes Quoit."

Tamsin Bran sat back, blinked twice, then rose.

"If you have no further questions, detective, I believe it is time for you and your injured colleague to leave. I am happy to help you however I can, for I loved Rebecca, as I do Tegan, but I will not be harassed. And as you make your way out, for I shall not accompany you, consider this: I have nothing to do with Dewes Quoit. There is no magic there. My spiritual center is the beehive chamber in the fogou of the Carn Dewes settlement and always has been, as it was my mother's. Good day and blessings on you both."

DAVIES WAS AT HER DESK in the overcrowded, open-plan CID office at the Penzance BCU later that afternoon when Bates approached. Davies had been pretending to study paperwork but was really grinding away at the damned witch's eerie telephoto lens into her history and her heart. It infuriated her to be "seen." Morgan did not care to be known. She'd shared her history and her heart with Max only, and look how that turned out...

Bates waited and Davies spun to face her.

"What?"

Bates smiled. She was getting used to working with "Miss Congeniality."

"Ms. Bran is correct. Horned god heads are readily available from, among other places, an online internet shopping site based just up-county in Plymouth called, 'Astral Play.'"

"Marvelous."

"Astral *Pain,* more like, Sarge; you wouldn't *believe* the stuff they sell! Skyscraper heeled boots, boned corsets built like torture chambers, spiked collars with matching leashes..."

"Terry?"

The young woman stopped immediately.

"Have you contacted them yet?"

"No ma'am; I thought you..."

"I'll do the thinking, you do the doing. That work for you?"

The young woman nodded once. "Ma'am."

"Get on to them. Got to be a customer service number. I don't imagine horned god heads are their fastest moving item. Get a list of buyers back at least two years."

"Do it 'dreckly, ma'am."

The detective's mobile rang.

"Davies," she barked.

"Calum here, Morgan."

"What have you got?"

"Has, 'Hello, Calum; how are you?' ever occurred to you, Morgan?"

"We're a little short on the social niceties down here in Penzance. Old pirate's and smuggler's culture, you see. We're just as likely to slit your throat as smile. Maybe both. Now, what have you got?"

"Damn all is what I've got. The bugs and pollen study says Rebecca Chynoweth died where we found her, or near enough. Nothing to suggest she was killed elsewhere and taken to the quoit. But forensics retrieved some hair samples from the remnants of the cloak, blond and black. They're examining them now."

"Bran's hair is black," Davies said. She told him about the interview at the witch's mill. "Place is a bloody museum of witchcraft. Packed to the rafters with all sorts of herbs and such, and bizarre tools like something from the Middle Ages. The woman somehow knew all about Bates's encounter with the horned beast, too, though Bates hasn't even spoken to me of it. Says she knows it from 'reading her,' but it could just as easily have been first-hand knowledge. She said something else that could be either a lead or a smokescreen; says the horned beast's head was a fake. Available online. Bates tracked down a source at an internet shop in Plymouth, though there are others."

"Want me to pop up there and have a look-see?"

"No, it's Bates's demon and I want her to run it down."

"You becoming a therapist, Morgan?"

"Just seeing what the girl's made of, Calum."

"Oh, Lord. Another DS Davies in the making?"

Davies laughed. "Only one of them, Calum. And don't say 'Thank God!'"

West paused. "I'd been about to say one in a million, but have it your way. Gotta run. Mister wants a visit. I'll fill him in. Cheers."

Davies looked at her mobile and finally punched the "End" button.

In a million?

Twenty-Four

AMANDA JEFFERS ROSE EARLY Friday, as she did nearly every day, weather permitting, pulled her work clothes on over her running togs, jogged the three blocks along the waterfront between their lodgings and the Penzance bus depot and caught the 7:40 toward Sancreed, the village closest to Carn Dewes. By 8:10, long before the rest of the team would arrive at the site, she had stuffed her work clothes in a small backpack and was pounding up the steep farm track to Chapel Carn Brea, the ruined Bronze Age stone fortress not far, as the crow flies, from Carn Dewes. She ducked under the low hawthorn shrubs that shielded the sacred well near the ruins of Chapel St. Euny and continued up to the summit. The view from Chapel Carn Brea was epic; you could take in both the Atlantic and Channel coasts and all the farm and moorland in between. On good mornings like this, the light on the water was incandescent.

Having caught her breath, she turned and ran hard down and across Tredinney Common, bounding over hillocks of sedge and grass, heading for Carn Dewes. She'd be there, sponge-washed, dressed and refreshed, by the time the students stumbled up the hill, barely awake, just after nine. The forty-five minute morning run was her greatest daily joy. And, in truth, the physical effort shaved some of her hard edges smooth, there being no other outlet for her intensity.

The footpath through the heather and gorse of Tredinney Common was narrow and rough. Wild ponies grazed so imperturbably as to suggest they were deaf as she hammered by. In several spots the path twisted between massive granite outcrops and the edges of the now-abandoned china clay mining pits that once had helped supply England's porcelain industry. She was just rounding one of these outcrops when a force she did not see launched her into the air above the deepest of the pits.

The last thing she saw was the blue sky spinning above her, like a kaleidoscope vision. After that, only pain and dark water.

HUNTER MUSTERED HIS TEAM at the operations tent just after nine to lay out the plan to begin closing down the site and gave little thought to Jeffers's absence. Certain she would appear shortly from her run, he issued assignments and the team began the task of restoring Carn Dewes to the condition in which they'd found it. Then he descended to the fogou and entered the corbelled chamber. The component slabs of the granite niche lay to one side. To keep the corbelled wall from collapsing, he'd inserted a short steel plate. Upon reconstruction, he would replace the angled stones and finally remove the steel support. They had taken great care not to scar or deface the stones, wrapping each of them in bubble-wrap. Now, with a care tinged with wonder at its antiquity, Hunter began rebuilding the niche as had the ancients; without mortar.

He had been at this task for only a few minutes when he sensed a charged energy in the chamber. Even as he tried to comprehend it, a white light burst from the niche and he felt in his bones, rather than heard, one word:

Amanda.

Though he was certain he had not moved, he found himself sprawled, as if thrown, against the wall opposite the niche.

Five minutes later, still stunned and struggling to act normally before the students he'd called back together, he broke up the group and sent them out to search segments of Amanda's usual running route. He stayed at the site to receive their calls, still expecting that any minute she'd arrive and wonder what the fuss was all about. The path up from Grumbla was found to be clear. The only thing searchers found at Chapel Carn Brae were the wild ponies. It was the group surveying Tredinney Common that noticed the disturbed earth at the lip of one of the clay pits. Far below, they could see a head, free of the water but immobile.

It was less than a kilometer over the high moorland between Carn Dewes and Tredinney and Hunter ran the whole way, a long coil of braided rope slung across his chest and right shoulder. Bent at the waist, sucking air like a beached porpoise, and feeling every one of his increasing years, he managed to punch into his mobile the now familiar number for the police, got a signal, and begged for technical help to pull his injured assistant from the pit. Arriving at the site where she had fallen, he called back the young men who were searching for a route down, threw his rope around an outcrop and, to the rest of his team's amazement, rappelled like a mountaineer down the dirty white clay face of the pit to the motionless body in the fetid water below.

Amanda Jeffers was breathing but unconscious. He checked her pulse but did not move her. In the water, he could already see a nasty compound fracture poking through the skin of her left forearm. It was the most natural thing to do in a fall, a reflex: thrust a hand out to fend off the ground. Even landing in shallow water, the drop was nearly thirty feet. Her good hand was caked with clay; it looked like she'd tried to pull herself free of the water before passing out from the pain.

He'd had time to wade around her body gently feeling for other injuries in the murky water when he heard the distant *whomp-whomp-whomp* of helicopter rotors beating the sky. Minutes later, a red and gray Royal Navy search and rescue helicopter from the Culdrose base barely fifteen air miles away hovered over the pit and an airman rode a caged steel stretcher down into the pit. Hunter left Amanda and grabbed the metal frame as it approached the surface of the stagnant water, pulling it to the muddy edge of the dark pool.

"Thanks, mate!" the airman cried out over the noise. "But leave this bit to me, okay? With a bit of luck, we'll get you both out of here straightaway!"

"Compound fracture of the left arm!" Hunter yelled. "Maybe spinal damage, too; I don't know!"

"No worries; we can get her in without shifting her much!"

The airman opened one side of the hinged stretcher, pushed it into the water and, while Hunter cradled Amanda's head, floated her body into the cage. Settling her there, the medic immobilized her head in an attached wire basket, checked her pulse, saw her eyes flicker, and called for her to be lifted.

Less than a minute later, a harness was lowered again and Hunter and the airman rose together to cheers from the students on the ground.

Twenty-Five

I'M LATE GETTING TO Tamsin's on account of my mum being with some guy I never saw before and waking up late. I never heard them come in.

She stumbles into the kitchen this morning in that gold Chinese kimono with the dragon on the back she wears, but with stockings underneath, like she's never changed from last night. She makes me tea and slides a bowl of Wheetabix in front of me, forgetting the milk, and then says she's not feeling too good and goes back to her bedroom. Next thing, this guy comes out of there. He's wearing jeans and a faded black tee shirt with "Slade" on the front, which I reckon is a rock group, but I never heard of it. Tattoos on both arms. Got his shoes on, too, he does. He smiles and pats me on the head, which is kinda nice, and walks right on out of the flat; never a word of "hello."

I get milk from the fridge, finish the cereal and tea, and look in on mum, who's starkers in bed but for the stockings, and snoring. I back out of her room, get my bike from the shed behind the terrace house our flat's in, and head for Tamsin's, hoping she won't be angry I'm late.

At Tamsin's, I put my bike up against the back of the mill as usual and go 'round to the door, open it and call, but she doesn't answer. And Desmond's nowhere to be seen. I look in back and see her old Morris estate is parked where it should be and wander up-valley through the gardens. I'm thinking maybe she's collecting herbs, which is best done in the morning.

Even though it's high summer, the stream is full, thanks to the strange afternoon cloudbursts over the high moors this month. Tamsin's explained that the clouds have to unload the weight of their rain to get over the tors, which makes sense to me; it's like the clouds have thumping great backpacks or something they need to shed to get over the tops. Anyway, that's why the stream has water running full and fast. I pass the herb garden but she's not there, so I continue upstream.

When you get far enough from the mill, the trees close in on the skinny valley. But they're not trees like you'd see maybe in Morab Gardens in Penzance, all grand and graceful. No, these trees are hunched and gnarly, their twisted branches hung with mosses that live off the morning fogs and dew. I saw a kid's book at the Morab Library sometime past. I don't remember its name, but it had these drawings inside by this old artist and his trees were just like Tamsin's—all twisty and bearded and like they were alive and had faces and could talk to you. But I've listened to these ones and they don't have much to say. To me, anyway.

Then I see Tamsin ahead in a bright clearing. It's quiet, except for the stream clattering over the stones in its bed, and I can hear her voice, like she's talking—or maybe singing—to the trees. I can't hear the words, but I can see the light and it stops me in my tracks. It's this shaft that comes slanting through the clearing like sunlight, only way brighter. I can't tell, like, if the light comes down through the trees or up from the ground. But it's brightest right where Tamsin sits, her long legs tucked beneath her and her arms crossed against her chest. I can make out that she's made one of her circles and now sits in the middle of it. She rocks gently and sings softly and the light dims and brightens as she does, like it's talking with her. Desmond's with her, too. He's sitting opposite her at the edge of the circle and he's sort of swaying with his eyes closed, like he's in a trance. He doesn't even know I'm there.

I back away, quiet as can be. I mean, I know she's a witch and all, but this is new. And the strange thing is, I can almost make out what the light is saying to her. Not like it makes a sound, you understand. It's just a knowing. It's peaceful and comforting.

I wonder what Tamsin needs to have comforted. She always seems so strong to me.

I decide I'll just go to work cleaning up the kitchen and see if there's laundry to be done, so I slip away from the clearing on tiptoes.

I'm just finishing the washing up when I, like, know I'm not alone. I turn and Tamsin's there, smiling. Desmond's beside her.

"It was kind of you not to interrupt, Tegan girl. Thank you."

I don't know what to say, really, and she steps forward and gives me a kind of sideways hug.

"I was talking to my mother, you see."

And here's the strange thing—I never thought about Tamsin having a mother, you know? Well of course she did. But Tamsin's just, well, Tamsin. Like the mill is just the mill. It just is and she just is and it's not like she's related to anything else in the universe.

And I guess Tamsin sees my confusion and she says, "My mother's name was Melwyn. She was the wise woman here in St. Euny before me. We come from a line of wise women as far back as anyone can remember. People depend upon us."

"You were talking with her?"

"Yes. When she died, quite some years ago now, I buried the urn holding her ashes in the middle of the glade where you found me. It was a special place for her, as it is for me. When I need her wisdom, I go there. She is always waiting."

What I want to do is ask what she needed to talk to her mother about when it hits me that I don't even question that Tamsin can talk to her dead mother. And right then, I feel something shift inside me and I think, *Tamsin's just told me about talking with her dead mother. Me. And she trusts me to understand that!* And suddenly, I feel happy and proud and grateful and give her the biggest hug I've ever hugged.

And she kisses the top of my head...

Twenty-Six

DAYLIGHT WEAK AS DISHWATER seeped through the dirty windows in the front parlor of the Belle Vue Terrace house Friday morning and left a smudge across the woman reclining on the only piece of furniture remaining in the abandoned room—a fly-blown, dust-encrusted Victorian settee covered in threadbare velvet the color of badly oxidized red wine.

Judith Chynoweth wasn't resting. A knife with an ornate black handle rose like an exclamation mark from just above her left breast.

Davies and Bates arrived at the front door of the squat just after nine. One uniformed PC stood at the threshold with a logbook. Another constable stood beside their patrol car. In the back seat sat Brendan Rice-Johnson, his head in his hands, a portrait of grief.

"Take a statement," Davies told Bates. Now the detective stood at the sitting room's threshold. But for the body on the settee, it looked like the room, and for that matter most of the floor, hadn't been used in decades. A layer of gray dust clung to every surface like mold. Her nostrils filled with the dull stench of abandonment. She couldn't credit houses like this being left to rot, but it was commonplace where towns were struggling to survive after their traditional industries declined.

From the doorway, she could see footprints tracking to and from the body. The medics, having confirmed the obvious, had already come and gone, leaving the corpse for the forensic team, so some of the prints—the smudged, bootied ones—were theirs. But they'd been careful to avoid the other, more distinct prints.

When Comms received the incident report they immediately contacted Penwarren, as well as Davies and West and the pathologist, Dr. Duncan. Davies did not enter the sitting room. She'd leave it for West's SOCO gang to examine first. From the doorway, the reclining Judith Chynoweth looked like a shabby version of a gentlewoman suffering from the vapors. Except for the knife in her chest.

A few moments later, Bates joined her at the room's threshold.

"You're not meant to be here. How'd you get past the PC at the door?"

"I badged my way through and said I was with you."

Davies looked at Bates. This woman's smile would get her anywhere. "What's his story?" Davies asked, nodding toward the squad car.

"Name's Brendan Rice-Johnson. Unemployed. A right lad, is our boy. Says he and the victim share the squat but he spent the night with another girl, came home about five and found the body where and as it is."

"Name and address of other girl?"

"Got it. Quick to give it, too, he was."

"No doubt. Get another response unit to bring her in."

"Already done."

An approving lifted eyebrow from Davies. "And tell our chaps out there to treat Mr. Rice-Johnson as a significant witness. Later we'll take him up to the interview suite at Pool. We'll do it by the book, but I'd like to know why he didn't call this in until it had nearly gone eight."

Bates nodded but hesitated.

"Yes?"

"With respect, ma'am, those PCs outside are my Penzance patrol mates. I don't think it right, me giving them orders."

Davies regarded the younger woman for a moment. Another reason to like her: ambitious, but wise. Not a posturer. "You're right, Terry. I'll attend to that. But first," Davies said, angling her head to the sitting room, "what's wrong with this picture?"

Bates looked into the room for only a few moments and smiled. "The floor, of course."

WEST'S TEAM ARRIVED just a half hour behind Davies and Bates. The first thing they'd done was to lay grated aluminum stepping plates down in the hall and along the approach to the body in the parlor, so as to protect the floor. While one of the men fiber-taped the parlor door and frame for hairs or threads and West took wide-angle photos of the interior, others began canvassing the rest of the house, taking prints, and checking the ground in back near the cellar entry. One of them found the woman's purse in the upstairs bedroom and recorded everything that was in it, finally bagging and tagging it all. The Tactical Aid Group men—West's "knuckle-draggers"—would be along soon to really take the place apart.

West lowered his camera when he heard a Tyvek boiler suit rustle behind him.

"You plan on spending all day taking pictures of corpses, Calum?"

"Doc! How'd you get here so fast?"

"I was on my way to a meeting at the hospital in Truro," the pathologist Jennifer Duncan said, "and came directly. Always rather spend a day with a body than in a meeting."

"Me too. Something dreadfully wrong with both of us."

"That's some knife," Duncan said, looking over West's shoulder.

"Care for a closer look?"

"Try to stop me."

Standing on the aluminum plates, the two of them bent over the body on the settee.

The pathologist manipulated limbs. "Rigor's well established. No sign it's going off yet, either."

Working slowly, their hands in surgical gloves, Duncan and West cut away Judith Chynoweth's clothes, bagging and tagging them as they went, but taking care not to disturb the knife. When the body was naked, Duncan took oral, vaginal, and anal swabs, slipping the swabs into plastic vials and marking them. Then West fiber-taped the body for any additional thread or hair traces. Duncan inserted a long digital thermometer into the victim's rectum to get a body temperature by which to estimate time of death.

After a while, she turned to West, shaking her head. "Less than twelve hours. Best I can do from here."

"No blood. Dead before she was knifed?"

The voice came from behind them and they turned to find Davies at the entry in her own Tyvek bodysuit.

"The absence of exsanguination tells us nothing, Morgan," Duncan said. "She could very well have been alive when stabbed. But because the knife remained, it can seal the wound like a stopper."

"Only knifings we see down here tend to be street fights or domestics. Stabbers usually take the knife with them."

"I know. This is odd. And suspicious. It doesn't look like suicide."

"Yeah," West agreed. "Nobody knifes themselves through their clothes; they always lift them."

"Not always, Calum. There are exceptions. You'll have to wait till the postmortem for a definitive cause of death, I'm afraid, Morgan."

Davies turned to West. "Undertaker's van is here, Calum. Your boys are ready with the body bag."

"We've got to improvise a barrier to isolate the knife," Duncan said.

West thought for a moment. "Got it. I've a small box in the car. We can place it in a sterile bag and sit it atop the knife. When the body bag's zipped, the knife will be protected."

"That'll suit."

"Oh, by the way, Calum," Davies said, smiling, "some of your most ardent fans are clamoring for you beyond the cordon."

"Bloody hell, already?"

She nodded. "BBC Cornwall, *The Cornishman*, *Cornish Guardian*, *Western Morning News*, among others. You're a popular lad."

"Why not talk to you? You're the detective!"

"Because they I know I'll just snarl at them; you're better at media relations. You'll treat them like the human beings they're not."

Watching these two, Duncan just shook her head and grinned. Like an old married couple, these two are, she thought. "I'll just see this lady to the van and be off to Truro, then, shall I?"

"I'm right behind you," West said. I'll have my lads mill about here as if they're doing something useful. Media vultures can get their photos and film that way. Then it's them and me with the same old same old routine: *Who is it, Sarge?* 'The victim has yet to be identified.' *Cause of death?* 'Yet to be determined.' *Time of death?* 'Sometime in the last twelve hours.' *Is it a murder?* 'We honestly can't say yet.' *Can't or won't, Sarge?* 'We'll certainly notify you if and when we can. That is all for now, people.'"

West turned to leave like a man going to a hanging. "Let's talk about the floor when I get back, Morgan," he said over his shoulder.

"Don't forget to smile," Davies called after him.

"And think of the Queen…" she heard him mutter.

"IF IT'S A SMOKESCREEN, it's a clever job, Calum," Davies said when West returned. She pointed. "So here's this room, practically ankle deep in dust, yeah? And a body on a moth-eaten settee..."

"And?"

"And the floor's been swept clean—or rather wiped since there are no brush marks—from door to body. The only dusty footprints—not in the dust, mind, but atop the bare floorboards—are those of our people and Mr. Rice-Johnson's trainers, tracked in clear as day. Did someone clean up when they did the woman in, or did Rice-Johnson kill her, then wipe, then add his own fresh prints, as if he'd just come across the body? Diabolical, this is. Could have been him either way."

West nodded. "By the way, speaking of footprints, the lads found several in the mud outside that cellar window entry. Judging from size, they're both male and female. They're taking castings now. Since this is a squat, I reckon they never entered directly from the street. Too conspicuous. Come in through the back. I'm off to the mortuary. You coming?"

"You're forensics; I'm suspects. Got my 'significant witness' in the car to interview. As soon as I have my little chat with Rice-Johnson, I'll come straight up to Truro to see what you've got."

He placed a hand on her shoulder. "Patience, love. It'll be hours before we know anything."

"Patience? Love?"

West smiled. "A very modest term of endearment, Morgan, common among working folk," West said as he walked down the stairs and ducked under the cordon.

And for the first time, something inside her let go—she could almost hear the snap, a tether released—and she believed him. He was looking out for her. No one ever had before, not even her ex. No one thought she needed it.

She didn't know how to respond. And anyway, he was gone.

Twenty-Seven

"MY CONSTABLES SAY there's no reason to think the American runner didn't just slip and fall. Then her colleagues trampled the site to mush. It's bloody useless. Dangerous area for running anyway. There are warning signs posted."

DCI Penwarren had taken the call from the head of the uniformed branch at Penzance because of the archaeology team's connection to the Chynoweth girl's case. But was it even related? A jogger slipped. Common enough. He tried to fit it into the other issues they were investigating but the puzzle pieces didn't match.

LIKE A FENCED ZOO ANIMAL, Hunter paced the waiting room outside the emergency surgery of the Royal Cornwall Hospital at Treliske, just outside Truro, part of him gripped by worry about injury to one of his own, part of him struggling with his feelings for this particular member of his team. He hadn't addressed or even admitted his feelings for his second in command, though they had been growing, and yet some part of him understood he had capitulated. He cared for her. Did he love her? Love her prickly strength? It was as if he'd been a boat adrift for years and suddenly, in part because of this attack, he had a tiller bringing him up into the wind. And it was due to Amanda.

After nearly an hour, a doctor emerged from behind the electronic doors.

"Dr. Hunter?"

"Yes?"

"Dr. Roth. It was a nasty fall, but I'm happy to say that the only serious injury is to her arm. It's a straightforward compound fracture. We've reset it."

"Her spine?"

"Fine. It was the concussion that rendered her unconscious; that and the sheer shock of the fall, I suspect. But the concussion was not serious. There is no evidence of hematoma. She's badly bruised all over, of course, but it's superficial. She is very fit; otherwise the damage might well have been worse. We sedated her while we reset the bone and sutured the arm. There'll be a scar, of course, but a small one. She's resting now. Would you care to see her?"

Amanda did not hear Hunter enter. She was still fighting off the effects of the sedation. It was the touch of his fingers brushing her brow that brought her into the present.

"Sweet, strong, Amanda," he said, and her eyes came into focus.

"Brad," she said, as if letting go of a great weight.

He leaned forward and kissed her forehead. "You are very dear to me."

She smiled. "That was nice. Do it again."

This time he kissed her lips.

She winced. "Careful. Tender."

He lifted the blankets covering her. Even in her hospital gown he could see bruises wherever her skin was exposed. She shivered, though the room was warm. He pulled the covers up to her neck and tucked them in around her, leaving the casted arm free.

"You were very lucky."

She laughed and immediately flinched from the pain. "Lucky? You call being flung into a pit *lucky*?"

"I meant your injuries."

"Don't feel so lucky just now."

"How did you fall? Do you remember?"

"I said *flung*, Brad. I was pushed! It came out of nowhere. I was running and then suddenly I was airborne. A shove from behind. Then nothing. Flying." She moved to shake off the memory and thought better of it.

"What is important is that you are okay, Amanda."

Her eyes flashed. "That's bullshit and you know it. What's important is finding who did this to me!"

Hunter looked at the woman in the bed but Amanda could tell part of him was elsewhere.

"Or what," he said finally.

"What do you mean *what*?"

"Has it escaped your notice that things have gone wrong from the moment we unearthed the Neolithic figurine? The body under the quoit? The weird poppet? Your fall...or whatever it was? Even the weather's turned evil; minutes after the helicopter lifted us out of that pit, the wind came up and the skies unloaded. Our people were drenched by the time they returned to Carn Dewes and part of the operations tent was torn away."

"Coincidence."

"Was it a coincidence that I, too, was flung this morning?"

"Huh?"

"As I began to rebuild the niche, a flash of white light threw me across the chamber and spoke your name."

"You're joking..."

"No. That's how I knew you were in trouble."

Jeffers watched him for a moment. "I think you have been under a lot of pressure, Brad."

Hunter waved the comment off and paced. "I think they want it back, Amanda."

"Back?"

"The goddess figurine. They want it back."

"Who does?"

"The spirits. The Annown."

"You honestly believe this?"

Hunter shrugged. "I just feel it. I know that's not how you think. And this fall..."

Amanda leveled a look at him that would have petrified wood. "I was *shoved*, dammit."

Twenty-Eight

"I CAN'T DO IT. It's too much."

As soon as she left the Belle Vue squat, Bates, in her role as family liaison officer, had driven across town to Penwith Gothica and given Kenny Chynoweth the news. She and another constable then drove him to the mortuary in Truro to identify his sister's body before the postmortem began. On the way, he said he'd taken a bottle of champagne to his sister's place the night before to cheer her up after the news of her daughter's death. As the police car sped north on the A30, he kept saying, "I was with her just a few hours ago…" It was as if, by repeating the mantra, he could alter reality.

Now he and Bates stood in a small room painted a soothing sage green. They faced a window behind which were heavy curtains in a darker forest green. He'd come gamely enough but now was resisting. It was nearly eleven and Bates needed to get over to the witness suite at Pool for Morgan's interview with Rice-Johnson.

"You will see nothing unpleasant, Mr. Chynoweth, I promise you," she said gently. "Your sister will be covered and the only thing visible will be her face, which will look perfectly normal, as though asleep. We simply need you to tell us if this is, indeed, your sister Judith."

"You know that already," Kenny insisted. He seemed now more truculent than upset. "You said her boyfriend already…."

"Mr. Rice-Johnson is not her next of kin, Sir."

"No shit. I'll lay odds he killed her!"

Bates was about to pursue this outburst but reminded herself she was only a constable. She'd report it to Davies later.

"Please, Sir," she said now in a voice so silky it was almost seductive. "She was your sister, your only surviving relative. She would want you to be the one to recognize her, to validate her personhood, now it's been taken from her. I promise, it will take only a moment. Surely you have the strength to grant her this small last thing?"

He paused and stared at the window. Bates took the pause as assent and signaled for the curtain to be opened. Brother stared at sister. She lay before him beyond the window wrapped in a royal blue velvet shroud trimmed with gold braid. As promised, only the face was exposed, pale as sand without her usual makeup, almost two-dimensional, like a faded Polaroid. The curtain closed immediately.

Kenny Chynoweth continued to stare, seeing only his own reflection in the glass, and Bates's.

Finally, he nodded.

IT HAD JUST GONE NOON when Davies entered one of the two witness interview suites that Devon and Cornwall Police had built in a private house in Pool, just off the A30 between Camborne and Redruth. Designed to be less intimidating than a bare-bones interrogation room at a police station, the suites were a bureaucrat's version of homey: upholstered settees and chairs, a coffee table, lamps. It was about as warm as a hotel room, but with state of the art digital recorders and cameras instead of a bed.

Davies and Rice-Johnson had ridden up together while a uniformed constable drove. The usual routine en route was to relax the witness with chat about inanities: cricket scores, favorite football teams, politics. Rice-Johnson had no opinions on any of these neutral topics, so the twenty minute ride from Penzance was spent mostly in silence. Now Rice-Johnson was slouched on the settee, his feet propped on the edge of the coffee table.

"Think you're at home, RJ? Sit up and get your feet off the table," Davies ordered as she swept in.

Rice-Johnson obeyed, but at his own, languid pace, making sure Davies knew he felt it was an imposition.

Davies sat in one of the upholstered chairs opposite the settee. In another room, a constable switched on the cameras and recording equipment. Bates had arrived just in time, entered the recording room, and watched the television monitor on the wall before her.

"Mr. Rice-Johnson," Davies began. "Or would you prefer your street name: *RJ*?'"

Brendan shrugged.

After the usual legal preliminaries, Davies said, "What is your occupation, Sir? Your job?"

"Got none. Had one—construction—got laid off, I did. The economy."

"And when was that, if I may ask?"

"While back, that was. Don't clearly recall. Been on the dole since, but still lookin'."

"I'm sure you are, and that the authorities will have a list of your most recent job applications. Am I right?"

Rice-Johnson shrugged again.

"But in the meantime, to keep home and hearth…" and here Davies pretended to look at her notes "…you've been running a few girls over Newlyn way."

Rice-Johnson puffed up. "Bollocks, that is. Somebody tryin' to set me up!"

Davies smiled. "And they would want to set you up because…?"

RJ caught himself and shrugged again. "Dunno, do I?"

"Dunno, *do you*?" Davies echoed.

"What you on about?!" RJ demanded.

"Don't play the idiot, RJ. Your latest Tom—your alibi for last night, in fact—has already agreed to assist us with our enquiries in return for immunity and another chance at a decent life. So let's us both move on to the death of your *other* girlfriend, your live-in partner, Judith Chynoweth."

"I got nuffin' to do with that."

Davies tapped the point of her pen against her notebook, a steady, patient beat like a pulse. She let time stretch out.

"'*Nuffin*'?" she said, finally.

"What I said, innit?"

She leaned across the coffee table. "Let's get something straight, RJ. You may live in an illegal squat and dress like a tramp, but you can drop the street talk. The word is 'nothing,' as anyone with your education and breeding knows only too well. Yes, thanks to the Internet, we know who you are and where you went to school. Member of the crew team at Eton. Very impressive. You may be a slob, RJ, but you're also a nob, so drop the act. Now, can we get on with this?"

Morgan's modus operandi with witnesses was antagonism. She bullied them until they revealed a weakness. Rice-Johnson was smart and wily. But was he tough?

For a moment, Rice-Johnson took her measure. A sly smile flickered. "I am at your disposal, Detective Sergeant Davies..."

Davies leaned back into her chair. "Disposal, RJ, is exactly what I like to do with scrotes like you, but let's begin with early this morning. You arrived back at the squat when?"

"Already told your people."

"Humor me."

"Sometime after dawn. Don't know when, precisely. Long night."

"With your latest. Yes, so you've said. What happened next?"

"I found her, didn't I? In the parlor. With that knife in her chest. Helluva shock, that was."

"I'm sure it was, RJ. Tell me, how long have you and Judith Chynoweth been living together?"

"Eight, nine months, maybe."

"Know her daughter, did you?" The question came out of nowhere.

"Becca? Nah, she done a runner. Jude claimed some witch spirited her away, if you can credit it."

"And why'd Jude decide to move in with you?"

"Lost her subsidized flat, didn't she? Practically homeless."

"I repeat: why you?

He smirked, "Asked her to; bloody marvelous in bed, she is."

"Was, RJ. *Was*."

The smirk vanished.

"Here's what I'm wondering, RJ. After the shock of finding her, what did you do next?"

"Looked for the killer, didn't I? In case he was still around."

"You assumed a 'he?'"

"Well, who else?"

"A rival for your affections, perhaps? Another woman wanting to take her place?"

Another self-satisfied shrug.

"Where did you look?"

"All over the house, I did, and outside, too."

"Were you airborne at the time, RJ?"

"Huh?"

"Airborne. You know: floating. Because, see, the thing is our scene of crime officers found the prints of those trainers you're wearing in only four places: the parlor, as you call it, the stairs, your bedroom, and the loo. If you spent so much time searching everywhere, being airborne is the only explanation I can think of for how you got around the rest of the house without making a mark."

"That's daft."

"Well-reasoned, RJ. Your education seems not to have gone completely to waste. It's daft, indeed. Now why don't you tell me what you really were doing between, say, six and eight this morning?"

Rice-Johnson looked away a moment. His face, when he turned back, was the picture of abject humiliation. "I got scared when I found her, okay? I ran out of the house and walked about a bit, didn't I? Then I got myself sorted and called."

Davies laughed. "Big, strapping lad like you, frightened? You amaze me, you do. Didn't take you for a sissy, but never mind. Anyone see you while you were having your little morning walkabout?"

"Like I said, it was early."

"Of course you did. But I'm thinking, you know, between six and eight on the last day of the week folks are getting ready for work, having breakfast, out walking the dog and so forth. Sure no one saw you?"

"Can't say, can I?"

"No doubt, given how 'shocked' you were."

There was a knock at the interview room door. Annoyed, Davies excused herself. West was in the hall.

"The TAG boys found a used Rizla filter tip under the mattress on the floor of the squat's bedroom..."

"You're interrupting an interview to tell me they were rolling their own ciggies?!" Davies had both hands on her hips and leaned toward West as if she were about to throttle him. He was unfazed.

"I said the filter was used; I didn't say it was used for tobacco. They also found a scorched bit of tinfoil in a closet."

Davies backed off. "Cooking up a little heroin?"

"And pulling it through the filter into a syringe, is my guess, though the lab will confirm that from the filter. So what I'm saying is…"

"That we may have evidence to charge him with a drugs offence," Davies said, cuffing West in the shoulder. It was as close as she could permit to giving him a hug. "You're a prince. Let the Crown Prosecution Service know. I'd love to hold him."

"PLEASE ACCEPT MY APOLOGIES for the interruption, Mr. Rice-Johnson," Davies said as she reentered the interview room.

RJ nodded with feigned graciousness.

"Let me see…where were we? Oh yes, the time gap. You were out trying to come to terms with your partner's death, is that right?"

"And looking for anyone suspicious."

"Of course you were. But that must have been a quite a walk—an hour or more, maybe two, during which no one saw you. Remarkable, that."

Watching the screens in the monitoring room, Bates said to the PC in charge, "She's really something isn't she?"

The PC smiled. "Trust me. She's just getting started."

Davies paused and looked at the ceiling for a moment as if struggling to think, then returned to Rice-Johnson.

"So, just to be clear, are you saying you didn't perhaps also use that time to do a bit of judicious housecleaning between your discovery of the body and your call to the police?"

He laughed. "Clean the squat?"

"I see your point. But I have another. You see, the pattern of your waffle-soled trainers in those few rooms was haphazard, like someone in a hurry. Jude Chynoweth was a junkie, RJ. She's been picked up several times in the past year and nearly died in hospital just this week. Did you know that?"

Rice-Johnson shook his head not in denial but as if bored with the question.

"No? So when she was being so 'bloody marvelous in bed' you never noticed there were more tracks on her arms and legs than public footpaths on a Landranger map? Of course, if you were her supplier as well as her pimp, then you'd want to make very sure the house was clean of drugs before our people got there after your call, wouldn't you? That might have taken a while, no matter how fast you scurried about."

"I done nuffin' of the sort."

"*Nothing,* RJ. Did nothing."

"Whatever."

Davies suddenly slapped her knee. "Goodness, RJ, I just thought of this: it must have cost you the earth to keep Judith high so she could be so 'bloody marvelous in bed' for her clients. Cocaine for fuel, heroin to calm her down; was she even earning her keep? Getting on in years for this game, wasn't she?"

Rice-Johnson crossed his arms and his face snapped from boredom to stony belligerence. "I don't know what you're talkin' about."

Davies smiled.

"Then it would probably come as a stupendous surprise if I told you that we've found a charred boil-up foil in your closet and a used Rizla filter tip. Only thing missing, really, was the elastic armband and the syringe. But you probably got the most obvious bits of your works disposed of before our people arrived. During that early morning interval, perhaps?"

Rice-Johnson was stony but his forehead was damp. "Nothing to do with me."

"I'm sure, RJ. Anyway the prints will sort that out."

"The prints?"

"Meanwhile, let's say for the moment it hasn't anything to do with you. Think back to the parlor this morning. Notice anything odd about it?"

"Yeah, Jude was dead in it."

"So we've established. Anything else?"

"Only thing I saw was her lyin' there, eyes wide open but gone."

"How did you determine she was 'gone'?"

"Checked her pulse, didn't I?"

"Notice anything else? Anything strange about the floor?"

"I told you, I was knackered from the night and shattered by findin' her dead. All I saw was Jude. You think I looked at the bloody *floor*?"

Davies leaned across the table again. "What I'm looking at, RJ, is a very clever murderer who stabs someone in a dusty room, then sweeps or wipes a clear path backwards from the body so evidence of his presence is erased. Then, because he's too clever by half, he deliberately walks back into the room with dirty shoes and makes fresh prints to make it look like he'd just stumbled upon the body."

"Why would he go to the trouble?"

"He wouldn't. He'd run. Unless he was you, creating an alibi in the dirt—covering his tracks with his own tracks, as it were. Genius, that would be...Eton-level genius."

Twenty-Nine

THE RAIL-THIN BODY of Judith Chynoweth lay naked and waiflike on a stainless steel trolley in the postmortem room at the Truro mortuary. It was just after noon. Scotty Thomas, the bearish mortuary manager, measured the length of the body, read its weight from the digital read-out at the head of the trolley, and called out the numbers to Jennifer Duncan, who stood at a side counter with a sheaf of forms on which she would register every step of her forensic examination. Above the trolley on a ladder, Calum West took top-down record photos. The knife remained embedded in the victim's chest like a giant party toothpick pinning together an obscene canapé.

"Mind you don't slip, Calum," Thomas quipped. "Ruin our day, that would."

Duncan laughed. "And not because of any injury to *your* person..."

"You are both cruel and unfeeling. My task is vital and precarious."

"Go on, then, admit it: you have a perverted passion for photographing naked women, and dead ones, at that," Scotty teased.

"Said that for years, but does anyone listen?" This from West's exhibits officer, Roger Morris, who was busy laying out an array of vials, swabs, containers, and tissue sample holders on another stainless steel table. As Duncan worked, they would take forensic samples and Morris would log them.

Down the center of the long, tiled room, three waist-high operating tables stood like albino soldiers at attention. Each high-rimmed white porcelain platform was shoulder-broad at one end, ankle-narrow at the other, and supported by stanchions thick as elephant legs.

While Thomas and West shifted the body, Duncan completed the case paperwork on the deceased. Then she took her place at the table, lifted a sterile scalpel, and cut a V-shaped incision down from each ear, around and beneath the jaw, finally meeting just above the sternum. From there, her scalpel ran straight and deep down the midline of the body to the pubic bone, detouring slightly around the navel. From the side, Calum marveled yet again at the absence of blood. Perhaps the soul, he mused, was nothing more than the throbbing flow of blood which animates us. When the soul departs, we stop bleeding. He flicked on the CD player in the corner.

"None of that bloody American jazz crap of yours, Calum," Duncan ordered. "Haven't we got an 'Adele' or something?"

"You are so common, Jennifer," West groused. "And so young."

He found Coldplay. It seemed appropriate.

DURING THE NEXT FEW HOURS Duncan, machine-like, removed Judith Chynoweth's vital organs and the team weighed, sampled, and logged each. She sawed open the skull, removed and examined the brain. West took record photos throughout. Tissue and blood samples were already en route to the lab. It was nearly five when Duncan stepped away from the porcelain table for the last time. Scotty was loading the organs back into the body and beginning the process of sewing up.

When they left the sterile zone, Davies was waiting for them in the staff room.

"So," she said after hearing their report. "We know what didn't kill her."

Duncan, slumped in her chair, didn't even open her eyes. "It's a popular misconception that the heart's on the left side of the chest. It isn't. It's only slightly left of the sternum. The knife nicked a rib, punctured the left lung sac, but completely missed the heart. No bleeding within the chest cavity, which suggests the stabbing was postmortem. Someone's both stupid and squeamish."

"Squeamish?"

"The knifer avoided her breast."

"Suggesting an intimate?"

Duncan shrugged. "That's for a forensic profiler, not me."

"Or maybe another woman?" West wondered.

"So, cause of death?"

Duncan sat up. "Unknown, Morgan. For now. She was a heroin addict, that's clear. There is a recent injection puncture inside her right elbow. One of the few areas where her veins haven't collapsed. Maybe she overdosed. Lab results could take a while, though perhaps if you put in a word…?"

"I'll talk to Mister. We've an MCIT a meeting with him tomorrow afternoon at Bodmin. Perhaps we can get some of the lab results by then."

"Will you be wanting me, Morgan?" Duncan asked.

"Mister, certainly will. I'm sorry, Doc."

Thirty

I'VE ONLY JUST SET my bike against the back wall of the mill early Saturday morning when Tamsin whips around the corner of the building, grabs me by the arm, and without a word, hauls me back toward the house, like I'm a dog or something. I never seen her like this before; she's that angry, and I'm too afraid to ask why.

Inside, she marches me around the kitchen and sitting area, still clutching my arm so hard it hurts.

"Look around, Tegan girl," she shouts, waving the other arm. "What's missing? What's missing?!"

I don't even know what to do, where to look, what to look for. There is fire in the golden flecks of her black eyes.

I look around the room, panicky, trying to find anything that's changed, but it's all a blur.

"I don't know, I don't *know*!" I yell back.

"My *athame*, dammit! What have you done with it? I told you never to touch it! Where have you taken it?!"

"I never…" I say, but then I'm just bawling. I never saw such fury in her before. It's like there's two people inside her and one is totally scary.

Then she blinks like she's coming out of a deep sleep, lets my arm go, and says, bright as sunlight, "I guess it wasn't you, then; I'll make tea, shall I?"

And I think: this is the time to run.

Only I don't. I stay.

Tamsin's all I've got.

Thirty-One

WEST ARRIVED AT BODMIN Saturday morning after having breakfast with his daughters. They both wanted to hear about his adventures the day before. He wondered when they'd be old enough to understand what he really did every day. He told them he helped solve crimes, which they thought was exciting, like something on the telly. He didn't tell them he was often at the gruesome end of that task.

West devoted every spare moment to being with them, but his spare moments were, well, spare. There were times they felt like strangers to him, his own daughters. But he knew he was the stranger.

After three years, he had reached the stage where he was grateful his wife Catherine's passing had been so quick and, but for the last week or two of her life, without obvious distress. The hospice care people had kept her comfortable with steadily increasing doses of morphine. As she faded from consciousness, it seemed to him she was speeding away into infinity. When she took her last breath, in his arms—her essence there, then gone—it was at least peaceful.

The persistent ache of mourning had evolved, changing shape and intensity over time. Now, more than anything, he missed the daily-ness of companionship: awakening together, rousing the girls for school, breakfast, the noisy four of them in the bright kitchen of their bungalow.

Catherine's mother had stepped in immediately. But he knew that for the girls it wasn't the same as having a live-in mum and, in an odd sense, he felt he was failing his daughters somehow by not providing one. With the discovery of Rebecca Chynoweth's remains, though, that worry was now overshadowed by the realization that his girls would always be in danger, from sources he might never identify, even after the fact. And that was just the beginning. Meagan and Kaitlin were never left alone now, but in a very few years they would be out in the world on their own. And then what? Who would protect them then?

WITH TWO ACTIVE CASES underway, the Bodmin SOCO office was fully-staffed despite the weekend. West dropped the evidence bag containing the knife removed from Chynoweth's chest on Beth Thompson's desk, asked her to log it in to exhibits, then headed to the gents' down the hall.

Thompson was waiting at the gents' door when he emerged, the evidence bag in her hand.

"Boss! This isn't a knife!"

West smiled. "Well, Beth, it has a steel blade and hilt with a black bone handle. If it looks like a knife, and quacks like a knife…"

"It's not just any knife, is what I'm saying..."

West tilted his head to one side.

"It's an *athame*."

"Would you like to continue this discussion here at the door to the gents', Beth, or shall we retire to the office?"

The young woman blushed, nodded, and strode down the hall. West followed.

In the SOCO Centre, the two of them settled into blue swivel chairs at a small round birch conference table.

"An athame, boss, is a knife witches use for invocations, consecrations, and to cast magic circles. The thing is, no witch would ever use an athame to harm someone. It is never used for cutting anything physical. It's a symbolic, ceremonial object and a practical tool."

"Symbolic of what?" West pressed.

"Of each individual witch's own power to call up the spirits."

"And you know this because…?"

"I'm a pagan. A Wiccan. I thought you knew."

West shrugged. "This a Wicca thing, then?"

"Oh gosh, no. It's ancient. It's mentioned in Italian, Hebrew, French, and Latin manuscripts centuries old, especially in versions of *The Key of Solomon*."

"Which is?"

"A *grimoire,* a book of magic. *The Key of Solomon* probably dates from the Italian Renaissance, though there may be antecedents. The spelling of athame has varied over the ages, and there are versions in several languages, but the knife has always been more totem than weapon."

West sent Davies a text on this latest surprise. Then something occurred to him.

"Beth, I may have something else for you..."

Downstairs in the locked, climate controlled exhibits room, West lifted a clear plastic bag from a steel shelf. "Any idea what this is? Penzance got a trespass call from the American archaeologists and brought this in on Wednesday. I hadn't thought it connected until now."

"It's a poppet, boss."

"Poppet?"

"A kind of doll. Used as part of a spell or remedy. But that thorn between the legs is a nasty bit of work. Never seen that before."

DAVIES AND BATES ARRIVED at the top of Causewayhead just before noon on Saturday. The sky above Penzance was dark as smudged mascara. The shop was empty. Cassandra was straightening stock on a rounder as they entered. She simply pointed to the ceiling.

They mounted the stairs and Davies knocked on the office door.

"'The hell is it now, Cassandra? I'm busy!" Kenny barked.

"Detective Sergeant Davies, Mr. Chynoweth," Davies announced as she entered. Chynoweth pounded the computer keyboard in front of him to exit whatever he was viewing. He rose slightly, seemed to think better of it, and plopped back onto the padded chair behind his desk. The chair complained.

"I thought we were done."

"Yesterday, at the mortuary," Davies said, "you told PC Bates here that your sister's boyfriend might have killed her. Can you tell us why you'd think that?"

"Bloody low-life, he is, that's why! Told her to steer clear, but did she listen? 'Course not. Shoot her up, did he?"

"Why do you ask? Was she an addict?"

"You're jokin', right? Check the police records. 'Course she is, thanks to him."

"Was," Bates snapped.

Chynoweth seemed to collapse into himself with this reminder.

Davies caught the edge in Bates' voice and wondered what was up.

"That Brendan bastard's been pimping Jude for nearly a year, as well," Kenny spat. "Ever since her little girl disappeared and she fell apart; kept Jude high to do it, he did…"

"Have you evidence if this? Had you tried to stop it, Kenny? Have you reported it?" Davies pressed.

His answer, as before when told his niece had been found, was the pitiful upturned hands that aimed to say, *I'm only her kid brother. What can I do?*

Davies let a moment pass. "Would this 'Brendan bastard' being the murderer also explain how your sister came to be stabbed in the chest with a knife?"

"What?"

"Double-edged, medieval-looking knife thrust directly into her chest."

With barely a moment's hesitation, Chynoweth lurched forward in his chair and aimed a pudgy, spatulate forefinger at Davies. "That witch! Maybe Jude was right all along! That Bran woman. Did she kill my sister?!"

"I thought you said Brendan gave her an overdose."

Kenny grabbed his head in both hands. "I don't know, I don't know. It's all too much."

What fascinated Davies were the questions that went unasked, the questions any family member asks: *Where is she now? What happens next? What must I do?* Instead, his responses were all about fixing blame, like his sister when told her daughter's remains had been found. Brother and sister. Davies wondered how they'd each ended up like this; what had happened to them as children to make both so immune to grief and quick to blame.

Bates got on with the formalities. "Mr. Chynoweth, as family liaison officer, it is my job to help you with the next steps, such as funeral arrangements."

"As this is a murder investigation, however," Davies added, "the Coroner will hold your sister's body at the mortuary until we've made an arrest, or until twenty-eight days have elapsed. Both the Coroner's office and, should we have an arrest, that suspect's counsel, have the right to order another independent examination, so what I'm saying is that it may be some time before we can release your sister's body to the funeral directors. Do you understand?"

Chynoweth nodded. He smiled weakly, as if he seemed to think that was required.

"I might suggest Alfred Smith and Son, on Clarence Street," Bates said.

"You get a commission or something?"

Bates glared at Chynoweth. "I suggest them, Sir, because they're just around the corner from Causewayhead and might be convenient for you…and for those in town who cared about her. Do you know if she had made any arrangements as to her demise—a will or final instructions?"

Chynoweth seemed confused by this question, as if it never occurred to him.

"She wanted to be cremated," he said, finally. It was obvious he'd plucked the first thing to come into his head.

Davies was surprised when Bates asked suddenly, "When you visited your sister to comfort her last night, Mr. Chynoweth, did you notice anything unusual or awry; something that might have given you pause?"

"I don't know what you mean…"

"Think back. She had just learned her missing daughter was dead. Did she seem grief-stricken, suicidal, or perhaps fearful? Did she seem wary?"

Chynoweth looked off toward the ceiling. "Jittery, is what I remember."

"Was she, do you think, expecting someone?" Bates pressed.

The upturned hands again. "Don't know, do I?"

"Then may I ask, Mr. Chynoweth," Bates persisted, "when it was that you and she finished the champagne you'd brought and you departed the squat?"

"Didn't finish the champers..."

"Sir?"

"She didn't want my comfort is what I'm sayin'."

"She threw you out?" Davies asked.

"Nuthin' that dramatic; just made it clear she wanted to be alone. With the bottle. So I left."

"And what time would that have been?" Davies asked.

"Oh, early that was. Maybe half seven or close to eight. Still light, anyway."

"Meet anyone, did you?"

"That neighborhood?" he snorted.

THEY'D LEFT CHYNOWETH and now stood on the pavement outside the shop.

"Let's have the CCTV cameras checked at the Co-Op and Tesco's on Market Jew Street to see if he actually bought champagne," Davies said.

"What about the wine shop on Bread Street?"

Davies laughed. "Think he'd buy the real stuff? I'm thinking cheap Spanish cava." She put a hand on Bates's arm. "You were good in there, but angry. You all right?"

"Wanker had a hard-on when we entered, Morgan. It's why he sat back down so quickly."

"Did he, now? Well observed, Terry."

"What did he have on that computer screen he was trying so hard to shut down, is what I want to know," Bates said.

Thirty-Two

THE CLOUDS WERE SO HEAVY on Saturday afternoon they seemed to lean on the hilltops for support. A steady mist cloaked the windscreen of Morgan Davies's Ford estate at a rate annoyingly too fast to be coped with by the wipers' intermittent setting and too slow to warrant full-on, which set the blades squeaking.

She'd just passed the slowly turning wings of the wind farm pylons north of Summercourt on the A30, en route to the afternoon MCIT meeting, when the weekend traffic slowed to a crawl at the big interchange at the A39. Davies groaned and slapped her left palm on the gearshift knob.

Two days after the buried remains had been definitively identified as those of Rebecca Chynoweth, and almost thirty hours after the same girl's mother had been found murdered, Davies was no closer to having a prime suspect in either case. Add to that the two Newlyn murders and yesterday's accidental fall or assault involving the American archaeologist, Jeffers, as well as last night's report from the Penzance BCU that the witch, Tamsin Bran, had reported a knife stolen from her home—apparently the same knife found in Jude Chynoweth's chest—and Davies would have a hard time making sense of things with DCI Penwarren. Somewhere in all of this was also the nighttime attack on Terry Bates. The pieces didn't hang together.

Brendan Rice-Johnson was Davies's pick for Jude Chynoweth's murderer. He had motive—Chynoweth had become a costly liability and he already had another girl at the ready. He looked to have had opportunity. She'd have to find out precisely when he and the other girl hooked up Thursday night. And was there a connection between Rice-Johnson and Judith's dead daughter?

As the traffic loosened past the A39 junction, her brain loosened too, with a question: *Forget the junkie mother; why would anyone want to harm a young girl?*

She yanked the Ford left to the shoulder and left it idling. *You imbecile! Rice-Johnson was putting Becca into the Life, into the trade, an early recruit eventually to replace her mother—cute, fresh-faced, virginal. Just like the new girl. Just like the dead girls in Newlyn. Only even younger. Were they all his fantasy of a schoolgirl tart? So RJ makes a move on Becca, maybe tries to rape her, but the girl resists. They fight and he kills her to keep her from letting on to her mother.*

She slammed her car into gear and roared out onto the highway again.

DCI PENWARREN LISTENED to her theory.

"Maybe it's a pattern, Morgan, but maybe it's not. The question, it seems to me, is whether Rice-Johnson had any contact with Rebecca before she disappeared. And does he know anything about witchcraft?"

"Doesn't have to," Davies argued. "He has the Chynoweth woman's stories and all the pagan lore that's part of the ozone down here, like the Golowan festivities last weekend. There's plenty of knowledge readily available. We've only just begun investigating the bloke. Slippery devil, he is, too. Eton boy. Plenty smart."

"Eton boy who lives in a squat and runs prostitutes?!" Penwarren seemed personally offended. The DCI was a Harrow School boy. He kept Harrow's signature straw-boater on a hat stand in his office, like a flag of office.

"Yeah, well…go figure," Davies replied.

"Before we have a sudden conflagration of class indignation," West said, "may I just remind us all that the chap says he never knew the Chynoweth girl?"

"Says he hasn't, but the bloke's a pathological liar," Davies answered. "She's dead and he'll lie. But I'm guessing some of the other girls at the Newlyn quays might provide some history, given the proper incentive."

Penwarren nodded in assent.

"I'm just wondering," West said, "how the witch, Ms. Bran, just happened to report the loss of her 'athame' the very day Judith Chynoweth was murdered? I know it hasn't been positively identified as hers yet but, with all due respect to my esteemed colleague," he nodded toward Davies, "I think we may be losing track of the obvious. Tamsin Bran is connected to everything we are investigating: the dead girl who was her understudy, the strange robe in which the girl was wrapped, the possibly not so crazy mother, now dead, the suddenly 'missing' athame, perhaps even the costumed attack on Terry. Plus there's something else, a crude doll used by witches for spells, found at Carn Dewes and now in evidence."

"Any of this related to the American woman's tumble?" Penwarren asked.

"No idea yet, Sir. Sorry."

"Yet she insists she was pushed, according to the report."

"Which is why I've sent my SOCO lads up there this morning to look closer."

Penwarren stared at the wall opposite for a moment, then switched gears.

"PC Bates escorted Chynoweth to do the ID on his sister, Morgan. Did Bates learn anything?

Davies told him about the champagne.

"Champagne?" Penwarren snorted. "Hardly a night to celebrate."

"Actually, cheap store-brand Spanish Cava from the Market Jew Street Co-Op," Davies corrected. "We've got him on CCTV. We asked him about his visit. Sounds like she threw him out and kept the bubbly for herself."

"Well, that explains a lot," Dr. Duncan interrupted. "Some of the lab results came in an hour ago. Judith Chynoweth had a blood alcohol level just under three hundred milligrams per milliliter. That's three times the drinks driver limit."

"Are you saying she drank herself to death?!" Davies blurted.

"No. She overdosed on heroin, as it happens. But the alcohol hastened it. They build upon each other."

"That's more like it," Davies snapped, as if the dead woman had passed some sort of test.

"Anything from the swabs?" West asked.

"Sex was about the only thing she hadn't had."

It was quiet around the table for a moment.

"So, I'm seeing this scenario," West volunteered. "Brother buys a cheap bottle of bubbly. Then he hoofs it over to his sister's place, figuring the bubbly will help her in her time of grief. She doesn't share well with others and gives him the toss. She's spent the previous couple of nights in hospital coming down from a nasty fix. She drinks herself to sleep. Our lad Brendan shows up before he swans off to his new girl, finds Jude out cold, sees his opportunity, shoots her up, and finally he drives the knife into her chest to throw suspicion on Bran."

"Are you backing off your position that Bran is the obvious link, Calum?" Davies asked. "And how does he happen to have a 'medieval' knife at the ready? Where did he get it and why this particular night? And when does he end up shagging that other girl, anyway? How early?"

"Okay, I grant you, a lot hinges on when he met the other girl."

"She'll tell us. She's terrified."

Penwarren looked around the table. "So here's where we are. We have the discovery of a long dead girl, the murder of her mother, the fall or attempted murder of an archaeologist near the site where the girl's remains were found, the alleged theft of a ceremonial knife which, though as yet unidentified by Bran as hers, may have been used in some fashion in the mother's murder. Oh, and the attack on Terry. And two other dead prostitutes. Am I missing anything?"

Silent head-shaking around the table.

"Then get the hell out of here and find me something I can use! The press is all over the mother's murder and the Chief is all over me. I've got a press conference in half an hour and all I've got is the mother's cause of death!"

The team rose as one, with variously mumbled "Sirs," and shuffled out. All but Davies.

"Something else, Morgan?"

"Guv, I can't hold Rice-Johnson long on what we've got at this point. On the basis of scant evidence the TAG boys found, I'm holding him on a drugs offence. There's a partial print on the foil which may be his. But maybe not. With his new girl's help, we might be able to keep him on evidence of running prostitutes. Any thoughts?"

"You check the mother's mobile for numbers?"

"It wasn't in her bag when West's boys logged its contents the morning we found her."

"Odd, that. For a woman with her particular occupation."

"Reckon somebody didn't want it found. I'm guessing Rice-Johnson, since, according to her brother, he pimped her, too."

"Go with the drugs offence. It's weak but it'll hold until he talks to a solicitor. See what you can get on the prostitution, as well. Where is he, Penzance?"

Davies nodded.

"Pay him a friendly visit. Tell him about the overdose and tell him we're getting the lab results on the filter tip and the charred foil. See how that sits."

Davies bristled. She hated to be told to do what she'd already arranged. She stuffed the annoyance.

"Sir," she said.

Davies was almost out the door when she heard Penwarren mumble, "Eton, indeed..."

Thirty-Three

LIKE THE UNIFORMED CONSTABLES from Penzance, the SOCO searchers had come up with nothing in the ragged scrum of footpath at the edge of the china clay pit into which Amanda Jeffers had dropped. But their team leader, Ronnie Long, had. He'd worked backward from the site of the alleged fall and found, caught on the rough, wind-eroded surface of a granite outcrop by the path, a single black strand of hair, complete with follicle, as if someone had caught it there while pressing against the stone to hide. He slipped it into an evidence bag and called the rest of his team back. Then he called West.

West, who was on his way across Bodmin to the century-and-a-half-old Lanhydrock Cricket Club where he coached a junior team on Saturday afternoons, received a second call almost as soon as he'd rung off from Ronnie Long. This time it was Dr. Duncan.

"Time you headed home, isn't it Jennifer?"

"No rest for the wicked, Westie."

"Oh, yes?"

"Don't go there. I've been thinking more about the Chynoweth murder."

"Which one?"

"The mother."

"About?"

"That knife blow. As I make it from the angle of entry, it came down and slightly left to right from the front."

"Which means?

"Maybe nothing, but maybe also a leftie."

DAVIES HAD PICKED UP Bates in Penzance after the MCIT meeting and they were on their way to St. Euny for another talk with Tamsin Bran when Bates suddenly ordered Davies to pull over. Normally, the less senior officer would be the driver, but Morgan wasn't about to cede control of her car. She also wasn't used to being ordered about by junior constables.

"What?!"

"We missed something entirely."

"Who's 'we'?"

"All of us."

Surprise trumping her annoyance, Davies yanked the Ford estate off the road into a layby.

"Give."

Bates was staring forward, as if reading something off the windscreen. "There's a Sherlock Holmes story," she began. "I don't remember which one anymore, but it's something to do with a horse that's disappeared. Holmes remarks about the 'curious incident of the dog in the nighttime.' The hopeless Scotland Yard detective he's assisting says, 'The dog did nothing in the nighttime.'"

"And Holmes says, 'That is the curious incident,'" Davies said, finishing the quote. I read it, too. Very clever. What's your point?"

"We have a curious incident, ma'am," Bates said, facing Davies now. "The champagne bottle."

"What champagne bottle?"

"Exactly."

The coin dropped and Davies cursed. "Bloody hell! Chynoweth takes champagne to his sister, she sends him packing, but our boys find no champagne bottle at the squat!"

"Yes, ma'am. That's the curious incident. And there's something else."

Davies lifted an eyebrow.

"That weird swept path in the parlor."

"Wiped. No broom marks."

"So where's the cloth?"

"Also missing."

"Yes, ma'am. So far, anyway."

Davies was chuckling as she pulled the car back onto the road. "I hate you, Bates."

Bates smiled. "Thank you, ma'am."

THEY TURNED INTO the drive to the mill and met Bran's diminutive, wood-trimmed old Morris estate wagon as it was coming out. The late afternoon light slanted through the gnarled trees along the drive and the damp mosses hanging from them glinted silver. Davies got out and walked to the other car. The girl, Tegan, was in the passenger seat.

"Going somewhere, Ms. Bran?"

"To the market in St. Euny, if that's not a crime, detective. Then I'm giving Tegan a lift home."

Davies saw the girl's bicycle protruding from the little wagon's rear hatch. "I wonder if we might have a brief word first about your missing...what's it called?"

"Athame!" the girl beside Bran piped up.

"Thank you, Tegan. We can do this here, Ms. Bran, or at the station. Up to you..."

They gathered in the kitchen. The three adults sat in the chairs by the hearth. Tegan stood, shifting anxiously from foot to foot beside Tamsin's chair.

"You reported to the Penzance station that a knife of yours is missing," Davies began.

"You say that as if it were something from my kitchen, detective. This is much more serious."

"How serious?"

"What is missing is an ornate ceremonial knife used in certain spiritual rites. It belonged to my mother. And before her, my grandmother. In fact, I have no idea how old it is."

"And you noticed it missing...?"

"Yesterday morning."

"And how did you come to notice this one item..." Davies looked around the room taking in the several dozen other artifacts on display, "...missing yesterday?"

"I had need of it," Bran answered without hesitation. "For my work."

"And that work would be...?"

Bran smiled. "Nothing of concern to you, detective, I assure you. But let me just say that I know you know where it is. I can read that in you."

Davies looked at the girl who stood beside the witch. "I imagine, Ms. Bran, that there might be something young Tegan here could be busying herself with while we continue this conversation…?"

"I was wondering, Tegan" Bates chimed in, "whether you could explain to me the special powers of the herbs in that lovely knot garden you've been working on outside with Tamsin?"

The girl looked a question at Tamsin and the witch smiled. "Off you go then…"

"Thank you," Davies said after the two had left. She pulled her mobile from her pocket and brought up the digital image West had sent her.

"Would this be your missing knife?"

Bran peered at the screen and pressed a hand to her breast. "Blessings upon you, detective. Yes, that's my family's athame!"

"I wonder if you would be surprised to learn that we found it early yesterday morning plunged into the chest of Judith Chynoweth, now deceased. Had you paid her a visit, perhaps?"

Tamsin Bran stared, her preternatural calm shattered, her face and body rigid, as if flash frozen.

Davies scrolled to another photo. "And are you also missing this crudely-made doll, called a poppet? We've got that as well."

Out in the garden, they could hear Bates and the girl chattering like busy sparrows about the herbs and their uses.

Tamsin Bran looked at Davies. "I believe it is time I consulted a solicitor. I have done my best to help you in your investigations. I shall say no more. And I dare say that if you had more evidence, you'd already have arrested me. This interview is over, detective."

Thirty-Four

"LAND ON HER A BIT HARD, did you?" Bates asked as they drove back to Penzance for the second interview with Rice-Johnson. The sun had appeared and the late afternoon light was lengthening. Across the meadows, grazing sheep looked like gold nuggets scattered upon a cloth of emerald velvet.

"Sometimes you have to, especially with someone as well-defended as our Ms. Bran."

"Chynoweth didn't die from the knife wound."

"Doesn't matter. What matters is whether Bran knifed her."

"That still doesn't make her the murderer."

"Unless she also gave Chynoweth the overdose. Maybe we were getting too close to Bran. Or maybe Chynoweth threatened her after the child's bones were found. Bran could easily have opiates in her witchy pharmacy. Herbalist? Druggist? What's the difference, eh? Who's to say she didn't find Chynoweth passed out beside a champagne bottle and stab her, not knowing she was already dead?"

"Then why leave behind the cherished athame?"

Davies looked at Bates and smiled. "So she could report it stolen."

"You don't believe that."

Davies shot her a look. "What, you're a 'reader' now, too? I think it is entirely possible our Ms. Bran is one person during the day and quite another, as it were, at night."

"You're saying, what? Vampire? Werewolf? That's idiotic."

"I'm suggesting multiple personality disorder. Or schizophrenia. Something that switches on and off. Normally, she is preternaturally calm. I don't trust that. And if you ever speak to me like that in the station, constable, I'll send you down."

"Can't send me down, ma'am. I'm a PC—about as far down as you can get."

Davies barked a laugh and pretty soon Bates laughed, too. Bates wouldn't be a PC long, Davies thought.

ON THE WAY BACK to Penzance, Davies called Penwarren, caught him before he'd left for the day, and filled him in.

"I'd have preferred we had her thinking there was someone else in our sights, Morgan. Sometimes it's useful to be indirect."

Davies looked at her mobile and made a face.

"There's something else, Sir. I know TAGs have done a house-to-house in Belle Vue Terrace."

"Of course. Turned up nothing."

"We need to do it again. Maybe someone who isn't as big and imposing as the usual lads, know what I mean? The few people still living there are probably old, easily frightened."

"What are we looking for?'

"Anyone who saw anything or anyone moving in or around the squat Friday night or Saturday morning—pedestrians, cars, anything. And have the lad check every rubbish bin in the neighborhood for that empty bottle of cava. The bins won't have been emptied on the weekend."

"I'll get on to the TAG before I leave. Anything else you'd like me to attend to for you this afternoon, Morgan?"

Davies laughed. "No, Sir. And thank you."

"Always happy to be of service..."

But Davies had already rung off.

"YOU GOT NO REASON to keep me here," Brendan Rice-Johnson complained, though with a remarkable lack of passion. He had been moved from his holding cell to an interview room. He lounged in his chair with his legs propped on the table before him, as if in a poolside chaise waiting for someone to bring him some fruity rum drink.

"Actually, genius, we do," Davies said as she took the seat opposite and brushed his legs aside. "Two so far: prostitution and a likely drugs offence. The lab's checking both the filter and the foil we found in your squat for DNA and prints as we speak. Miss them, did you, when you did your little bit of housecleaning Friday morning? I don't suppose someone with your pedigree has much experience as a charwoman…

"Where's your solicitor, by the way?" I told you you'd need one, or are you formally waving your right?"

Rice-Johnson sighed, as if about to succumb to terminal boredom. "Don't need a solicitor. I already said…this is all nothing to do with me."

"As you wish, but under the rules of the Police and Criminal Evidence Act, I must inform you that this interview is being recorded so your solicitor may use it in your defense. As for whether this is nothing to do with you, the lab analysis will confirm or refute that shortly."

Davies glanced at a sheaf of notes which had nothing to do with this case, stalling for effect. "Oh, and did I mention," she said without looking up, "that we've discovered your former partner died from a heroin overdose? Combined with the other possible drugs offences you face, that's not looking good for you."

Rice-Johnson rocketed to his feet.

"Jude was dead when I found her! I had nothing to do with it!"

"Sit down!" she ordered. "Do you honestly expect me to believe you didn't cook up a lethal fix for your aging and increasingly costly girlfriend when you found her drunk Friday night, administered it, and then stabbed her in the chest to cast suspicion elsewhere?"

"That's preposterous!" Rice-Johnson was shouting now.

"Goodness, that's a four-syllable word. I'll wager you really did go to Eton."

"If she overdosed, she did it to herself! She was that far gone in the habit, she was!"

"Well, you of all people would know, because we reckon you're not just her lover and her pimp, but also her dealer.

"I've nothing to do with this!"

"You will need very skilled legal assistance to prove that, RJ. Shall I have someone assigned to represent you? This is moving on to the Crown Prosecution Service."

Thirty-Five

JUST AFTER TEN on Sunday morning, Calum West and two members of his team stood in the cobbled forecourt of Bosun's, the renovated stone shipping warehouse where Hunter and his expedition team had their lodgings. Hunter had mustered his students outside. West explained they'd found a strand of hair on a rock near the site where Jeffers had fallen and they needed to take DNA samples from the expedition members.

"But we were down at the site," one student said.

"Or at least on our way there," said another.

West held up a hand. "Please, we are not suggesting guilt on anyone's part here. This is simply normal procedure. Inconvenient, but necessary. My assistants here will be taking your name and quick swabs from the inside of your cheek."

While they worked, West took Hunter aside.

"I'm sorry to ask this, professor, but has there been any sign of animosity toward Ms. Jeffers by any of the students? Any bad blood?"

"None that I'm aware of, detective, though Amanda can ruffle feathers. I think it's fair to say they all hold her in high regard. She's a consummate professional."

West wondered if Hunter was being completely candid, but he nodded anyway.

When they returned to the group, the SOCO staff were just finishing bagging and tagging each sample. West thanked the students and they shuffled back into the residence in various states of discomfort, suddenly wary of their own.

Hunter was glad the expedition was nearly completed. His team was fracturing.

"YOU KNOW THAT PARTIAL DS Davies found on the edge of the farm track west of Carn Dewes, Boss?"

It was Beth Thompson, West's staff archeologist, calling on his mobile. He'd just cleared the roundabout west of the Penzance heliport on his way back to Bodmin.

"It's Sunday, Beth. You should be home with family."

"What family? And besides, you're not…"

"All right, guilty. What about the footprint?"

"The lugged pattern of that farm track print matches one our boys took outside the cellar window of the squat on Belle Vue."

"Check the data base for a brand match of the sole pattern, will you? Worth a try, anyway. And well done!"

West punched a number into his mobile.

"Where are you, Morgan?" he asked when she answered.

"Been clearing the cobwebs from my head with a walk along the Southwest Coast Path. I'm in Treen, a few miles from Land's End, at the Logan Rock Inn." She glanced at the half-empty pint of Tribute ale before her. "You've just interrupted my lunch."

"Lunch sounds lovely. I'm in Penzance. Be there in fifteen."

"Had I invited you?"

"Got something for you, love."

She looked at her mobile for a moment. "All right, if you must…"

Morgan took a sip from her pint and smiled. Calum would like the Logan Rock, but not because of its flower basket-hung, four hundred year-old granite exterior, or the cozy low-beamed bar, or the publican's Jack Russell terrier asleep by the cold summer hearth, dreaming of a winter fire. And not for the beer or the food, both of which were very good. No, he'd be bonkers because the pub was practically a museum to cricket, its walls festooned with memorabilia. West was growing on her. She wondered if she could live with a sports fanatic. Sweet bloke, and smart, too. But cricket? She stared out through the deep-set window by her table, shook her head and chuckled. *Get a grip, girl!*

* * *

"The weather hadn't yet gone nasty when you saw that print below the quoit; lucky break, that, Morgan," West said between bites of a disgracefully healthy mixed salad topped with fresh local crab. She worked on another pint and a bag of ready-salted crisps. West had spent nearly half an hour ogling all the cricket news-clippings, souvenirs, and signed photos on the walls in the pub's snug as ardently as if they were pictures of those naked Page Three girls in Rupert Murdock's tabloid, *The Sun*. He was happy as a kid in a toyshop.

Davies's eyes narrowed. "Logic, Calum, not luck. There had to be another route to the quoit besides the path from the farm at Trerane or Terry's attacker would have been seen climbing the tor. But I'll grant you the print was lucky; the rest of that path is nothing but granite rubble."

"You reckon the print's from the night Bates was attacked?"

"I'm going after a magistrate's order to search the witch's place tomorrow. Bran's still the only solid link we have."

"Morgan…these boot prints: they're a man's."

"Bugger!" Davies slammed a fist on their table and Calum's salad jumped. At the bar, the publican paused, hand and bar towel raised as if in stop-time.

"Okay, that brings us back to Rice-Johnson."

"Which means…"

"Which means we have to find out whether he's lying about having never known Jude's daughter. Bloody hell! I wish I'd known this earlier. I put the fear of God into him yesterday afternoon. He'll have a solicitor by now. I don't think we can get a search warrant to check the squat again, but I'll ask Mister.

"Meanwhile, I think I'm going to have to do a bit of streetwalking tonight. The other girls around the quays at Newlyn might know when RJ and Jude got together. If it was a year ago, he'd have known the girl."

Thirty-Six

CONSTABLE NIGEL CHACEWATER didn't fit West's "knuckle-dragger" stereotype for the guys in the Tactical Aid Group. Baby-faced but approaching thirty, he was slender, almost slight. Unruly ash blond hair fell from his forehead like a schoolboy's, framing eyes so blue they seemed kiln-baked by the Wedgewood china works up in Stoke-on-Trent. There was nothing the slightest bit threatening about him, which made him ideal for house-to-house interviews near crime scenes.

Sunday should have been ideal for catching families at home, but Chacewater was having little luck on Belle Vue Terrace. He had to laugh at the street name. It was true, cut as it was into a steep hillside, that it had a partial view to the east toward Mounts Bay. But the "vue" on the street itself was anything but "belle." The road was only one lane wide and dead-ended in a cluster of haphazard padlocked garages and workshops that huddled together like mangy feral dogs. Half of the connected terrace houses on the street were empty, their faded and flaked, two-story Victorian facades staring blankly out at the world like a row of old men with cataracts. The tiny walled front yards were either weed-choked or paved in concrete. A few appeared to be occupied but no one responded to his knock.

At one of the houses, just a few steps away from the empty house Judith Chynoweth and Rice-Johnson had occupied, which was still encircled with police tape, Chacewater saw movement behind a curtain. He knocked again.

"Good afternoon," he cried out in his cheeriest voice. "Neighborhood watch officer. Just calling to check on your safety, if I may?" He wished he was in uniform.

The curtain moved again and he caught the profile of a ferret-faced elderly woman. He held up his warrant card.

"Good afternoon, ma'am! I hope my visit is not too inconvenient."

The curtain dropped and the door, once painted in a shiny royal blue enamel but now chipped and creased like alligator skin, opened a crack. He saw it was chained.

"About time someone came around," a voice thin as air rasped. "Been calling the Council for weeks, I have."

"I'm terribly sorry, madam. Different department from mine. I'm police. Might we chat?"

"You think I opened the door to let the cat out?" She unhooked the chain.

"Of course not, madam."

It was the sort of interior Chacewater imagined filled terrace row houses like this throughout the length and breadth of Britain—overstuffed with ill-matched furniture too big for the living spaces, carpeted in patterns that bore no reference to the upholstery fabric or curtain designs, a patently fake electric fire where a hearth should be, and every horizontal surface littered with porcelain knick-knacks, none of which seemed to post-date the end of the last World War. Here and there, faded framed photos of family rose above the clutter as if struggling for air.

The old woman pointed to a chair and Chacewater sat. She sat opposite.

"Now then, Mrs….."

"Constantine. Flora Constantine."

"Mrs. Constantine, then. I wonder if you could tell me whether there have been any untoward movements or events along the terrace in recent weeks, activities which might have given you cause for concern as to your safety?"

The tiny woman's bright lavender eyes fixed him with a look. "You're joking, right?"

"Well, of course I know there has been some police activity this week."

"Not talking about that, young man, though I could have predicted it. You've no record of the calls I've made to the County Council these past few weeks?"

Chacewater tried to look chastened. "It's as I said earlier, ma'am, not my department, you see. I'm not with the Council." He flashed her a klieg-light smile. "But I would be delighted to learn what's troubled you."

The ferret-woman warmed to him. "Fancy a cuppa?"

"That would be splendid, Mrs. Constantine."

"Well then, come through to the kitchen. We'll chat there…"

Chacewater followed her as she scurried down a hall of worn black and white ceramic tiles to a spotless kitchen that looked little altered from the Fifties.

"Now then," Flora said a few minutes later as she poured coffee-black tea from a flower-print porcelain pot, "it's these comings and goings a few doors down."

"Yes?" Chacewater prompted, helping himself to milk and sugar.

"Mostly just this tart and her man, but sometimes others. Think I don't see them. But I do."

"I'm sure you're very observant, Mrs. Constantine."

"Someone has to be. Hardly anyone left on the street anymore."

"And this house would be?" Chacewater took out his notebook.

"Two doors down. The one the police visited. Empty for years, it's been. Till these lot showed up."

"Can you describe 'these lot,' ma'am?"

"Well, of course I can. Tart's skinny, has short spiky bleached hair. Pretty, I suppose, in a used up sort of way, if you get my meaning."

"And the bloke?"

"Big, broad-shouldered chap. Dresses like one of those homeless people but has a posh accent. Spoke with him on the street, I did. Then there are these others who come and go. Don't use the front door, mind; they all go to the top of the street and round the back. See them from my bedroom."

"What about their cars?"

"Oh, they don't usually have motors, these people; they walk. Except a car did visit a couple of days ago. Yes. Thursday evening it was. Been here before, it has, too. Usually goes up to the top of the street to the workshops. Black BMW. Three series."

"You knew the brand and model?" Chacewater was amazed.

"'Course I did! Watch that Jeremy Clarkson and his 'Top Gear' mates on the telly every week. Hilarious! Ever see it? Why this week they were racing old double-decker London buses around a track like they were bumper cars at Blackpool. Ever been to Blackpool?"

Chacewater smiled and shook his head. "Do you happen to remember what time you saw the BMW?"

"Arrived before eight, I should think. Maybe earlier. Still light, anyways. Didn't leave till after dark, though. Saw its headlights—those bright bluish new ones. Not like the warm yellow ones on the Cortina my Bert and I used to have."

Chacewater had what he needed. "And these comings and goings, they're what you've been trying to tell the Council about, Mrs. Constantine?"

She put a hand on his forearm, her eyes bright. "Please, call me Flora."

"Flora, then, ma'am. And no one from the Council's come around?"

"Oh they came, all right, awhile back. Midday. Knocked on the front door those people never use, got no answer and swanned off, job done. Bloody idiots, 'scuse my French."

Chacewater drained his cup and rose. "Thank you so much for your company and the cuppa, Mrs. Constantine. Be assured that I shall speak to the Council as soon as their offices open tomorrow morning."

"Leaving so soon, then?"

"Yes, so much to do, you see. But may I look in on you from time to time…Flora?"

The old woman almost bounced from her chair, took Chacewater's arm, and led him back down the hall to the front door. "I'm sure you're a very busy young man and I'm the least of your concerns, but yes, you may certainly stop by again! Tea cakes next time?"

"That would be lovely, ma'am. In the meantime, here's my card. If you see anything more, just ring this number and ask for me. Okay?"

Flora Constantine straightened to attention. "You can count on me, officer," she said, as if being sent on a dangerous mission.

Out on the pavement, Chacewater scanned the street for wheelie-bins, but empty houses don't create rubbish. He drove up to the dead end to turn around and, by the garages and workshops, he found one. Beneath empty plastic motor oil containers, various crumpled crisp packets, and a dirty towel, he found a heavy green bottle. An empty Co-Op brand Spanish cava.

He flipped open his mobile and had Comms notify the SOCO team. Then he settled into his vehicle and waited. It would have been a simple matter to lift the bottle and place it in an evidence bag, but that wasn't how the system worked. The scene of crimes people had to photograph the bottle *in situ*, along with everything else in the bin. Only then would it all be taken away in evidence.

THE MARY WILLIAMS QUAY in Newlyn was quiet on Sunday evening. Davies walked out to the end and, for a moment, relished the salt air. The girls Jude Chynoweth had been with days before were nowhere to be seen.

Under the lights, a young man still wearing the yellow rubber bottoms of his heavy weather gear, straps crossed over two broad shoulders, sat on a bollard and checked over the blue nylon nets beside his wood-hulled beam trawler, called the "Lady B." The ship had seen better days. She reckoned the young man was just starting out on his own, hopeful this was the first of an eventual fleet. He looked up, took Davies's measure, noted the absence of the usual tart's garb, and returned to his work. Davies guessed there was a live Lady B waiting at home and felt the slightest pang of envy.

"I wonder if I might have a word," she said, approaching the fisherman. She pulled her warrant card from her bag.

"Reckon you can," the young man said, eyeing the badge.

"Your name?"

"Brian Tregarren. What's this about?"

"Tregarren," Davies said. "I know that name. Had some good hauls lately."

Tregarren nodded, proud.

"It's no problem with you, Brian. I'm looking for a woman called Jude." She didn't know any of the other women's names. "I understand she's down here with her girlfriends most nights."

"Ain't seen her."

"But you know her?"

"Aye. Most of us do," he added, nodding in the direction of the silent boats moored on the quay. "Her girlfriends as well. Some of the men, well..."

He seemed almost embarrassed.

"I take your meaning," she said quickly. "Any idea where they go once the boats unload?"

The young man, who looked barely old enough to drive, much less captain a fishing boat, already had a weather-roughened face. And the act of perpetually squinting through the windows of his vessel's bridge had begun etching crow's feet. He lifted his handsome, unshaven chin toward Fore Street along the waterfront. "The Seahorse, sometimes. Or the Star. So I hear..."

SHE FOUND BOTH of the girls at the Seahorse Inn, a whitewashed, black-trimmed pub hardly wider than an alley. It was a Spartan affair conveniently situated directly across the road from the quayside ice house. The floor was bare wood and there were a few battered tables and chairs that looked as if they might have doubled as weapons in fights. A short bar was presided over by a petite but remarkably foul-mouthed platinum blond publican of indeterminate but not inconsiderable age. Davies knew her.

"Hold yer fuckin' water, Jamie; I'll get to you soon's I take care of Burt here. He's bigger'n you anyways! Meaner, too, ya' wet bastard!" she bellowed, amid accompanying laughter.

Until they noticed the stranger.

Roxy Pennard looked up from the pint of Doom Bar she was drawing when the quiet fell. She reached over the counter and shoved the men gathered there apart. "Come on now, Morgan, don't be bashful! What'll it be, dear? Take no notice of these louts. Hell, you've probably arrested half of them!"

Davies had always wondered if the woman was capable of speaking below a shout. "I was looking for Jude," she lied.

"Anybody seen Jude tonight?" the blond yelled.

"Try the back room," one of the men suggested. The others around him laughed.

She froze them with a look and strode to the rear, her low heels thudding like drumbeats on the bare floor.

The back room held a pool table and a small crowd of drinkers gathered around it hooting encouragement and insults while an old man quietly and methodically humbled his young opponent, ball by ball. The air was thick with cigarette and marijuana smoke. Off to one side, she saw one of Jude's girlfriends straddling the lap of one of the men, her mouth clamped against his like a lamprey and one hand working rhythmically between his legs. The other girl hung on another chap's arm watching the action. Davies approached the one who seemed least busy. The girl recognized her.

"I ain't doin' nothin' wrong," she growled. Her man pulled away and acted as if the girl had suddenly become invisible.

"Jude's dead."

The girl blanched. Then her back went up. "Nuffin' to do with me," she hissed.

"Did I say it did? I'd like a word. Outside. Now. I'm not here to make trouble for you. It's just a question and, as you say, nothing to do with you, personally."

The girl shrugged and nodded to a side door leading to a steep alley, the same one that led up to Morgan's house.

"Got a fag?" the girl asked outside.

"No. What's your name?"

"None of your business."

"You wouldn't tell me the truth anyway," Davies said, "but I may get back to you. How long did you know Jude?"

"Dunno, do I?"

"I'm going to make a leap of faith and assume you have a brain. Why don't you try using it, just for a moment."

The girl looked up at a blackening sky still tinged a dusky rose by a long-weary sun and concentrated, her head nodding as if counting backward. After a moment she said, "Year maybe? Maybe less. She's really dead?"

"Really."

"She OD or something?"

"We're not certain yet. She was found in the squat she shared with Brendan Rice-Johnson. I assume you know him?"

The young woman frosted over instantly. "I ain't sayin'."

"No, of course you're not. He's running you."

The girl looked away.

"Do you recall whether Rice-Johnson knew Jude before her daughter disappeared? You heard about that?"

A nod. "She talked about it all the time. Said some witch done it."

"Was she involved with RJ then?"

The girl's shoulders sagged. "Look, I just don't remember. Only, I don't think so, 'cause when she moved in with RJ she was really full of it. The chosen one, you know? Silly cow. That was sometime last summer. Maybe July or August?"

Davies jerked her head toward the door. "What about your friend in there? Would she remember?"

"Her? Nah. Midlands girl, she is. Got off the train maybe a month ago."

" 'Got off the train?' "

"End of the line it is, Penzance."

Thirty-Seven

JUST AFTER NINE on Monday morning, Terry Bates pulled several pages from the fax machine in the Penzance CID office. She tried to suppress the thrill that she had been reached at CID and not the uniformed service office down the hall.

The fax was from Astral Play, the mail-order pagan, medieval, Goth, and Steampunk emporium in Plymouth, and it listed all the customers who'd ordered goat-headed, horned god headdresses during the past two years. The list was longer than DS Davies had predicted.

The timing of most of the orders coincided roughly with the huge Glastonbury pagan festival up in Somerset. But on page two she found what she was looking for: an order from Penwith Gothica. To her surprise, however, the order had not been placed recently, but in late May of the previous year.

"THE QUESTION," DAVIES SAID, "is why Rice-Johnson hid the champers bottle."

"And wiped it clean," West added.

The two of them stood in the evidence room at the Bodmin Operations Centre. It was as spotless as a surgery. Body parts and other organic matter lay packaged in quietly humming refrigerated units. Other items, including the Spanish cava bottle, were arrayed in carefully labeled exhibit bags on gleaming steel shelves.

"Bugger," Davies snapped.

"Indeed. To me, the puzzle isn't why it was wiped. It's why Rice-Johnson bothered with the bottle at all. You'd think he'd see it as helping his alibi. It was nothing to do with him. And then hiding it up the street? What was the point?"

"Neat freak?"

"In that hovel?"

"I was joking. What if the Bran woman took it?"

"I thought you had Rice-Johnson in your sights."

"I do. But Bran gives me the creeps; she's otherworldly."

"Isn't that her job, as a witch?"

She shoved West gently with her shoulder. "You haven't met her. You don't know what she's like. She tells you things she couldn't know. Plus, it's her knife in Chynoweth's chest. And—lo and behold—she suddenly reports it missing. Too many coincidences around that woman."

"Okay, but how does Bran even locate Judith Chynoweth? It's not like she has a postal address."

"She follows her."

"From where? How does she even know where to find her to follow her?"

Davies slid a look at West. They'd never worked so closely together before and she was enjoying it, if partly because his brain worked like hers, constantly examining actions and their motivations. They were like two safe crackers, their ears pressed against the locked door listening for the slightest click for the next bit of the combination.

"Let's remember that Jude made Bran's life miserable by claiming she spirited Rebecca away. I'd keep an eye on someone who'd done that."

"Okay, but there's the matter of her prints. If she knifed the woman, why wouldn't she have wiped the weapon afterwards?"

"Same reason she reported it missing—to throw us off." She looked at her watch. "Just gone nine; too early for such discussions. You got a decent cup of coffee upstairs?"

West laughed. "Is the Pope a Catholic?"

"I thought he was a German."

"You're not only lapsed, but fallen. He's Argentinian now."

UPSTAIRS IN THE light-drenched SOCO headquarters, Davies sat at a small round table and watched dust motes dance through the rays of sun slanting through the windows while West brought their coffees.

Beth Thompson gave him two photos of the boot prints. He could tell she was excited about finding the match.

Davies bent over the photos, nodding as she examined the pattern. "Yes," she said, "they match. But what they match is anyone's guess. We need to get back into the squat, check out whatever shoes are there."

"Not going to happen anytime soon," West said. "Can't get a warrant. I tried. Magistrate's office says that while you're holding Rice-Johnson on two charges—both of them tenuous, according to them—neither has to do with your significant witness ever having been at or near Dewes Tor to leave a print. No way to tag him with being both there and at the entrance to the squat, and therefore no warrant to search the squat again."

"Bugger!"

"So you said earlier."

BATES WAS IN THE Penzance CID office writing up her report on the horned god head shipment to Penwith Gothica to take to the eleven a.m. MCIT meeting when she was called to reception.

"Thank you for seeing us," Brad Hunter said, as they stood in front of the bullet-proof glass partition in the security area. Amanda Jeffers, her right forearm encased in a fiberglass cast, was less gracious.

"What's the status of the investigation into my attack at Tredinney Common? What's happening? Anything?!"

"Let's step into an interview room, shall we?" Bates said. "I can bring you up to date."

This appeared to mollify Jeffers. Bates nodded to the officer behind the security glass, the door buzzed, and the two visitors trooped down the hall behind the young PC.

In the room, Bates gestured to two chairs beside a simple steel table. Her visitors remained standing.

"As you know," Bates began, "the initial investigation of the site of your fall..."

"Assault," Jeffers corrected, her eyes sharp as weapons.

"...alleged assault, was highly compromised by the very people sent to look for you. It's made it very difficult..."

"But Sergeant West's people collected DNA samples yesterday morning," Hunter said, "presumably because he was looking for a match with something found at the site."

"Yes, and the samples have been sent to the lab for testing and a comparison will be made. But, as perhaps you know, doctor," she said nodding toward Hunter, "DNA testing takes time, normally a week, though we've put a rush on it. It's only Monday morning. You'll have to be patient for a bit. And we do have a murder investigation underway as well."

"I could have been murdered!" Jeffers pressed.

Bates took a breath. "And, thankfully, you were not, Ms. Jeffers. All we ask is that you trust that we haven't forgotten you. Are you still staying at the apartments at Bosun's?"

Hunter nodded.

When they left, Bates looked at the officer in reception, Rhonda Wise, a graying veteran, and lifted an eyebrow in question.

"Well, who else, Terry?" Rhonda said. Once again, Bates's heart filled with a sense of belonging.

BY THE TIME HUNTER and Jeffers reached Carn Dewes, it was nearly noon. Hunter had completed the painstaking task of rebuilding the mortarless niche the previous afternoon. Tomorrow they would break down the operations tent and ask for a site inspection by English Heritage.

While Hunter prowled the grounds looking for any remaining evidence of the team's presence, Jeffers checked the fogou.

Hunter, who was at the upper end of the settlement, heard her shout his name. When he entered the beehive chamber, Jeffers pointed with her good arm. The two of them stood in the gloom, dumbstruck.

The principal parts of the niche Hunter had only just replaced in their original positions now lay splayed out across the earthen floor—the plinth, the two upright pillars, and the stone slab that had formed the false back—as if they'd been blown outward. Somehow, the thick horizontal stone that formed the niche's lintel, and which supported the inward-curving wall above it, was still in place, albeit tenuously.

Hunter was furious. "Why the fuck would anyone do this? Why would they bother?!"

Jeffers left his side, went out to the fogou's tunnel for a moment, and returned.

"Brad, the only footprints in the tunnel are ours. No one's been in here since last night."

"That's impossible."

"No kidding."

Thirty-Eight

AS USUAL, Desmond rockets round the corner of the mill as I ride up on my bike Monday morning and today he's talking up a storm. I truly wish I understood cat talk, because he always seems to have so much to say to me, especially today.

During the school year I hate Mondays, the start of five totally boring days of stuff I can't imagine ever needing to know. But this summer, working for Tamsin, Mondays are like a door opening to new surprises and, of course, Tamsin's company. Yeah, sure, there was that scary moment with her, but I believe in her, and I've let it go.

But when I go through to the kitchen with Desmond at my heels, Tamsin's not around. There's stuff piled in the sink to clean and dusting to do, but she's gone. I head out to the garden and call for her but get no answer. Desmond's looking at me like I'm bonkers. Then I twig what he's saying: *No Car!* And he's right. I didn't even notice. The Morris estate is gone.

I finally find a note by the sink: *Off to Carn Dewes to attend to a client. Back sometime after lunch. Tidy up as usual. See you soon!*

She signs the note with a little line drawing of a raven, which she's told me is what her Celtic surname, *Bran,* means. I really think that's cool and try to think of what I might draw for my own name.

Desmond jumps up on the counter while I'm doing the washing up, chatting away, his tail flicking jerkily this way and that. I finish at the sink and grab the feather duster from its hook by the herb shelves and start whisking away at the glass jars, not that it looks to me like they're all that dusty. The dustiest place is always that big cauldron hanging in the hearth. Even though it is summer, the soot drifts down through the big, gaping stone chimney like black snow and settles in the bowl. It's the devil to keep clean.

I'm just moving around the area where Tamsin keeps her most important things—the chalice, the bowl, the two brooms—when I come to the empty place where the athame should be. It makes my heart lurch, I can tell you. I dust the space anyway and then my vision starts to change. I'm still seeing the shelf around the corners of my eyes, but in the middle where the athame should be there's just this dark spot I've seen before. I know something's coming and I honestly want to turn away, but I can't. It's like I'm glued to the spot.

I don't know how long it takes, but then the dark spot clears and I can see Tamsin's athame exactly where it should be. It looks different, though, like there is a light inside it. The light glows and fades, like a beating heart, and then I see a shadow cross over it. I look hard as I can. I try to be a searchlight, but when the shadow passes, the athame is gone. I turn quickly to follow it and suddenly feel nauseous as I spin. That's when I see him—the back of a man slipping out the front door. I run, but I trip over Desmond, who seems stiff as a statue. It's like everything is frozen in time and I'm the only one moving—me and the man. When I throw open the door, though, my eyes come clear and all I can see is the front walk, the drive, and the lawn stretching down to the mill stream, all of it shimmery in the sunlight.

The man is gone. And I know that he wasn't there at all, not in the here and now anyway, but I try to see more of him. I know him somehow. I keep staring down the empty lane, trying to "see" him.

And I finally remember.

Thirty-Nine

"SO LET ME SEE if I've got this right," Penwarren said.

This was an ominous opening. The team was in the incident room at Bodmin again. It was just past eleven.

"We have, thanks to the TAG officer, a champagne bottle found in a bin in Belle Vue Terrace which has no prints and which Kenny Chynoweth's already said he took to his sister. It is an interesting discovery which tells us absolutely nothing, other than that someone unknown, for reasons we don't know, has wiped it clean and disposed of it...yes?"

Nods.

"And we have matching boot prints from both the squat and somewhere on or near Dewes Tor but we have no idea whose they are and no way, legally, to ascertain whether they belong to Mr. Rice-Johnson."

More nods.

"Or that, even if they are his, the one near Dewes Tor was made the night Terry here was attacked and by the same person."

Davies interrupted. "The print had to be coincident with the attack. The weather afterwards deteriorated but a faint print survived."

"And before?"

"Even worse, Sir; I checked with the Met Office weather records."

"Thank you, Morgan. At least someone here is on top of her game. And, not to diminish the attack on Terry, but we all understand, don't we, that none of this helps our cases with either the girl or her mother?"

West spoke up. "Actually, I've just received mitochondrial DNA profiles from the lab for the hairs found on the buried girl's cloak. The light one is definitely hers. It's been matched with her tooth DNA.

The other is black..."

"Rice-Johnson?" Penwarren asked.

"Unlikely, Sir," West said. "His is sandy brown."

"Tamsin Bran's hair is black," Davies said.

"Kenny Chynoweth's hair is black, too," Bates added. "Dyed is my guess."

"All of which suggests," Penwarren continued, "that someone other than sandy-haired Rice-Johnson was involved in the girl's death."

"But does not rule him out as the mother's killer," Davies insisted.

"Exactly, Morgan. Which makes knowing when Rice-Johnson and his latest girl 'hooked up,' as they say now, all the more important. Lisa Ames is her name? What's her status?"

"Gone to ground. Poor girl is terrified, as well she should be. I've had watchers on her. She's hiding out at a girlfriend's."

"Where?"

"Teneere housing estate."

"Lovely refuge. One of the most crime-ridden council housing estates in the county. Let's bring her in to Penzance. We've only got one question for her, no need to haul her up to the interview suites in Pool. Terry, can you handle that? Get a concrete answer on when they met that night."

"Sir."

Penwarren paused to consult his notes. "And what's this about a horned god headdress?"

"Worn by the person who assaulted me, Sir, and ordered by Kenny Chynoweth from a mail order company in Plymouth more than a year ago..."

"Hang on, Terry. Chynoweth is in business to sell such products. Do we have any evidence to suggest that this particular costume was worn by any of his customers during your attack?"

Terry suddenly felt out of her league. She had no experience wrestling with someone as senior as Penwarren but she was damned if she'd be found wanting.

"The question, is whether he ordered it for a customer, like any other product, or for himself. I suggest we check his sales records."

Penwarren smiled.

"I'll get on that," Davies said, "while Terry interviews the Ames girl."

"I APPRECIATE THE TRUST you place in me by calling, professor." Bran, Hunter, and Jeffers were in the beehive chamber at Carn Dewes.

"I think desperation might be a better term, and in any event it was Amanda's idea. We are beyond our depth here."

Tamsin Bran touched the cast on Jeffers's arm. "You've had a fall."

"I was..."

"Pushed. Yes. But you are healing quickly."

"How...?" Jeffers began, but Bran had turned her attention to the blasted slabs in the beehive chamber.

"This has always been my special place. My mother's, as well. We never quite understood why, but now, I think, it's clear."

"The figurine," Jeffers said.

Bran nodded. "Goddess worship dates from at least 20,000 BC in several places in Europe. The images of figures from that period emphasize the hips, the sagging breasts, the heavy belly, all aspects of the primal Mother Goddess, the universal symbol of life-giving and renewal. Interestingly enough, no similarly totemic male figurines exist from that period. There is no evidence of a father god. In the same way, there are few images from that period representing warfare. The images and figurines were all about fecundity, life-bearing, fruitfulness."

"This image looks wizened," Jeffers said, "and it's white."

"Yes, the Crone."

"But the other day," Hunter said, "you talked about how Wiccans recognize both a horned god and a priestess, and your own practice sees them as two sides of the same godhead."

"Duality came much later, perhaps 2500 BC, in the Bronze Age. It was a marriage, of sorts. The people who arrived here from the eastern steppes were patriarchal and worshipped the sky, the thunder, the lightning. I believe the co-equal male and female deities that we see in later pagan societies were an attempt to harmonize those two opposing belief systems. Before that, there was goddess worship."

"So this goddess figure?" Jeffers pressed.

"May predate that period."

"But how...?"

"How does it end up in an Iron Age settlement? It had to be carried along by goddess worshippers through the ages and this is simply where it ended up."

"But what about this?" Hunter asked, pointing to the scattered granite slabs.

"To understand this," Bran said, "we have to make a leap: that this is not just the last place the figurine ended up, but that this place is a portal to the Annown, where the goddess reigns still—something my mother always believed."

"Oh, come on," Jeffers said.

Bran lifted her hands. "Look, if you have a more persuasive analysis, professor, I should like to hear it. The question is why this has happened now and not some other time in history and I believe the answer stands beside you: Dr. Hunter is a spirit channeler, even though he does not know it."

"What?" Hunter said.

"You may remember my blacking out briefly when you visited me?"

"Yeah, that was weird, frankly."

"No, it was your power. You were channeling a message from the Annown directly to me. You just didn't know it. I've heard of it before, but it was a first for me and, as you say, strange. I think what is happening here in the fogou is that you are channeling messages from the Annown, and that more than anything else, they are signaling that they want the figurine replaced. Ignore that and I think you can expect more mischief."

Forty

"LAST YEAR'S ORDERS? We don't keep records that old," Kenny Chynoweth said between bites of a Cornish pasty and swigs from a beer bottle. The pastry flakes littered his paunch. "Bin the paperwork after twelve months, we do, after reporting to the Inland Revenue. Plus, we're always ordering at least six months ahead of each fashion season: spring orders for fall, summer orders for winter, fall orders for cruise season, and so on."

"Cruise? What is that, black leather bikinis?" Davies said.

Chynoweth smiled. "It's a term of art in the garment industry for early spring, Sergeant," he said looking her over, "though perhaps you've missed it."

Davies said nothing but her eyes burned two holes into Chynoweth's forehead.

"Why d'you want my records anyway? My filings with the Inland Revenue are current and in order."

"A constable was attacked one night last week up on Dewes Tor by someone wearing the costume of a horned goat. As it happens, you ordered just such a headdress last year from a mail order firm in Plymouth called 'Astral Play.' Have you any recollection of that order, Kenny?"

"I order lots of things from them."

Davies smiled. "But only one horned god costume, Kenny."

"Yeah, I ordered the headdress. So what? I wanted a pagan window display for the week before last year's Golowan festival. Town's crawling with pagans then. Somebody bought it for the festival parade, didn't they?!"

"Did they indeed? Can you prove that Kenny?"

"Like I said: binned the records. And what the hell are you doing messing with my business when you should be locking up Jude's killer?"

"And that would be...?"

"That Brendan bastard!"

Davies had to admit, it was a deft change of subject. "Not to worry, Kenny. You'll be happy to know he is in custody and we have his prints and DNA. And we're on our way to see Ms. Bran, the other person you suspect in your sister's murder. Maybe your sister was right about Bran all along. Think about it: our constable is attacked by someone in a pagan costume at Dewes Quoit, your niece is found wrapped in a pagan cloak beneath Dewes Quoit, and your sister is found with a pagan knife in her chest."

"Exactly what I mean. Jude knew. Maybe she knew too much."

"I thought you said 'that Brendan bastard' killed her?"

DAVIES FOUND CALUM WEST leaning against her car on Causewayhead holding a large shopping bag.

"What the hell are you doing here?"

"Always that gracious greeting..."

"I repeat," she said as she opened her door.

"Mister wants a fresh DNA swab from the witch."

She dropped into her seat and West climbed in the other side.

"How'd you know where to find me?"

"Instinct...and the ever helpful receptionist Rhonda at the station. I parked there and walked over. Thought we might visit Ms. Bran together. Get anything new from Chynoweth?"

"A headache. Says he's got no records confirming his purchase of the horned goat's head or its alleged sale to a Golowan reveler last year. I suspect the first claim is true, the second not." She put the car in gear and eased out of Causewayhead, making for the A30 and St. Euny. "What's in the bag?"

"Thought I do a bit of shopping while you were upstairs with the Godfather of Goths. The lovely Cassandra was very helpful."

"No doubt. Let me guess; is it one of those close-fitting black mesh vests to show off your pecs?"

"Something far sexier, my black-hearted lovely..."

"Your *what?!*"

West laughed. "Bear with me; I'm getting into my dark side." From the bag he pulled out a cardboard box from which he removed a tall, silver-studded black leather boot.

"It's so you," Davies said.

"This is, I'll have you know, the latest from Old Rock, the premier Goth boot company. Pair cost me more than a hundred quid, mind you, but look at this: calf high, with not one but four metal buckles in addition to the laces, not to mention the metal skull image spread across the toe box—which is steel reinforced, by the way—and the metal flame pattern on the back of the heel. This is art, this is. Plus, check out this inch-thick lugged sole!"

Davies glanced at it and abruptly yanked the car to the verge. "You found a match to the bloody print, didn't you, you bastard."

West grinned. His soft-featured face looked like a happy child's.

"Don't be so pleased. You're forgetting something."

"I know; the fact that he sells those uglies doesn't mean Rice-Johnson owns a pair."

"Or anyone else in Penzance with bad taste in shoes," Davies said as she pulled back on the highway.

Forty-One

"THANK GOODNESS YOU'VE COME!"

It was not the sort of greeting Davies had expected from Tamsin Bran.

"She always waits for me, you see," she said. "But she's not here. I rang her mother but she was drunk, I think, or anyway incomprehensible. Then I called the police. Where is she? Where's Tegan?"

Davies considered the edge of hysteria in the witch's voice. She had heard this voice before, the voice of mothers of missing children, the voice of panic and despair. But this wasn't a mother. This was a woman whose previous girl helper had been murdered, the woman whose knife had been found in that same girl's mother's chest, the woman whose latest helper she now claimed was missing.

"May we come in?"

Bran simply withdrew and let them follow. She stood at the kitchen sink and stared out the window to the garden. Her hand fluttered to a piece of paper on the millstone table behind her.

"I left her a note saying I had gone to Carn Dewes to help the American archaeologists and that I would soon be back. She left that on its other side."

Davies bent over to look at the note but did not touch it. *I saw who took your athame and have gone to fetch it.* It was written in clumsy block letters and beneath it the girl had drawn an eye.

"What's this bit?"

"I sign my notes to her with a line drawing of a raven; she's come up with an eye to sign hers, I imagine, because of her seeings, her clairvoyance. I imagine it's also a play on her surname, *St. Claire*. She's very clever." Tamsin covered her eyes with both hands, dragged the hands down her cheeks, and looked at the ceiling. "This is my fault. There have been forces I should have recognized. My mother even warned me, but I could sense no imminent danger."

"Your mother has been dead for years, Ms. Bran."

"Only to the rest of you; not to me."

"You were at Carn Dewes because..."

"Because they asked me to come to sort something for them."

For the first time, Bran registered West. "You're new. You've come for something from me. That's why you two are here. It isn't because of my call. But I am sorry, Sir, for your loss; you are nearing the end of that pain."

West blinked and struggled to regain his mental footing. "Detective Sergeant Calum West, ma'am; I'm a crime scene manager. And I'm afraid my job is to take a swab from inside your cheek. And...um...thank you for your sympathy."

Bran didn't hear this last. "Am I yet a suspect in Becca's death, a full year later? Or is this about the mother?!"

"Neither, Ms. Bran." West said, in a voice warm as the summer air. "It's to rule you out that we take this sample."

"To help with your enquiries? Yes, I've heard that euphemism before, Sergeant, the last time I was a suspect."

"You are not a suspect, Ms. Bran," West said, his voice deep and gentle.

Davies was disgusted. She could see what was happening. West had already succumbed to this handsomely exotic beauty. She reckoned Bran was used to having this effect.

"Let's be clear, Ms. Bran; you were never a suspect in Rebecca's disappearance," she said. "You were simply a person of interest. Second, you are a person of interest in the mother's case now. And how could you not be? It was your knife found in Judith Chynoweth's chest."

Bran did not respond.

West cleared his throat. "I wonder if I might just do what I was sent here for, ma'am?"

"Of course," Tamsin said, her voice dropping to a near whisper. "Of course you may."

She opened her mouth for West's swab and then signed the consent form.

Davies pointed to Tegan's note while pulling a sealable plastic bag from her jacket pocket. "May I take this?"

"What for?"

Davies slid the note into the bag without waiting for permission. "When two pre-adolescent girls suddenly go missing while in your employ, Ms. Bran, it begins to look like a pattern."

"But not one I have designed!"

"Or conjured?"

West stepped in. "Ms. Bran, why don't you tell us what Tegan's usual routine is and why today seems unusual."

The woman looked at him and relaxed slightly.

"She arrives by bicycle from St. Euny at about nine, depending on how bad things are at home for her, and they often are difficult. She is punctual and precise, a rare thing in a girl her age."

Davies could barely contain her impatience. "Was she even here today, Ms. Bran? Is there any evidence?"

"Of course! The kitchen and work spaces are spotless."

"You couldn't, perhaps, have accomplished that yourself?"

"I was with the Americans. What are you suggesting?"

"And so today, while you were out," West continued, "she carried on in your absence and then what would normally happen next?"

"She would have waited, given my note. We always spend afternoon time together."

"And instead?"

"She was not—is not—here!" The panic rose again. "And she says she's gone after my athame!"

"I might remind you, that your athame," Davies said, "is in our custody, as an exhibit in a murder investigation."

Bran grasped her hair in frustration. "She doesn't know that!"

West said, "I have heard about your skills, Ms. Bran, and I wonder why you did not perceive this event?"

Bran pushed the fingertips of her left hand against her left temple. While she massaged that spot she regarded West with exhausted futility. "Sergeant," she said, "I am not a seer. I can read those who are in my presence, like yourself, and therefore know about your loss. But I cannot see things beyond me, the way Tegan can. I did not, and could not, anticipate this."

"Ms. Bran," Davies said, taking charge again, "Tegan St. Claire is connected, however tangentially, with at least two and possibly three criminal investigations we have underway. If she has truly gone missing, I can promise you will have the full support of the Penzance force in the search for her. But isn't it entirely possible that you two have simply missed each other and that she is cycling home even as we speak?"

The witch looked away for several moments, then turned. "Her home, detective, is not exactly a haven. She stays here as long as she can."

"Could she have gone elsewhere? Penzance, perhaps, to look for your athame?"

"She would need transport. The bus perhaps? I just don't know. Where would she look, anyway?"

Davies felt herself softening. But how much of this act was simply savvy witchery? Was Bran protector or predator?

"LOOK, I'M JUST GOING TO say this and you can tell me to piss off if you want, but I think your prejudices are boxing you in," West said. They had just reached the end of Bran's drive and Davies had called Comms to put all available Penzance staff in search of the girl. She'd got a picture of the child from Bran and would email the image to all the other squad cars in the area when she could scan it at the office.

Davies spun around in her seat. "You're just mesmerized by her."

"No, you're blinded by her."

"You're telling me you don't find her attractive? And persuasive?"

"Stop."

"What?"

"Don't turn into the lane. And listen to me. For a change. I find you attractive. I find Bran persuasive. There's a difference. And I think it is time you got that straight and recruited her."

Davies was trying to digest West's first comment as she struggled with his second.

"Recruited her?"

"She has a skill, which she has proved in several interviews now, as I understand it. She reads people; she read me. Okay, so that's inadmissible in court, but don't you think it would be worthwhile to give her a shot at Rice-Johnson?"

'That's bloody daft."

"Compared to...what? Come on, Morgan, you've got a quarter century of experience on the force. As I see it, as you must see it, and as Mister certainly will see it, you haven't yet got the evidence to make a case against Rice-Johnson, though he is clearly our main suspect. You have made no case against Bran, either. Lots of circumstantial; no case. So why not ask for her help, eh? Might just flush her out."

"You're nuts."

"Yeah, but that's why you love me."

"I do?"

"Something else you might want to think about."

"Bran's left-handed."

"So am I, Morgan. It doesn't make me a suspect."

Davies stared at him a moment then rammed the gearshift of the Ford estate into reverse and backed down Bran's lane.

Some There Are Who Learn

Forty-Two

"MS. BRAN," Davies began when the surprised woman reopened her door, "you and I have not had the warmest of relations, for which I offer you my apologies. You have always been gracious. I have not. What's more, I should like to acknowledge the accuracy of your insights into my own past. I was unable to do that when you read me. Maintaining distance is, I suppose, the nature of my job."

"No, detective, it is simply your nature. It's how you've survived. And it's completely understandable given your history."

West looked at Davies.

Davies took a breath; she was struggling upstream in a rampant flood of contrary instincts.

"I confess that your apparent abilities go against everything I believe. They violate every principle of rationality and reason that has shaped my life."

"I know."

"But I find I can't dismiss them."

West could hardly believe his ears. He cleared his throat. "We should like your help, Ms. Bran," he said.

"In finding Tegan?"

"Not exactly," Davies said. "I want to take you to the Penzance station to consider a man we have in custody," Davies said. "Your skills as a reader might help us, however informally. I will be taking him into an interview room for questioning. Legally, I cannot permit you to participate or observe that interview. However, I think we can arrange for you to pass him in the hall when I've finished with him. Would that be enough time?"

"Very possibly, if I meet his eyes. Do I know him?"

"Almost certainly not. And he will not know you."

"Will this help us find Tegan?"

"I'm not sure, to be honest. But it may. They are connected, we believe. In the meantime, we have all available staff searching for her."

LISA AMES SAT ACROSS a small table from Terry Bates on a hard metal chair in an interview room at the Penzance BCU. Brendan's newest girl had come willingly enough when Bates collected her from the Teneere council estates, as well she might have given her girlfriend there had an out of control screaming toddler in the flat.

Without the makeup and the tart's outfit, the girl looked as she should: like a dimple-cheeked young checker at Tescos supermarket, perhaps, working a summer job before returning to school.

"Miss Ames…may I call you Lisa?"

A nod.

"This is not an interrogation, okay? There are no cameras or recording devices. I just have a question or two to ask you, the answers to which might help solve a serious crime. You are not in any way a suspect. Do you understand?"

Another nod.

"You are safe here. No one wants to hurt you. Quite the opposite, in fact. I think when all is said and done we may be able to help you. I'd like that. Would you?"

A third nod, just once. Lisa studied the scarred surface of the desk between them as if there were an escape route mapped there.

"I'm going to begin, Lisa, with a hard question, but this one is just between us girls. You don't even have to answer it."

No response.

"You're just off the train, aren't you Lisa? What brought you here?"

The girl's head did not lift.

"As far as I could get, innit?" she said finally.

"From what, Lisa? Were you in danger?"

No movement, then finally a look to one side, as if to another county altogether, and then a shrug.

"Listen carefully for a moment, and look at me directly, Lisa. Were you being abused?"

The girl did not respond. She straightened her slender back, proud and strong. And then a single tear escaped from the outer corner of her right eye and threatened to trace its way down her face. She scrubbed it away. Nothing else about her changed. Bates marveled at her strength.

"I'll take that as a 'yes'," Bates said softly. "And then you found Brendan, or he found you, yes?"

A nod.

"How?"

Lisa laughed without the slightest amusement. "You watch the other girls on the street or down at the quays. You learn who's in charge. You show up. One of them told RJ, I guess, and he came 'round looking for me. Said he had a special client for someone young-looking like me."

Bates watched the girl for a moment and tried to place herself in the same position. Bates, too, had been abused, by an uncle long ago, but her path had been different: she chose law enforcement. She loved the discipline, the rules, the order. Most all she loved the search for truth—like the truth those who should have protected her as a girl would never acknowledge.

"May we talk about that night with Brendan?"

The girl squeezed her eyes closed for a moment.

"Please?"

"He's an animal," Ames said in a whisper.

"Can you talk about it?"

Lisa shook her head and did not look up.

"Look, Lisa, I care about you and what's happened. I don't expect you to believe that, but I do, so I'll just say it. I'm not only a cop; I'm a woman. And I've been there. I've been abused."

Lisa lifted her head and peered at Bates.

"Okay," she said.

"I really only have one question—and it is very important in ways you won't understand just now. Will you help me?"

A nod.

"I need to know exactly when Brendan Rice-Johnson came to you that night. I won't ask you what happened, though that's something we—you and I—might talk about privately sometime. Can you remember when he collected you in Newlyn? Were you already drugged?

"No. That was later."

"When, then?"

"I'd only done one turn; a bloke who stank of fish. It was early yet. I'd gone back to the Seahorse. Brendan, he took me off for fish and chips at a stand near the docks. Just what I wanted to smell again, you know?" She shook her head.

"What time, do you reckon, luv?"

"Nine maybe, possibly later. The light had just failed. The evening light over the docks was a wonderful dusky rose color like I never seen where I came from. Anyway, then he took me to the flat we use. The flat I used earlier."

"And where's that flat, Lisa?"

With the certainty that she would never return there, the girl said, "Tewarveneth Street. Number Twelve. In the back."

There was just the fraction of a moment of self-control, and then tears came again. And though it was completely out of order, Bates rose, came around the table, and embraced the girl, cushioning her shudders like a human duvet and building a fearful hatred for Brendan Rice-Johnson.

RICE-JOHNSON WAS SITTING upright at the interview room table when Davies entered the room.

"I see a little time in a cell has improved your posture."

"Place is inhumane. Nothin' but hard surfaces, mattress included."

"Pretty cheeky complaint, for a squatter. I don't see your solicitor, by the way."

"Don't need one."

"Is that confidence, or just a con?"

"What do you think?"

"I ask the questions here, RJ, but I'll tell you what I think for free. I think you're perfectly happy to occupy one of Her Majesty's guest rooms because it's too dangerous for you right now on the outside. It's dangerous because you're not the free-agent pimp and small time drug dealer you pretend to be. You're part of something big time, and you have drawn far too much attention to yourself. A murder in the very squat you deal from—complete with media coverage—cannot be welcome to those who control you, now can it?"

Rice-Johnson shrugged and stared across the room, avoiding Davies's eyes, but his color had faded.

"Don't know what you're talkin' about," he said finally.

"Well, either you are the youngest case of Alzheimer's on record or you're lying through your teeth, because we have a reliable eyewitness who has watched the comings and goings at the squat for months. Oh, and I forgot to mention that your Ms. Ames is underage, so we've got you under Section 6 of the Sexual Offenses Act of 1956."

Rice-Johnson shrugged. "Then she lied to me."

"She's fifteen and looks it."

He stared at the ceiling, avoiding the detective's eyes. "Said she was seventeen. I believed her."

"A girl that young and innocent, a girl that petite, a girl who looks almost prepubescent? You believed her? Or, is it actually the case, RJ, that she was exactly what you were looking for? A godsend. Not for you, of course; you've already proved you like them older, so long as they're 'bloody marvelous in bed'. But for someone else. Someone, perhaps, you fear?"

Rice-Johnson stiffened like a poorly-dressed shop mannequin.

Davies leaned back in her chair and smiled. The edge was off her voice. "Then again, I might be able to help you out of the spot you're in, RJ. In fact, I'm almost certain I can. And I can see the charges already against you greatly reduced.

She saw a twitch in the corner of his right eye, the rigidity easing almost imperceptibly.

"It all depends upon your willingness to help us expose those who control you. We put them away, and you are no longer in danger. It's that simple."

"What about the Section 6?"

"Perhaps Ms. Ames did lie to you, RJ."

He nodded.

"Here's the first thing you can do to help yourself: I know you got the squat clean of drugs—though not as carefully as you might have, perhaps, what with Jude dead in the parlor. But I'm also thinking you didn't go far with them, given the time you called us. So I'm going to have our Scene of Crimes people do a sweep of the entire neighborhood. Care to help us narrow that search?"

Rice-Johnson's face was as expressive as a slab of Cornish slate.

"Right then, have it your way, RJ. But fair warning, eh? We're searching the flat in Newlyn your girl used. You see, two other very young Toms, now dead, are on our radar. We'll be checking for their DNA, too."

"WHAT *NOW*, DAMMIT?!"

Cassandra poked her head in Kenny's office. "Young lady here to see you, boss."

Chynoweth's smile was still in its infancy when a little girl marched in and announced, "I was Becca's best friend, and I saw you at Tamsin's house."

Tegan had finished the tidying up at the mill by early afternoon and had just enough time to cycle back to St. Euny to catch the bus to Penzance. It was something she and Becca had done sometimes, not that they were supposed to. They liked to pretend they were shoppers.

It was nearly two-thirty when she bounced out of the bus in Penzance town center and began striding up Causewayhead, a girl on a mission.

Kenny rose, the half-formed smile still in place and ushered his manager out. "Thank you, Cassandra, I'll carry on from here…"

"Now, Miss…I'm afraid I didn't catch your name," Chynoweth said returning to his seat.

"I'm Tegan St. Claire and I saw you take the athame. I've come to fetch it back."

"The what?"

"Tamsin's athame. Her ceremonial knife."

Chynoweth folded his hands over his belly and, with an effort, completed his smile. "I'm afraid you've made a mistake, young lady." The girl was lovely; strawberry blond hair below her shoulders, green eyes, her limbs already beginning to grow out toward womanhood.

"I saw you. You were wearing the same kind of black clothes you have on now and had your hair in that ponytail."

He forced a paternal chuckle. "You came through my shop, yes my dear? You may have noticed that almost all the clothes on offer here are black and I sell them to a lot of women, as well as men, with ponytails, as ponytails are popular just now. So, did you actually recognize me, or just someone who may have looked like me in similar clothes when this thing…this, what…?"

"Athame."

"…went missing? Did you, for example, see my face?"

"Didn't need to. I had one of my seeings. And I knew it was you, Becca's uncle. I remembered you."

Kenny had no memory of ever having met Tegan St. Claire. "A *seeing*, is it! Goodness! Are you a witch like your friend Tamsin?"

"Me? I don't know, but Tamsin says I have potential. 'Cause of my seeings."

"Does she, now; well, that changes everything! Do you know why?"

Tegan shook her head and her hair danced.

Kenny leaned slightly toward her. "You don't know who I really am, do you?"

"You're Becca's uncle."

He dropped his voice to a confidential whisper. "I am that, indeed, but I am also *Bucca*, the High Priest of Penwith, King of the Pagans in the whole of Cornwall. What do you think of that?"

"Tamsin's never said that name."

"Do you know why?"

Again, her hair flew.

"Because my existence is the greatest of great secrets. And that is because no one can become a witch unless I have initiated her in the wise ways."

"Tamsin's mum trained her. She told me."

"And who do you think trained Tamsin's mum?"

"Her mum's mum?"

Another warm chuckle and a beckoning finger. Tegan leaned a little closer, mesmerized by his rumbly voice.

"The Bucca trains them all. The Bucca, you see, is ageless. I have always existed; I shall always exist. I transcend time, you see, as do the wise ways."

"Like a vampire?"

Chynoweth waved the notion off. "Of course not. Vampires suck life out of others so they may continue to exist. The Bucca gives life and infuses his initiates with his essence, his timeless wisdom."

He let this sink in for a moment. He glanced toward the door and then leaned forward again, "Shall I tell you a secret?"

"Sure. I won't tell."

"I was training Rebecca before she went away."

Tegan's pale eyebrows leapt. "They found her, you know," was all she could think to say.

"Found her worldly remains, yes. Word has come to me, as it always does. But they did not find her spirit, because it is alive in the spirit world. And like all of my initiates who have gone over to the spirit world, I can communicate with her whenever I wish."

"You talk to Becca?!"

"All the time. I am also her uncle, remember. Although 'talk' is perhaps not the right word. I hear her thoughts, and she hears mine."

"You hearings are like my seeings!"

"Quite right. Tamsin is correct. You are a very promising young witch. Of course Becca told me this long ago. I am honored that Becca has brought you to me at last."

"She did?"

"Of course! Who else? I think it may be time for me to have a word with dear Tamsin about your training and initiation."

Tegan's heart felt suddenly swamped with excitement and hope.

"But first," Chynoweth whispered, drawing her close again. "We must address the matter of this missing knife."

"Athame."

"Yes. And here is my worry; if someone took the athame as you say, and I have no reason to doubt your great gifts, then the knife may still be in his or her hands. Not only that, but they may be pretending to be me, perhaps to confuse your seeing."

"I'm sure it was a man."

"Good, though the fact that the thief could mimic the clothes I sell here at the shop is troubling."

Chynoweth sat back and regarded the ceiling, his eyes blank as the plaster. Tegan held her breath.

"Thank you, Becca," he said finally, focusing on Tegan again.

"You heard her?"

He nodded. "And she heard me. She made a very wise observation. Becca says that so long as the athame is at large, you are in grave danger because your power is known to someone dangerous. She is right, of course, as she so often is, the dear girl. She says we must do two things: report the theft of the knife to the police, and find a safe place for you until the police have found the knife and arrested the thief. She says you are in danger at home, but also at Tamsin's where he's sensed you before. Becca has made a suggestion which I think very wise, and we shall discuss it on our way to the police. Fortunately, one of the detectives there, a Sergeant Davies, is a friend of mine."

"I know her, too! She came to the mill." She frowned. "She wasn't very friendly..."

Chynoweth nodded, sage-like. "What you must understand, my dear, is that it is not her job to be friendly; it is her job to solve crimes. That's hard work. Almost as hard as mine. Now then, are you ready? Becca thinks you are. She's very proud of you and your courage."

He rose, opened the door, and bowed. Tegan St. Claire skipped through and down the stairs.

Forty-Four

WHEN DAVIES WAS FINISHED with him, a uniformed constable led Rice-Johnson back to his cell. There was a blockage in the hall where Bates and Bran pretended to be in conversation. They broke it off as Rice-Johnson approached. A striking woman, Bran caught Rice-Johnson's eye. She smiled, he tilted his head and nodded, and then passed on.

A moment later, Davies joined the two women.

"He has not taken a life, but he is in fear for his own," Bran said to the detective.

Davies smiled. "Thank you, Tamsin. My thoughts exactly."

Bates answered a call on her mobile and waved to stop Davies from continuing to her office.

"When?" she said into her phone. "Good. This is from Comms? Yes, she's just out of an interview."

"What?" Davies asked.

"The shop manager at Penwith Gothica..."

"The Cassandra woman?"

"...says a young girl calling herself Becca's best friend showed up demanding to talk to Chynoweth this afternoon. Described her."

"Tegan!" Bran exclaimed.

"What else does she say?" Davies pressed.

"That after a private chat, Kenny whisked her out of the shop."

"Let's get over there; you're with me Terry. May we ask you to stay here, Ms. Bran?"

Bran nodded. "Please find her. Blessings on you both."

Bates driving this time, Davies made a quick call to Penwarren.

"Mister's on his way from Bodmin," she said after snapping shut her mobile. "MCIT meeting here in an hour or so. Put the strobes and roof lights on; Causewayhead will be crowded at this hour."

"WHY ARE YOUR car windows dark?" Tegan asked as Chynoweth maneuvered through the one-way traffic pattern in central Penzance.

"Because the Bucca must not be seen by those who could harm our witches. We can see out but they can't see in."

"Who'd want to harm us?"

Kenny heaved a theatrical sigh. "There are many who fear us. It has been so for centuries. We have been captured. We have been tortured. We have been killed. All because we have the wisdom of the wise ways. There are evil ones who hate us."

"They watch us? Tamsin lives alone. Is she in danger?"

"All of us are who have the special gifts."

"Me, too?"

"Oh yes, my dear, especially you because they sense you are among the chosen, because of what Tamsin calls your potential. But that is also why you found your way to me, to the Bucca. I know how to protect you. Your friend Becca gave me a plan."

"I miss her."

"We all do, and yet she is still with us if we know how to connect with her. Would you like to connect with Becca?"

"You can do that?"

"Of course I can. Is that what you truly desire? To be an initiate like Becca—to be like her?"

"Yes, but we need to find the athame, too. For Tamsin."

"I'm sure the Tamsin I know would give you permission to speak with Becca before we visited with Sergeant Davies about the knife."

"Athame."

"Yes, of course. I have a special place where Becca and I communicate most easily. I keep some of my most important magical tools there. It's just ahead. Shall we go there to speak with her in my magic room?"

"Yes, lets! I have so much to ask Becca."

"Then, after that, we'll go see the police, okay?"

"Uh-huh."

"LOOK, I MAY DRESS LIKE a cheap slag for this job, but I've a degree in fashion merchandising from the Plymouth College of Art, only no one was hiring, okay?" Cassandra said to Davies. "Except Kenny. And the pay for running the shop is brilliant. But there's other stuff that goes on here. Upstairs. Drugs, I reckon, because I reckon the shop doesn't make enough to support the two of us, or that flash car he owns."

"So you look the other way," Davies said.

"I gotta live, don't I? Economy sucks."

"And in the process, people die."

Cassandra squirmed behind her sales register. Her only customer had vanished as soon as Davies and Bates entered. Bates was in uniform, and Davies clearly didn't belong.

"I stay out of it, okay? But him walking outta here with that girl was just plain wrong, you know? What was she, ten maybe? So I called. I have my limits."

Davies smiled. "As an accessory to a possible drugs business, that's always good to hear. Why did she say she was here?"

"Said she'd seen him at Tamsin's, whoever that is. Said she was his dead niece's friend."

"How did he respond?"

"Don't know; he hustled me out. They were up there for quite a while."

"Any idea where they were going?" Bates asked.

Cassandra shook her head; her silver hoop earrings slapped her cheeks. "Only he took the car."

"We'll need to have a look upstairs," Davies said.

"Be my guest; reckon I'll lose my job anyway."

Davies looked around the cramped, windowless office. Slipping on a white latex glove, Bates hit the "Enter" key on Kenny's keyboard and brought his computer out of sleep mode. He'd been in the middle of placing orders when interrupted and hadn't signed out. On a hunch, she clicked the "Favorites" tab on his web browser.

"Bastard!" she spat, slapping the monitor so hard it shifted an inch across the desk.

"What?!"

"There's six kiddie porn sites on this list!" Bates was trembling with fury.

Davies came around behind the desk and peered at the screen.

"Put it back where it was, Terry. We can't acknowledge we've seen that, but if we get him we'll seize this."

Bates hammered a few keys and sleep mode was restored.

"But thank you, Terry. Thank you very much."

The two of them were almost out of the office when Davies stopped and turned.

"Terry. Look around. What's missing?"

"Excuse me?"

"Where's his inventory, his back-stock? There's no room here for storage. No boxes. There's someplace else."

"Yes, we get our deliveries here but he takes any overstock in a minivan to a storage space he has somewhere," Cassandra explained. "No idea where, honestly."

"You never see the invoices?" Davies pressed.

"No!" she said. She was pleading. "I just merchandise the shop and sell. That's it. Nothing to do with the rest of it!"

Forty-Five

AS THEY DROVE BACK to the station through a persistent rain that had shoppers scurrying along the shiny granite pavements, Davies called Comms to increase the alert on Tegan St. Claire from missing person to probable abduction. But there were precious few response units available and it was a big county. She had another plan, however, and just before the five o'clock emergency MCIT meeting at the BCU, she had Rice-Johnson moved to the interview room again and had the tape and camera activated.

Rice-Johnson sat on his steel chair. Davies leaned against the door.

"Still no solicitor, RJ? Well, never mind; I probably should release you, anyway."

She watched his body tense.

"I had you for Jude's murder, RJ. Had you wrapped up in a nice neat package: the body at your squat, the overdose, the time gaps in your story, the drugged new recruit giving you a convenient but bogus alibi? Perfect but for one thing: we have no solid forensic evidence to warrant naming you as our prime suspect, much as I'd like to. And no connection to the death of those other Newlyn girls, though we're still waiting for forensics, mind."

Rice-Johnson's smile was very nearly a sneer.

"On the other hand, I do have you, by the balls if I may be so indelicate, on a sufficient number of lesser charges: drugs possession, running prostitutes, sex with a minor..."

He shot upright: "You said you believed me about Ames!"

"Changed my mind, didn't I? Although, that could change again. Way I look at it, I can put you back on the street and let whatever happens to your sorry arse happen, or I can get you locked away for a good long while. It's a choice I have to make, you see."

She tried to stifle a smile. RJ looked like a fox treed by hounds.

"On the other hand, I might be able to arrange to have Her Majesty continue to provide you with three gourmet meals a day and a safe, if Spartan, hideout here for a while, if you will provide me something in return."

Rice-Johnson stared at the ceiling, as if seeking guidance there. "What?" he said finally.

Davies smiled. "Let's return to our last interview, shall we? There's someplace close by the squat, I reckon, where you keep the drugs stash…on behalf of someone else, of course. And I believe we now know who that someone else is. Thankfully for you, he is in much bigger trouble than just for supplying drugs to a punter like you, which means you are in a powerful position to help us without being fingered for doing so. Nice, eh? You might finally get out of here and not get yourself killed when you do."

Rice-Johnson stared at Davies, blinking several times, as if doing complex mathematical sums in his head.

"There's a large purpose-built garage he uses as a warehouse," he said, finally. "Top of Belle Vue, number 34. Concrete block with a slate roof. Poshest and biggest in the cul-de-sac. Automatic drive-in garage door. It's why we lived in the squat down the street: to keep an eye on it."

"For?'

"For Kenny fucking Chynoweth, like you didn't know! Part of the deal was Jude living with me. Keep an eye on her, too, and have her earn her keep while we're at it. A bit too much of a loose cannon for him, she was."

"And the other girls?"

"Part of the cover. An enterprise to shield an enterprise. A loss-leader, those girls are."

"Excuse me?"

"Loss-leader. You know, like the discount bins in the center aisle at the Tescos. They draw you in with the value and get you to buy other stuff at full price. Don't earn their keep, really, the girls; just a cost of doing business. They pull in the new customers for the main business."

Loss-leaders. Davies resisted the urge to strangle him.

"Why'd you keep at it, RJ?"

"Fell for Jude is why, innit?! Couldn't help it. Something about her."

Davies said nothing. For the first time, Rice-Johnson seemed genuine; his breathing was momentarily ragged, but he got himself under control.

"He killed her. Had to have. His own sister, for Christ's sake. Then he tried to set me up for the job."

"And you believe this because…?"

"Needle mark inside her right elbow, that's why. Saw it when I found her. That vein hadn't collapsed yet because she was right handed and was clumsy with her left. Shot up her left arm first and when those veins finally collapsed, she used her legs and feet. So somebody else had to have shot her up inside that right elbow. Who else was there that night, but that slimy fucker?"

"Besides you. Why not you, RJ?"

"Could never have done it. Tried to get her to wind it down when we met, but she was already too far gone, thanks to Chynoweth. I never shot her up. Never. That was all about her. And like I said, I wasn't there. Until it was too late."

"But you still haven't told me why you continued to work for the 'slimy fucker.' You could have taken Jude away."

Rice-Johnson stared at the floor and shook his head.

"Chynoweth made his connections years ago and he works hard to maintain them, okay? A good soldier in a big army, he is. But he's dumber than shit about business. Knows what he knows, does what he does, and no concept of management. Meanwhile, I've been skimming a small fortune off the top. I was gonna have us slip away soon, me and Jude. He's got no idea. But I figure at some point Jude threatened him somehow. She was crazy when she was lit. Killed her to shut her up, he did. Kill me, too, if he gets the chance."

"A 'small fortune' you'd have to share with Jude sounds like a powerful motive for you to murder her, RJ. No sharing that way." She pushed off the wall and turned to leave.

"Tell you something else, okay?" Rice-Johnson blurted. "Guy's a perv. Always wanted me to find him some little girl he could have just for himself. That's why I recruited the Ames girl; she looks so young. Like a schoolgirl."

"*Is* so young, RJ. *Is* a schoolgirl, or should be. Just like the other two we found in Newlyn a few weeks ago. Young. Very. But not as young as his niece, Rebecca."

Rice-Johnson's mouth opened but he was speechless.

BATES WAS WAITING for Davies in the hall.

"You okay Morgan?" she asked when she saw Davies's face.

"I hate the bastard, but I think Bran's right. He hasn't killed anyone, though he had both opportunity and motive."

"Listen, I checked Astral Play's shipping date for the horned god costume. It would have reached Penwith Gothica about a week before last year's Golowan festival, like Chynoweth said."

"And that helps us how?" Davies snapped.

"Stay with me for a minute; Golowan's not the same dates every June; it varies according to the weekend closest to the longest day. This year the parade date was the twenty-fourth. That was the night I was attacked. Last year, though, it was the twenty-fifth."

"And?" They'd just reached the door to the CID office.

"The twenty-fifth was the night Rebecca Chynoweth went missing last year. The mother reported it morning of the twenty-sixth. Maybe Rebecca was waiting on Causewayhead that night for Tamsin to get out of her meeting and met someone else, like her uncle. And so I'm thinking it isn't a coincidence that the horned god was at Dewes Quoit this year, right where the girl was buried, on the very night of the parade; I'm thinking it was an anniversary visit. I'm thinking he wore the outfit a year ago as well."

"That's sick."

"No shit, Sarge."

Forty-Six

THE GARAGE DOOR LIFTED as the BMW approached 34 Belle Vue Terrace and the inside lights came on automatically as the car purred into its place.

"Wow, that's cool!" Tegan said as the door closed behind them. Chynoweth got out, circled the rear of the car, and opened the passenger door with a bow.

The walls of the warehouse were stacked high with boxes and at one end a stainless steel counter held dozens of small plastic-wrapped packages laid in neat rows.

"This is your magical place?" Tegan asked as she got out.

Chynoweth heard the edge of worry in the girl's voice and chuckled. "Oh, no, my dear. That's in the next room, the special place where Becca likes to talk with me. Are you ready to see it?"

Tegan nodded.

Chynoweth fit a key into the lock on one of two doors along the back wall of the big garage. Opening it with a flourish, he flicked a light switch and swept Tegan inside.

The room, roughly twelve feet square, was aglow from the fairy lights that edged the perimeter of the ceiling. On the oxblood red walls, spotlit by halogen tracklights, there were prints of occult scenes: a ring of naked dancing maidens in a forest glade, another topless maiden, arms raised before a ceremonial fire, and a tinted photo of Dewes Quoit, among others. In the center of the space, upon a deep purple carpet, a table draped in black velvet supported a tarnished silver candelabra holding five red tapers. Beyond it was a tufted black leather Chesterfield settee. A fur-trimmed red gown was draped across it. In another corner, mounted on a short stand, hung the goat-shaped head of the horned god, wrapped in another red cloak. Beside it, arranged as if it were an altar, was a cabinet holding a crystal orb and a single candle. A thickly braided curtain enclosed the opposite corner of the room.

Tegan St. Claire stood just inside the door and marveled at the magically illuminated room. It was like looking at a shop window Christmas display, only better. Everywhere she looked there was some new surprise.

"No wonder Becca likes to come here to talk!" she said. "It's way better than Tamsin's kitchen!"

Chynoweth closed the door behind her and said, "Shall we invite Becca to visit us?"

"Yes, lets!"

"Ah, but we have a ritual to perform before she will come, my dear."

"Tamsin does them all the time."

"Of course she does, but this one is special. It's to call on Becca!"

"What do we do?"

"First, we must dress in our ceremonial gowns. Yours is that one with the fur trim. You may change behind the braided curtain, and while you do I shall change into mine.

Tegan emerged a few moments later in her robe to find Chynoweth had donned the horned god headdress and cloak.

"That's really awesome, but also kind of scary."

"You needn't worry; this is the Bucca's ceremonial dress, but I am still Becca's uncle inside. Now we light all the candles and put on the music that acts as the channel through which Becca comes to us. Has Tamsin never told you about the Horned God?"

Tegan shook her head.

"I must speak to her. The Horned God is how the Bucca shows himself to his initiates, those young ladies, like yourself, who are ready to learn the wise ways. He is the male half of nature; you are the female half, as Becca was before you, and Tamsin before her. He puts on his headdress and then he honors the new initiate, which is to say you, in that special fur-trimmed gown. It all happens in silence.

"But that is in the future; today we aim to bring Becca to us, and to do that we drink a small potion—I'm sure you've seen Tamsin prepare potions..."

"She lets me help her!"

"She does that because she believes in your potential. The potion is small, hardly a thimbleful. It's something Becca likes and which summons her. We both sip this, you and I. And when we are done, the door is open for Becca to join us. Sometimes we have to wait a bit, but she always comes. Isn't that exciting?"

"She'll really be with us?"

"Oh yes, absolutely. Because she so much wants to, you see. Because she loves and misses you. You will see her, and hear her. You will be like sisters."

"What have I got to do, then?"

"Let me prepare the potion first. Are you ready to welcome her back into your heart?"

"Oh, yes!"

Chynoweth lit the candles, dimmed the lights, and switched on a small CD player near the cabinet. Barely audible Gregorian chant filtered through the room. Then he bent and opened the small cabinet and withdrew a fluted cordial glass, a cut crystal flask of orange-infused Russian vodka, and a small plastic container. With his back to Tegan he removed one white Ambien pill from the container and crushed it with a black basalt mortar and pestle, shifting the powder to the glass. Then he added a measure of orange vodka and swirled the emulsion. He placed the glittering glass upon the velvet topped table, raised his arms to the ceiling, and then brought his hands together as if in prayer, remaining motionless for a moment. In the glass, the pill had dissolved.

"Come, my dear," he finally said to Tegan. "It is time to begin inviting our Becca home. Are you ready to hear her?"

Tegan nodded.

"We will each sip from this lovely glass in turn: first me, then you, until it is empty. The vapors may tingle your nose and the drink may feel sharp in your throat, but that is just part of the ritual, and what Becca loves about it."

Chynoweth took the glass to his mouth and pretended to sip. Then, holding it in his hands like a chalice, he tipped it to Tegan St. Claire's lips. As expected, she coughed.

"It's kind of hot and greasy-feeling on my tongue," she said, wiping her lips on her sleeve after catching her breath.

"You are absolutely right, my dear; that is as it is intended to be, but it is smooth as you sip it, with that nice taste of orange, and it warms your tummy. Becca told me you would sip with me to bring her to us."

He put it again to his lips and then held the glass for the girl. This time she drank more deeply and stifled her cough to be brave. She would do anything for Becca.

After two more exchanges, the glass was empty.

They listened to the music for a while and soon Tegan said, "I feel a little sleepy or something."

"Me, too; our spell is working. This is what always happens when she's coming. She wants us to feel completely relaxed, you see."

"Um-hmm."

Tegan was struggling to stay awake; Chynoweth watched her carefully and put a hand on her slender leg. "It's okay to close your eyes during the spell, dear; you will hear her anyway. It won't be long." And it wasn't. Tegan St. Claire was asleep in a matter of minutes.

Chynoweth laid her out on the settee and opened her robe. To his surprise, she had taken off all her clothes. Angelic, she was. So chaste. Her skin clear and fresh as a baby's. As always in situations like this—with Becca, with the other young girls—he saw his father and his pre-adolescent sister thrashing around in bed and felt his desire grow like a fire in his skull. He wanted the girl now, right now, as she slept, and struggled with the wanting. But that was not in his grand plan. Instead, he closed the cheap robe and retied its sash. Soon, oh yes, soon, but not yet. And not here.

As he gazed at her slumbering form, her unformed chest rising and falling ever so slowly, he wished she'd found him a week earlier, during Golowan. That would have been perfect. That would have been an anniversary: she and Becca; just a year apart. But this would have to do.

And unlike Becca, this one would not be an accident. This one was too dangerous to live.

Like Jude.

Forty-Seven

DCI PENWARREN WAS MOMENTARILY SPEECHLESS when Davies and West walked into the cramped Penzance CID room with Tamsin Bran in tow. But when they explained the help she'd already provided, and the fact that she was no longer a "person of interest," Penwarren relented. At that moment, Rhonda Wise slipped in the room with a message. Davies glanced at it.

"Morgan?"

"It's from Nigel Chacewater, Sir: one of our TAG men. He befriended that elderly woman on Belle Vue Terrace I told you about yesterday. She reports a black BMW drove up the street and into a garage in the cul-de-sac at the top a little over an hour ago. Says it's the same car that left the night Jude Chynoweth was killed."

"He's already told us he was there."

"Except that Mrs. Constantine says the BMW didn't leave until well after dark that night, which is to say after Judith was killed. Kenny told us he left while it was still light." She handed him the message.

Penwarren looked at it, but without actually reading it, then acted. "Right, then. That's it. We move our people in on the garage immediately, but with care. We can't afford to frighten the man. West, I want you there, too, in case we need you particular skills, yet again. How quickly can you get the SOCO team and some more TAG boys here?"

"Fifteen minutes, guv; I called them down before the meeting just in case. They're already past the Hayle roundabout."

"Nice thinking, Calum."

"Morgan's idea, actually."

Penwarren looked at Davies and shook his head. "I'm beginning to feel like a figurehead." He walked to the large street map on the wall of the office that had been his for so many years.

"Belle Vue's got only one outlet but there are alleys. I'll have uniformed units stand by on both Rosevean and St. Mary's streets. We'll box him in. No lights, no sirens." He looked at the witch. "Ms. Bran, you're with me."

KENNY CHYNOWETH RAN A THIN LINE of coke on the stainless steel counter in the garage and inhaled it in swift short snorts, without implement, his left nostril pressed against the steel, his right compressed with a pudgy finger. He unlocked the second door in the back of the garage. Inside was a white minivan. Back in the magic room he snuffed the candles, gathered the sleeping girl in his arms, carried her to the van, and tipped her into the back. He stroked her downy cheek, then covered her with a brown tarp. He relocked the building's interior doors and, when the rear garage door opened, eased the minivan down a rutted gravel track wedged between the walls of two semi-detached terrace houses facing Rosevean Road. A sharp right onto Empress Avenue, connecting to Coombe Road, and in minutes he was at the Treweath roundabout on the A30 and heading west toward the high granite spine of the peninsula. Out clean and fast; he could feel the coke high coming on. He could feel the magic.

FIFTEEN MINUTES LATER, the TAG boys pried open the small door beside the front garage entrance. It had just gone six. Unarmed as usual, Davies stepped through, called Chynoweth's name, but got no response. The garage was windowless and dim but in the shaft of grey light bleeding through the opened door she could make out the BMW. Damp tyre tracks led under the garage door from the wet cul-de-sac.

Davies found the light switch. Noting the doors at the back, she called out again, with the same negative result. Using gloves, she tried both knobs but found them locked. She backtracked to the front door where Penwarren and Bates waited. West and two TAG men stood behind them, already suited up in Tyvek.

"I just checked," Bates told her, "and he does indeed have two vehicles registered: the BMW and a white Ford minivan, W11 plate."

The back doors in the garage were steel, but it only took one of the TAG officers a few moments to force the lock to the "magic" room and flick on the lights.

"Clear," he called. "Looks like bloody Halloween in here. Candle smoke, too."

Davies stayed just outside but Bates lurched toward the room when she saw the spot-lit horned god headdress. Davies yanked her back.

"That's it! That's what attacked me!"

West was still in the garage leaning over the steel counter. "There's some residue here; coke I think." A large, burlap-lined box at one end of the table held stacks of clear plastic packets that he was certain contained heroin. Beside it, several other boxes held prescription painkillers—oxycontin, Ambien, hydrocodone, and more.

Davies came up beside him. "Bloody full service pharmacy, this is..."

"Hang on," West said. "I've seen this fabric before. Boss?" he called to Penwarren. "We have an exhibit at Bodmin, a crude doll. The Americans found it in the chamber at Carn Dewes one morning last week. It's covered in this material, which I'm guessing is what his heroin is shipped in."

"He makes dolls?" Penwarren said.

"It was female and had a thorn thrust between its legs."

"Jesus Christ," Penwarren said.

A moment later, another of the TAG boys had the second back door open. "Empty," he called. "Fresh auto exhaust, though."

Penwarren radioed Comms. "I want every response unit we can spare looking for white Ford minivans in the Penzance area. Pull every bloody one of them over, regardless of registration plate. We're looking for a man, early- to mid-thirties, described as having a ponytail. A young girl may be in the vehicle. And scramble Oscar 99 immediately. We don't have many hours of light left and we need that chopper. A child's life is at risk. If the Superintendent has a problem with this, put him on to me immediately."

Penwarren turned to Tamsin Bran.

"Ms. Bran, if you have any insight into what may happen next, please let me know."

"Let me into the room."

"Touch nothing."

Bran nodded.

"HE HAS CREATED A private world," she said when she emerged a few moments later. "It is a mirror of his soul, that room. And it is readable, as if he were still here."

"What's that mean in plain English?" Davies demanded.

"The man is a charlatan. He wraps himself in the mystery of witchcraft but has no real knowledge, no skill, no connection with the Old Craft or with Wicca. It is a masquerade for him, like the horned god headdress, a way to attain other objectives."

"Meaning?"

"Girls like Tegan. Like Becca. Perhaps others as well…"

"Tamsin!" Bates interrupted. "The other day you talked about the sexual union of the horned god and the goddess."

"The Great Rite, yes."

"That's what he'd planned! The bastard's a pedophile and he uses this mumbo jumbo to seduce these girls. He tried it on Rebecca and she panicked. That's the scream the old farmer below Dewes Tor heard that night. He attacked her, struggled to shut her up, but ended up strangling her instead!"

Bates was trembling with fury. Davies put a hand on her shoulder. Bates shook it off.

Davies gestured to the steel counter. "I suspect he's drugged her."

"And he's high himself," West added.

"Where would he go next?" Penwarren asked.

"To Dewes Tor and the quoit," Bran said. "He sees himself in the midst of a mystical ritual. I think Tegan is still alive, but we need more help to save her, Inspector…"

"I already have everyone at my disposal on this!" Penwarren's patience was fraying.

"That's not what I mean. Listen to me, all of you: we do not have much time. Last week the American archaeologists at Carn Dewes found and removed a stone figurine, which may be the most ancient representation of a version of the earth goddess in all of Cornwall, and perhaps Britain itself."

"And?" Penwarren pressed.

"This figurine is one third of the triple aspect of the goddess…"

"The what?!"

"The goddess comprises the three aspects of a woman's life: the maiden, the mother, and the old crone. These aspects represent fertility, birth, and decline, or seeding, abundance, and harvest, following the cycle of all living things. We will need the power of all three for me to help free Tegan."

"Is Tegan the maiden?" West asked.

Bran nodded.

"And the figurine is the mother?"

"No. The crone."

"Then who's the mother?" Davies demanded.

"I am."

Davies broke the silence. "How can you be?"

Bran looked at Davies and the detective saw her soften: "I lost my daughter, in childbirth, Sergeant. Ten years ago."

Forty-Eight

ONLY FIFTEEN MINUTES LATER, while West's team was still investigating the "magic room," Penwarren got a call from Comms.

"Oscar 99's got a white Ford minivan heading west at speed on a single lane road out of Sancreed. Requests orders."

"Tell Oscar 99 to back off," Penwarren barked into his phone, "and thank him. If we're right, that's our man and we don't want to crowd him. We'll take it from here."

"Wait!" Bran cried. "We still want the helicopter. The figurine the Americans found at Carn Dewes is at the museum, in Truro. It has power and the Americans will confirm this. I need it! *We* need it!"

Penwarren considered the woman before him, this "wise woman," and finally acceded: "Comms, get on to the Royal Cornwall Museum and its director, Hilary Gracefield. Friend of mine, she is. Tell her to get the Carn Dewes figurine to Victoria Gardens, the park uphill from the museum. Tell Oscar 99 he can land there."

He turned to Morgan. "Clear this with Hunter, now; it's his discovery."

"Sir."

"I need him at the tor as well," Bran said. "He's our channel to the Annown."

"He's *what*?" Davies challenged, but Bran waved her off.

"It would appear that the best we can hope for here is a hostage situation," Penwarren said, pacing the garage. "Media will eat that up. We'll need to get in a police negotiator."

"That would be me, Sir," Davies said, turning from her phone. "I've had the training. I've done it before."

He regarded his sergeant for a moment, wondering if he could trust his resident renegade to dissuade a killer, then decided he had little choice. There simply wasn't enough time.

"All right, he's yours. Strategy?"

"Most important, Sir, is encircling the tor. If the boot prints I found are his, Chynoweth knows the faint and very private path from the west. He'll have a job getting the girl up there. Let's get everyone we can to secure the perimeter and very slowly advance to the ridge top, tightening the noose. Remember, he doesn't know that we know where Tegan's been taken or why. That gives us a temporary advantage. If he goes to the quoit, he won't be able to see the farmyard, though he'll be able to see to the west. No cars on that side until I'm up there and no sirens on any side. I want to surprise him, but I don't want to frighten him. We'll need an ambulance from West Cornwall Hospital, but again, no sirens. We also should have an armed response unit team high enough to make an incursion if necessary. Bottom line is we want to avoid using them; that's when people get hurt."

"Armed Response are already on the way," Penwarren said. He was watching Davies carefully and was pleased with what he saw.

Comms was on the phone again. The museum director hadn't yet left for the day and was on her way to Victoria Gardens to meet the helicopter, which was fifteen minutes out.

When Penwarren rang off, he looked around the garage. "Where the hell is Morgan?!"

A car engine fired in the cul-de-sac and a vehicle screeched away.

"CHRIST, MORGAN, you're gonna get us both killed!"

They'd cleared St. Euny and were racing along the single lane road to the farmyard beneath Dewes Tor. The hedges, higher than the Ford Estate, were nothing but a blur of dark green.

"Supper time. Farmers at home. No tractors out at this hour."

"What, you're clairvoyant now, too?"

"I want this bastard."

"I do too, but it would be really brill to live through it."

They'd already checked the road to St. Just and had spied the white minivan high up the farm track leading to the west slope of Dewes Tor, tucked behind but not quite fully obscured by blossoming gorse bushes. Davies was thankful that her Ford estate was unmarked and nondescript. The landscape up here was so barren Chynoweth would have seen a Panda car. She reversed course at Grumbla and headed east to the lane leading to Trerane.

Barely idling, this time, Davies avoided the farmyard and parked behind an outbuilding. The mist had not let up all day and cows had turned the ground around the farm to the consistency of a rank pudding.

"You're in the car," she said as she pulled on her boots.

"What?!"

"Look, Terry, a few days ago you were pounding the pavement in Penzance, okay? You're good. You'll rise fast. But negotiation is technical and I can't risk you being there. But you're my lifeline, okay? I'm in trouble, I ring you on the mobile; you're my backup and my link to the rest of the force. Are we clear?"

"Ma'am," Bates answered, with only a touch of petulance.

Davies grabbed one of the pre-packed kit bags she kept in the back of the car. It held energy bars, water bottles, torch, and a metallic foil "space blanket" for warmth, among other items. She hoped they wouldn't be needed, but there was no telling how long the negotiating might go on.

THE POLICE TAPE MARKING the cordon around Dewes Quoit was gone. In the slanting light from the western sky, the tree-thick granite legs of the quoit high on the ridge looked weirdly magnified. Davies stayed low and well away, only occasionally peering above the crest of the slope from her place of concealment, but she saw no movement between its uprights.

A few minutes later, though, the silhouette of a human shape moved into the dim light behind the western edge of the quoit, someone struggling under the weight of a burden. The shape swayed for a moment and slid the burden to the ground beneath the capstone, then raised its arms as if in triumph. She had no doubt it was Kenny Chynoweth and that the burden was Tegan St. Claire. What she didn't know was whether the girl was alive or already dead.

As she watched, Chynoweth circled the perimeter of the quoit, gesturing and calling something she could not make out. When he ducked under the capstone again, Davies moved quickly. Within seconds, she was at the edge of the bare ground around the quoit, but still in its shadow.

"Kenny Chynoweth," she called, using the least threatening voice she could muster under the circumstance. "I know how sacred this place is to you. But you must not harm Tegan St. Claire."

"Who dares to interrupt the Bucca and his initiate?!" he roared.

Chynoweth was clearly in another reality. "A protector of the innocents!" Davies called. She had no idea what she was talking about.

"How shall I know you?!" he demanded.

Davies struggled for a moment to recall the story Bran had told them. "By my equal power."

"There is no power equal to the Bucca!"

"Oh, but there is. There is the equal power of the goddess, the mother god of all creation. Surely you know this, Bucca; the goddess is your consort!"

Chynoweth disappeared again but Davies did not approach. She knew it was only a matter of time before his coke high crashed and his mystic fantasy imploded. In the lengthening shadows of the lower slopes of the tor to her left she could see a scattering of constables, as well as some of West's crew, picking their way uphill through the dense thickets of heather and thorny gorse. Behind her, Penwarren and Bran were just ascending the main path. Below them, in the car-packed farmyard out of Chynoweth's sight, a white-haired old man leaned on a walking stick beside an immobile border collie. Far to the west, a clear weather front was developing at the horizon, a slender band of pale blue pushing eastward the low overcast that had hung over the peninsula all day. As the lowering sun slipped out of the cloud bank and into the clear sliver of sky, Chynoweth emerged as if backlit, dragging Tegan by the furred collar of a red gown clasped at her throat. Morgan slipped into the deeper shadow the late sun created.

"Bucca," she called out. "We are healers; we cause no harm!"

"Give it up, Sergeant. I recognize your voice! Approach me, and I will slit the girl's throat, I promise you. I've nothing to lose."

So, she is still alive…if he isn't lying. Davies watched Chynoweth haul Tegan St. Claire along the footpath to Carn Dewes as if the girl were a sack of coal. In his right hand was a box cutter, the blade exposed. She pulled out her mobile. "Bates, tell Comms to get the climbers on the north side of the tor to move quickly; he's heading for the Iron Age settlement with the girl."

A few moments later, as she followed Tegan's dragged heel marks her phone vibrated.

"North side is a series of outcrops and cliff faces, Morgan," Bates reported, "but the men say they are moving as fast as they can around them."

"Shit."

When Davies finally reached the settlement compound, Chynoweth and the girl had vanished. Either he'd continued down the west side of the tor, in which case he'd be captured, or he was holed up in the fogou. She crept to the tunnel entrance and heard a scuffle and muffled cries. Tegan was definitely alive. She backtracked to the settlement entrance and pulled out her mobile.

"Bates, the bastard's gone to ground in the fogou and the girl is alive and resisting. Where's Mister?"

"Right here, Morgan," Penwarren said, stepping out from behind the granite pillar that marked the entrance. Bran was behind him.

Davies jumped. "Jesus, boss!" she hissed.

"Would have been here sooner, but Ms. Bran needed to stop at her house to gather some things. The climbers are on hold around the summit. Oscar 99 will be here in minutes. Media 'copters enroute, too. What's your plan?"

"I'm going down into the tunnel. I'll be able to talk with him without showing myself at the entrance to the chamber. That's good, because it doesn't constitute a confrontation. It's like being on the phone in a more conventional hostage situation. He'll feel less threatened. We'll talk. The 'copter will unnerve him; I'll say it's medevac."

"Excuse me for asking," Penwarren said, "but are you all right going down there, Morgan?"

She shrugged. "I'm fine."

"All right, you're in charge here now. But Ms. Bran here believes she can help you."

Davies lifted an eyebrow.

"There is a powerful ritual that invokes protection and defense through the Annown," Bran said. "I have in mind, Morgan, that we work together on Tegan's behalf. You below, me above. I will be on the ground directly above the chamber. They will have no knowledge of my presence. But perhaps I can make my presence known with a rite that will summon the energy of the goddess on behalf of the girl."

Davies looked at Penwarren.

"I suggest that we enlist every assistance available to us, Morgan. I misjudged Ms. Bran a year ago. I'm not making that mistake again."

"Sir."

Off to the northeast they could hear Oscar 99's rotors throbbing.

"I need to let Chynoweth know what's happening," Davies said.

"I'll tell Comms to warn off the media 'copters. Keep your mobile on and open."

"Blessings be, Morgan," Bran whispered.

Forty-Nine

"KENNY? This is Sergeant Davies. Can you hear me?"

Davies was crouched in the muddy tunnel that ran roughly perpendicular to the five-foot long entrance hall to the beehive chamber. She knew he could hear her, but there was no answer.

"I'll take that as a yes, shall I Kenny? I have no intention of entering your space here. I just think we should talk a bit about this situation that's occurred. Most importantly, I want to make sure everyone stays safe, okay?"

"What's that noise?" Chynoweth shouted.

"That's a medevac helicopter, Kenny. It's just a precaution in case any of us requires medical assistance. The light out here is fading and I suspect he'll circle and hover a bit in order to find a safe place to land before it gets too dark. It's for your safety, and of course Tegan's as well."

There was a pause, and a muffled, "Be still!"

"Keep the 'copter here." Kenny called, finally. "I'll be wanting it."

"Of course, Kenny. We'll do anything we can for you. But first, you need to let me know Tegan's safe. Can you do that, Kenny? Can you let her say hello to me?" Davies kept her voice solicitous.

There was another small scuffle and finally a faint, "Hello?"

"Hello back, Tegan. It's Sergeant Davies. You'll remember we met at Tamsin's. Are you and Kenny both okay?"

"It's dark in here. I'm afraid!"

"Hey, I can fix that! Tell you what, Kenny, I have a torch here with me. I'm going to toss it to you, okay? I promise that's all it is. It'll soon be black in there and you'll need it."

Another pause. Then, Chynoweth answered, "Yeah. But no funny business."

"None at all, Kenny. I have no interest in harming either of you. Here it comes. I'll roll it in." She knelt in the shadow beside the entrance and propelled the torch cylinder into the chamber, hoping it would roll far enough through the entry portal. A moment later, light flashed around the chamber and then at the door.

The helicopter hammered closer.

"Okay, Kenny, let's just take a break while this pilot looks for a place to land. We won't be able to hear ourselves think while he does. After that, we'll talk some more about what you need, okay? Why don't you think a bit about that? Think about what you need. I'll be staying right out here."

Oscar 99 hovered above the settlement and lowered a net in which nestled a simple brown cardboard box. Bran took it and waved the bird off. It lifted fast and was soon a distant murmur.

"Where'd he go?" Kenny yelled. "I want him close!"

"He is, Kenny; he is. Just going to land in the meadow by Grumbla farmhouse down the hill. You know where that is?"

"Yeah. Good."

"Now, Kenny, this has been a horrible week or so for you, hasn't it? First, your niece is discovered dead and then your sister. It's an awful lot to take on board, isn't it? I can only imagine the weight of your grief. You must be shattered."

"Horrible, is what it is," Kenny said, without the slightest emotion. The coke high gone, he was gaming her.

"I hear you, Kenny. And then Miss Tegan shows up, looking for all the world like a miniature of your very own Becca, doesn't she? Was it too much, Kenny? Was it just too much?"

"Too right it was."

"I can certainly understand your wanting to bundle Tegan away and up here to this...well, this is a kind of sanctuary for you, isn't it, Kenny? A peaceful place. Am I right?"

"Peaceful. Yeah."

"I have to wee," she heard Tegan say.

"Shut up."

"Kenny? When we girls have to wee, it's not like guys, you know? It's hard to hold it in. Do you think you might be able to let young Tegan out to wee while we talk?"

"Not bloody likely!"

"Well, then, Kenny, you'll just have to let her go right there next to you. Is that what you want?"

Chynoweth's chuckle was deep, salacious, frightening.

Tegan reacted immediately. "I can wait!"

Davies scrambled for advantage. "Right, then, Kenny, how can we help you out of this situation, eh? After all, you have done no harm to Miss St. Claire, and that is very good. No one has been hurt. Right now, all you've done is spirit her away from your shop. Maybe you thought that was best for her, so she didn't get into the Goth culture, which is pretty dark, let's face it. That would be very thoughtful."

"Yeah."

"That counts for a lot, it does, and we all appreciate that. We do. It means we can all come out of this safely—you, me, and Tegan. So the question is, Kenny, what is it you need next? What would make that safe outcome happen?"

ON THE TURF ABOVE the chamber, Tamsin cast a circle with her staff, divided it into the four cardinal quadrants, placed lit tea candles at the edge of each, and whispered her blessings to north, south, east, and west. Then, she walked the circle clockwise three times.

Coming to the center, she raised her staff in a clockwise arc high above her, then bent and swept it through a downward arc, by these two circles thereby describing an imaginary sphere, a universe half below the surface, half above.

Erect again in the center, she whispered, "I conjure this circle as a place between two worlds, as a time out of time, as a channel between the other world and this one."

From a small backpack she withdrew two antique mirrors—like those from old makeup compacts—darkened by age, their silvering gone almost to pewter. With a lead pencil, she sketched the profile of a man with a ponytail on a scrap of white paper. Then she sandwiched the image between the faces of the two round mirrors. Finally, she wrapped the package in black cloth and bound it with black cord both vertically and horizontally, mirroring the quadrants of the circle.

She glanced behind her and saw that Hunter and his assistant had arrived. Silently, she beckoned to him.

"Dr. Hunter," she whispered when he reached her, "I need your power as a channeler. I have never before performed this rite, though my mother did. I believe you can be the vehicle for the girl's release, by channeling her predecessor, Rebecca. You may be emotionally shattered by this afterward, but the girl's life is at stake and you will recover. Will you trust me?"

Hunter nodded. She took his hand.

"I DON'T HEAR THE CHOPPER," Kenny called.

"Well, no, Kenny; it's landed at Grumbla, on the north side of the tor."

"I don't hear it!"

"No, you wouldn't; it's standing by, Kenny. Conserving fuel, you see."

"We need to leave here."

"I couldn't agree more, Kenny, but if we make the helicopter available to you, we will need something from you in return, won't we?"

"What? Who are you to make demands?! I'm in control here!"

Davies was struggling to maintain her cool. "No, Kenny, no one is in control here, not you and not me. We simply are having a conversation, plain and simple. We're trying to make the best of an awkward situation, in which you, Kenny, have been most cooperative so far, for which I thank you. But you're in a tight spot, aren't you? With someone less sympathetic outside your door, someone different from me, for example, one could say you were trapped, actually. So, let's talk more about what you need to get out of here."

Silence. Then muffled noises from the girl. He obviously had his hand over her mouth. Which meant he was behind her, using her as a shield. She tried to imagine which hand held the box cutter. His left, almost certainly. The right arm would be weaker.

"Where would you like the helicopter to take you, Kenny? When you're ready to leave here. Have you a plan?

Another silence. He hadn't thought that far out yet.

"France," he said finally. "I want it to fly us across the Channel."

"Well, Kenny, there are two problems with that plan, if I may mention them…"

"That's what I want!"

"…and the first is that the helicopter has only one spare seat, besides the pilot's. And the second is that it hasn't the range to get you there. Not enough fuel capacity, you see. Is there somewhere else the pilot could take you?"

Davies wondered whether he'd chosen France because that was where his drug suppliers were, where he could disappear. There were countless secluded coves on the Channel side of Cornwall where fishing boats or pleasure boats from France could slip in contraband undetected. It was a time-honored tradition. Centuries ago, it had been French brandy. Today, it was heroin, cocaine, marijuana and, lately, methamphetamine.

"The girl doesn't need a seat!"

"Actually, the seat isn't the real issue; it's the weight limit. It's a two-person 'copter, Kenny. It can't lift off with three."

"You're lying."

"I can get you the specifications from the pilot in a few minutes, if you'd like. Would you like that, Kenny? I'm happy to arrange it for you."

Davies couldn't crouch anymore. She sat down in the mud and rested her back against the mossy granite wall of the fogou. The tunnel was darkening quickly and she was grateful it was a warm evening.

"The girl stays with me!"

"I don't see that as a very realistic option, Kenny, if you want the 'copter. Is there something else you'd like us to do for you?"

"Yeah, have the 'copter take us up to Newquay. And get a plane from the airport to take us from there."

"Where to, Kenny?"

"France, like I said!"

"If we can find someone to fly you there, and that's a big 'if,' they'll need a flight plan before they can take off. Can't take off without a flight plan."

"Why would I tell you that?"

"So you can get off the ground?"

"Fuck."

"It's out of my control, Kenny. I'm sorry."

Another pause. "There's a small airport just north of Brest."

"In Brittany?"

"Yeah."

"Let me see what I can do. Hang in there, Kenny. You, too, Tegan. I just need to make a few calls."

Fifty

CALUM WEST WAS WAITING for Davies at the entrance to the fogou. Penwarren was there, too. She unkinked her back as she emerged and took a deep breath. Her trousers were caked with mud and her hands were shaking. She hated being in the tunnel. Even more, she hated that Penwarren knew it.

"You're in charge here, Morgan, but I'd like you to consider an option," Penwarren said, "something that might bring this situation to a quicker close."

"Hostage negotiation is slow, boss. You know that. We wear them down with solicitude leavened by demands. It's glacial, but it usually works."

"I know, bore them into submission. But Calum has a proposal. He is, after all, the crime scene manager."

She bristled. West smiled.

"Among other things, Morgan," West said, "I'm on the national anti-terrorism squad, right?"

"Yeah, that's how you got that flash Volvo of yours."

"That's not all I got."

"What?"

"I have light grenades."

"Huh?"

"They're simple perforated canisters. You pull the pin on one, toss it, and there's a deafening noise and a flash of light so blinding in a confined space that the person inside is stunned to immobility for between five to ten seconds. We go in and cuff him."

"What about Tegan?!"

"She'll be stunned, too, but it won't harm her; the canister doesn't explode and scatter metal shards. Someone whisks her away while we subdue Chynoweth. Simple."

Davies looked off across the shadowy moorland. She could see the lights in St. Euny and the cars twisting along the A30: the normal world.

"I can see how it might work in this situation," she said finally, "but I want more from him. I want confessions. I'll bet my career he's good for the murdered Newlyn girls, too."

"Morgan," West said gently. "Are you willing to risk Tegan's life to get those confessions?"

Davies looked at her colleague for a long moment and softened. She was after blood, yes. But not the girl's.

"Let me talk with him a little more."

DAVIES HAD NO INTENTION of arranging a plane for Kenny and she'd got Penwarren's okay to press on. She settled herself in the tunnel outside the chamber entrance again, feeling the invisible pressure from the roof above, thinking of her brother, always that brother, buried beneath the slag in Wales.

"I'm back, Kenny," she said, finding her voice again. "Are you two okay in there? It's getting late. Can I get you something to eat?"

"We won't be here that long. I'm giving you ten more minutes!"

"Well, to be honest, it's taking a bit of time to find a pilot who's willing to fly you to Brest. Not everyone is interested in helping the police, you see."

"No shit."

"Can you let me hear from Tegan again, please, Kenny? I want to be able to tell everyone out there we're all safe and sound."

"Who's everyone?"

"The media, of course. We've got reporters from *The Cornishman* and the other local papers, as well as film crews from BBC Cornwall and ITV in London. We've told their 'copters to stand down and leave us be, but they're like jackals, these boys."

"You *called* them, you bitch?!"

"Of course not, Kenny, and that's no way to talk to someone who's trying to help you out of this fix, if I may say so. Media's got their ears everywhere and with the Internet, nothing stays secret long. You're a star, Kenny! Now, how's Tegan?"

"Tell her you're okay," Kenny ordered.

"You said you were the Bucca and you were going to teach me the wise ways!" The girl's voice was high and strangled.

"Shut up."

Davies could hear shoes scuffing and Tegan's voice strengthened. "Did you tell Becca that, too?"

"Shut *up*, dammit!"

"You're a courageous girl, Tegan," Davies called, "but I think it would be better for all of us if you could calm down. You hear me, Tegan?"

"Damn right; girl doesn't know what she's talkin' about," he called.

"On the other hand, it does seem an odd coincidence. You see my point?"

"You don't have one. Look, the girl came with me voluntarily. We were going to perform a simple rite in the hope that it might help her communicate with her lost friend, my niece."

"Is that right, Tegan?"

"Yes, but he gave me a potion that put me to sleep…"

There was another brief scuffle and the rest of the girl's words were muffled. Davies could imagine the scene in Kenny's "magic" room: he puts the kid to sleep, violates her in whatever perverse manner pleases him at the moment, with an urgency he cannot control, and later must figure out what to do with her. She pushed the vision out of her thoughts.

"Well, there you are, Kenny; there's your way out! You see, since she came with you voluntarily, at least to some degree, this whole matter would be very difficult to prosecute. I can see an argument in which you are simply trying to help the girl with some of your magic. Maybe you did give her a potion and she unexpectedly passed out. Maybe you became frightened. Or maybe you thought that when she awakened she would be thrilled you'd taken her to the place where her best friend was found and you'd both commune with her. But then we showed up and you panicked. Am I right, Kenny? Maybe you just got scared and panicked? No dishonor in that."

There was a long pause. She could almost see him working through the scenario.

"Yeah. You scared me. I was trying to help her."

"I hear you, Kenny, I do. And if we did, indeed, frighten you—if we boxed you in—then you have my apologies. We were just trying to find a missing girl. I'm sure you can understand that, having lost your own niece. So the way I see it, the next steps are pretty simple: you release the girl, Kenny, and then you come out voluntarily. We will take you safely into custody on a suspicion—a *suspicion*, I want to emphasize—of illegal abduction, and then, with the help of your solicitor, you'll get to tell the true story. How's that sound, Kenny?"

"Like fucking bullshit. The girl stays with me and you get us out of here!"

"Kenny, Kenny. Calm yourself. Why would you risk committing a far greater crime, with far worse consequences, when so far all you've done is commit an error of judgment? That just doesn't make sense."

"What makes sense to me, lady, is that you've run out of talking time. Either get us an escort out of here or I slit this girl's throat, and then my own."

Davies understood that Kenny Chynoweth believed, as only someone who is guilty would, that they already had him for the murders of Rebecca and Judith, and possibly the Newlyn Toms as well.

"All, right; I hear what you're saying, Kenny. Can you give me a moment to climb out of this tunnel to see what's been arranged for you?"

"Use you're damned mobile and stay here!"

"Sorry, Kenny; no signal down here."

"Three minutes! That's what you've got!"

"I'm on it, Kenny! Hang in there."

IT WAS NEARLY DARK, even this high on the spine of Cornwall. The sun had plunged below the watery horizon. Calum West divided his attention between listening to Morgan's negotiations below and watching Tamsin Bran's movements directly above. Just as Morgan emerged he caught Tamsin's eye and she nodded. She was nearly done.

Brad Hunter held both of her hands as they stood at the center of the circle she had drawn. There was a tiny glowing fire of incense and fragrant herbs between them and the ancient white quartz figurine lay beside it.

Morgan found Calum with two armed response officers in full SWAT gear.

"He thinks we have him for the murders and has nothing to lose," she said. "He'll kill the girl; he's got used to killing. We go with your plan, Calum, but I go first into the tunnel. You got that? My signals."

Calum nodded to the woman he so admired and then he and his team crept into the tunnel from the opposite end. Davies settled near the chamber entrance again.

"I've got your transport to France arranged, Kenny," Davies announced. "Are you listening, Kenny? I'll call the 'copter in as soon as you tell me to do so." Out of sight to Chynoweth, she motioned for Calum's people to move into position.

At that same moment, Tamsin's voice roared out of the darkness:

"I call upon the power of the three-fold Goddess—the Maiden, the Mother, and the Crone..."

"Tamsin!" Tegan cried.

"And call all present to bind all negativity generated by Kenwyn Chynoweth and thereby ensure no harm comes to Tegan St. Claire, our friends, and me, in thought or deed!" Bran thrust her horned staff deep into the turf immediately above the chamber.

"What the fuck?!" Kenny yelled.

Davies signaled for West to toss the grenade.

A deafening explosion of white light flashed from the chamber, blinding everyone and echoing across the moors.

Kenny Chynoweth felt a force rise from beneath and fling him away from the girl, leaving him blind and convulsing, his limbs twisted and beyond his control.

"Got him!" West yelled inside the chamber. "He's down!"

Davies crawled out of the tunnel, still struggling to regain her sight, dragging a screaming, nearly naked Tegan St. Claire. Above her, Tamsin Bran waited, arms open.

"It was Becca! I saw her!" Tegan screamed.

Bran pulled the shuddering girl to her breast and whispered, "Hush, child, hush. You're safe and that is all that matters."

Like spent fuel, Hunter collapsed beside Tamsin and the girl. Jeffers wrapped her arms around him.

Bates pulled the foil space blanket from Davies's kit and passed it to Bran for Tegan.

Davies sat on a low wall of the Iron Age settlement rubbing her eyes back to life. West knelt in front of her and put a hand on her knee. "Well done, Morgan, you dear lady."

"We should use those light grenades of yours more often in these situations, Calum," she said as she tried to get her bearings.

"Only one problem, love."

"What?"

He held out his hand. The undetonated light grenade was cradled in his palm.

Fifty-One

"THE TRIAL'S A LONG WAY OFF, but I'm certain we'll get a conviction," DCI Penwarren said. "Thanks to you lot. Well done, all of you."

"We got lucky is all, boss," Davies said, staring at the table top.

No one seated around the conference table in the Major Crime Incident Room at Bodmin Tuesday morning—West, Bates, Duncan, the armed response unit leader—none of them, disagreed with her.

"We make our own luck, Morgan." Penwarren said. He was leaning against one of the windows that ran the length of the room, willing the warmth of the morning sun into the increasingly arthritic bones of his spine. It was one of the reasons he didn't go out into the field much anymore, but he preferred his people to think he wanted them to lead.

"With respect, Guv, that's bullshit. The bastard convicted himself. We had nothing on him."

"Has it occurred to you, Sergeant," Penwarren replied, "that calling your senior officer's opinions 'bullshit' might not be the fastest way to advance your career?"

Stifled laughter.

"But do go on."

"Okay, start with the buried girl, Rebecca: even if the DNA of the black hair follicle found on the shroud matches the swab we took from Chynoweth, and I expect it will, he sold those robes in his shop. Could have got the hair on it then, since his hair's already falling out. It's all we had to connect him to the buried girl."

Penwarren nodded. "The mother?"

"He told us he'd brought the cheap champagne for her, so the

CCTV tape that proved he did gave us nothing. Nor did the discovery of the bottle in the bin near that garage, when we—or rather Terry—noticed it missing from the TAG's inventory of the squat. He said he left it with her. Anybody, including Bran or Rice-Johnson, could have binned it there. Wiped clean. Worthless. And nothing else to place either person there at the time of the murder. The boot prints? Yes, TAGs found matching prints outside Chynoweth's squat, but unless there's a matching soil sample from the sole, which also remains to be demonstrated, there's no way to put him on the tor when Bates was attacked."

"What about Flora Constantine?" West asked. "She put him there much later that night than he said he was."

"Memory of an old woman? Come on. The defense would eat her alive. And the drugs equipment that pointed to Rice-Johnson? I wouldn't be at all surprised if Chynoweth himself had squirreled them away that night to cast suspicion and RJ just missed them in his panicked clean-up the next morning. The knife in Judith's chest? Had it not been for Tegan, we'd have had no idea Chynoweth had stolen it. And no court would take seriously the 'seeings' of a ten year old clairvoyant, even if you assume she is one. Then again, it wasn't the cause of death anyway."

"The poppet," West said. "It's made of the same burlap we found in the storage garage."

"So what? RJ had access. He could have made it."

"Why would he?"

"Doesn't matter; all that matters is that it can only be linked indirectly to Chynoweth."

"Excuse me!" Bates erupted. "The guy's a bloody pedophile! We have his computer records now to confirm it. He preyed on little girls, and underage women like Lisa Ames who looked like girls. Isn't the pattern pretty clear here?!"

"Pattern, yes, Terry, proof, no," Davies answered. "We have no evidence he violated Rebecca, only that he may have strangled her. He appears to have had no time to abuse Tegan, though given she was unconscious for a time, her doctor will have to confirm that. And Ames? Okay, legally underage, but already an admitted prostitute. And what Chynoweth views on the Internet doesn't convict him of anything but being a perv."

"That's an outrage," Bates snapped.

"That's the law, Terry," Davies said, her voice dropping to a tone soft enough that everyone heard as affectionate. Penwarren heard it, too, and smiled. He pulled away from the window and folded himself into a chair at the table. Though neither the chair nor the table fit him, he managed to make the move seem graceful.

"Morgan's right. We had nothing on Chynoweth. He's convicted himself. What matters here is that our man knows none of this, and neither does his solicitor. We may never get him for murder, but we have him for criminal abduction and I have no doubt that the fluted glass Calum's team found in his 'magic' room will prove Chynoweth drugged the girl. We also have him for possession of a very large shipment of illegal drugs. We can prevail upon Rice-Johnson for drugs distribution evidence against his boss in return for a reduced charge. Depends on how helpful he is. We've got a twenty four hour watch on RJ now he's been released, and he's cooperating. Even if the Crown fails to pin these murders on Chynoweth, he's going away for a very long time. And of course word he was a pedophile will make his life inside most unpleasant."

No one was pleased, but no one dissented.

"What do we have on the attack on the American archaeologist, Calum?"

"The shopkeeper, Cassandra, has given a statement that Chynoweth saw her at the shop and that she had been asking about the pierced poppet."

"I figure he decided she knew more than was safe, and studied her morning routine," Davies said. I'll bet my badge the hair the SOCOs retrieved up on the Common matches his DNA swab."

Penwarren regarded his sergeant with veiled pride. Renegade or no, her analysis was flawless.

"All right, people," Penwarren said, "Morgan will interview Chynoweth this afternoon in the presence of his hastily-arranged solicitor. He already thinks we have him for the murders. I have every confidence that our sweet-talking DS Davies will break him, armed with the evidence—however circumstantial—you all have amassed. I have a meeting with the chief and a press conference tomorrow morning. I am proud of the work this team's done and of being your SIO. I think we're done here."

"Not quite, boss," Davies said.

Penwarren sighed. "Yes, Morgan?"

"I hate to admit it, but we owe a debt of gratitude to Bran."

"And an apology, I should think, too. But that'll be my job," Penwarren said. "And my pleasure. Off you go then, people."

They all rose.

"Morgan, you'll remain, however," Penwarren ordered as they turned to leave.

"Oh Christ, what have I done now?"

The rest of the team filed out. Penwarren remained standing.

"Please sit. Coffee?"

"Vodka? A day off?"

Penwarren took his seat again.

"Sergeant, you are a perpetual thorn in my side, but I find I like the irritation. You are the sand in my oyster shell that produces pearls and I respect you. I would like you to be here at Bodmin, permanently, as one of our major crime incident investigators. And I should like to recommend you for promotion to detective inspector as well."

Davies lifted an eyebrow, revealing nothing. "I don't know, boss; it's pretty comfy down there in Penzance. A few domestics here and there, the occasional break-in. Not much pressure. Decent hours, too, mostly. What's my incentive?"

Penwarren struggled to keep from laughing. He put on the most serious face he could arrange.

"After she has additional training, I'll give you Bates.

Morgan stared her boss down for a moment and then smiled.

"Done," she said.

TWO WEEKS LATER, at midnight on a new moon, Royal Cornwall Museum director Hilary Gracefield, standing in the candlelit interior of the beehive chamber at Carn Dewes, handed the white quartz figurine to Brad Hunter. Hunter, in turn, handed it to Tamsin Bran.

On the perfectly round floor of the chamber, the witch had cast a circle with her staff and divided it into the cross quarter directions: the east road, the south road, the west road, and the north.

Placing Hunter, Gracefield, Jeffers, and Tegan St. Claire in the center around a tiny brazier of smoking herbs, Tamsin now walked three times around the circle sinistral, or anticlockwise, the pattern which would permit her to slip between the two worlds and gather in the powers of the Annown.

The gathering done, Tamsin then stood at the back of each quarter, and at each she called:

> *"I conjure the spirits of this road, keepers of the flame of enlightenment and the blade of cunning. Hear the call, hail to thee, awake, arise and here be!"*

Having completed the quarters, she walked the round in a rapidly accelerating dextral, or clockwise, circle until she was nearly running, the purpose of which was to raise the gathered spirits that called Carn Dewes home.

Having completed this, she stood at each quadrant, her arms in the air, her fore- and middle fingers raised like horns, and called:

> *Bucca Gwidder and Bucca Dhu,*
> *Horned one and Goddess both,*
> *Shrine, hearth, and vessel of all dualities,*
> *I dedicate this rite to thee!*
> *Guide me upon the path of all wisdom,*
> *And by the light betwixt the horns,*
> *Accept the return of this holy one,*
> *And release us from all harm!*

There was silence then, in the candlelight. No one moved. At last, Tamsin lifted the figurine and placed it in the vulva niche. It nestled there and, to their astonishment, momentarily glowed. Then the light was gone.

Epilogue

MY NEW ROOM is at the western end of the mill house, under the eaves, looking upstream toward the glade where Tamsin goes to talk to her mother. She's been there a lot lately, asking her advice, I reckon. The room's tiny, but cozy. It fits me just fine. My bed is tucked under the slanting oak rafters, big as trees, and there's a little pine table and a cushioned chair where I'll be doing schoolwork in September. Opposite the bed, there's a small chest of drawers for my clothes, some of which are brand new. Tamsin took me shopping at Marks and Spencer's in Hayle. I'm saving the new stuff. I don't know why. She even got me my own mobile phone. She says she doesn't ever want us to be lost to each other again.

I was scared stiff what would happen next when the Social Services came and took me away from my mum. They said she wasn't fit to raise a child, that I was in danger which, I don't know, was maybe right, you know?

Mum was drunk in the kitchen the morning they came. Nothing new there, really. I don't know when she'd come home. She hadn't changed and was at the table where we eat, smoking a fag and drinking whisky straight from the bottle when I came out to fix something for breakfast. She didn't even look up. There was a swollen purple bruise just below her left ear.

I opened the door when they knocked. A silver-haired gentleman in a nice suit and a plump younger woman with short blond hair who carried a briefcase asked to speak to mum.

Mum flew into a rage when they said why they were there. She fell over when she tried to get up from her chair. The older man had to help her. But the plump lady, she pulled all these legal papers from her briefcase and explained a lot of things and that was pretty much that. Mum called them a lot of names as they led me out of the flat, but she didn't get up from her chair.

That was maybe a month after the craziness up at Carn Dewes. On that night, after some questions at the police station, they tried to take me home but mum wasn't there. So Constable Bates, who's also a family liaison officer, whatever that means, took me to her own place and gave us supper and we talked a lot. I slept there. It was really nice. She's brill.

Last week there was what's called a hearing, which is not the same as a seeing at all. There were questions from some woman who was a judge or magistrate or something, and people answering, and lots of talking. This was in the big granite courthouse up in Truro, right in the center near all the shops. Really old building, it is—the hearing room had tall ceilings with lots of fancy plasterwork around the edges. The walls were pale blue, the carved plaster white, and the windows were the longest I've ever seen. I don't know how they cleaned them; I could never reach. Tamsin was there. Mum didn't show. I don't know why, but I was glad to have Tamsin sitting next to me. It took a while for me to realize the whole idea was that I wasn't going back to mum. The whole idea was that I would go and live with Tamsin. A lot of people said really nice things about Tamsin, including Detective Davies and Detective Chief Inspector Penwarren, and eventually someone handed the woman in charge a piece of paper my mum had signed. Then, it was basically all over.

Anyway, that was last week, like I said. Since then, I've just been trying to get used to being here at the mill house full time. Tamsin keeps me busy, like always. But in the evening I don't have to leave. We have supper and later she reads to me before bed. That's really nice, I have to say.

I haven't had any Becca seeings lately. Maybe she's happy how things turned out.

There's still a lot I don't know.

THE END

Keep reading for an excerpt from the next book in the Davies & West Mystery Series!

Acknowledgments

PERHAPS BECAUSE I'VE WRITTEN so many nonfiction books, I tend to be obsessive about factual accuracy, even in fiction. In researching and writing *Harm None,* I have had the generous help of a large team of "expert advisors," to whom I am deeply grateful.

On matters of police investigative procedure, I am indebted to Crime Scene Manager Detective Sergeant Martin South and his Scene of Crimes team in Bodmin; Detective Sergeant Tessa Adams, formerly with the Criminal Investigation Division, Devon and Cornwall Police; and Detective Sergeant Glenn Alvsaker, Devon and Cornwall Police. On forensic science and autopsy procedure, I thank Dr. Amanda Jeffery, forensic pathologist serving the Devon and Cornwall Police and Kevin Hammett, Mortuary Manager at the Royal Cornwall Hospital in Truro.

Ancient archaeological sites play a key role in this story, and on that subject I was capably guided by James Gossip, senior archaeologist at the Historic Environments Service of the Cornwall Council; his team of volunteers from the Meneage Archaeology Group who generously invited me to carry buckets of rubble at the excavation of a fogou in Cornwall; Hilary Bracegirdle, Director of the Royal Cornwall Museum in Truro, and Jane Marley, the museum's Curator of Archaeology and World Cultures; and finally members of the Cornish Ancient Sites Protection Network (CASPN), who invited me to help with their work on the sacred well in Sancreed.

As guides to the deep and continuing culture of pagan beliefs in Cornwall, I thank Sarah Vivian, artist and CASPN member, who invited me to the Penwith Moot of the Pagan Federation of Devon and Cornwall;

and to witchcraft scholars and practitioners of both the Old Craft and Wicca in the UK, including Vikki Bramshaw, Gemma Gary, Cassandra Latham, Cheryl Straffon, Lana Jarvis, and Gerry and Vanessa Greenslade.

Not for the first time, I am also grateful to Graham King, Director of the Museum of Witchcraft in Boscastle who gave me access to the museum's extensive library. Finally, thanks to Bryan Rescorla, Deputy Harbormaster, Newlyn Harbor, for guidance on the fishing industry and Nigel Waller for providing me a splendid home base in his renovated granite warehouse, Bosun's, on the harbor in Penzance.

That's a lot of help, but it doesn't mean I've got everything right. Moreover, I may have adjusted some facts to suit the story, though these instances are rare. As always, I must say that if there are errors, they are mine alone. I trust my friends, for these advisors have become friends, will forgive me.

I am especially delighted to thank the principals at my new publishing house, Booktrope, Ken Shear and Katherine Sears; my project and book marketing manager, Stephanie Konat; cover designer extraordinaire Annie Brule and her partner Phil Bevis; proofreader Hunter Richards, and all the other members of my creative team at Booktrope. An author could not ask for more responsive and enthusiastic partners.

Finally, my deepest appreciation to my family: Susan, Eric, Baker, Nancy, and Tom. They understand that when they talk with me, some part of me will always be AWOL—working on the latest book. Thank you all for your patience and love.

WILL NORTH
April 2014

Author's Note

AS A NOVELIST best known for writing stories about people at middle age finding second chances in love and life—it may come as a shock to my fans that I am now killing people.

But I make no apology. And, by the way, killing people is hard work. Where does this murderous impulse come from? Let me tell you a story. Once upon a time, in a far off land just north of the New York borough of the Bronx, a boy who was often sick and had lots of time to read, began reading Sherlock Holmes stories. And they changed him forever. Why? Because they taught him how to think, how to reason, how to make sense of a world around him that often made no sense.

In Arthur Conan Doyle's story, The Sign of the Four, Holmes says: "When you have eliminated the impossible, whatever remains, however improbable, must be the truth." It's the fundamental principle of deductive reasoning. Reading that, the boy felt like he'd been struck by lightning. Suddenly, everything was bright and clear. Suddenly, there was a method for making sense of the world around him.

As time passed he became a fan of the authors in the Golden Age of English mysteries: Dorothy Sayers, Margery Allingham, Ngaio Marsh, and also of contemporary English mystery writers, like P.D. James, Peter Lovesey, and Scotland's Ian Rankin, as well as American novelists writing mysteries set in England, like Elizabeth George and the hilarious Martha Grimes.

Though the boy, as an adult, went on to become an award-winning author of nonfiction books, including a series of travel guides to the British countryside he so loved, it never occurred to him to write mysteries. Until one day it did.

Harm None is my eighteenth book, my fourth novel, and the first in the new Davies & West Mystery Series. The next installment, *Too Clever By Half,* is already in the works and there will be more to come.

Excerpt from
TOO CLEVER BY HALF

The next book in the Davies & West Mystery Series!

Available later in 2014

For updates, go to www.willnorthonline.com.

One

ONE MINUTE Archie Hansen was jouncing across the stony field in his aging, rust-red Massey Ferguson tractor, doing a shallow weeding of his Maris Peer potatoes. The next minute he was airborne. Like a stumbling horse, the lurching tractor pitched him right out of its cab.

"Son of a bitch!"

Right shoulder wrenched, his side bruised by the jagged granite shards that studded his ancient field on Cornwall's Lizard Peninsula like a crop of their own, he struggled to his feet. The tractor, still in gear, labored helplessly to move forward, its big rear power wheel turning uselessly because the right front wheel was deep in a hole.

Archie Hansen, on the wrong side of fifty and beginning to show it, was rawboned as a goat but for a developing paunch that spoke of too many nights spent downing pints of Doom Bar ale at his local, the New Inn at Manaccan. He fetched his cap from the ground and slapped it on a skull that was as bald to its crest as a half-peeled orange. He offset this tonsorial desert with a graying beard which, fastidiously trimmed to a sharp point at the chin, gave him a vaguely Mephistophelian air. The leader of a local group of Druids, he'd lately been straying from the faith and experimenting with spell-casting and darker magic. The devilish beard was, he thought, only appropriate.

Hansen climbed up to the cab, shut off the motor, and cursed himself for not owning a four-wheeler that could have pulled itself out of this dilemma—not that he'd ever spring for something that pricy. Depending on the year and the field he was rotating during Cornwall's mild winter months, Hansen cultivated daffodils, cauliflower, early potatoes, and followed with grains—barley or wheat—in the spring. He was as successful as any farmer in Cornwall could say he was these days, but he was tight as a Shylock, and therefore better off than his neighbors.

Now he knelt beside the sunken wheel. The ground he'd farmed for years here on the Lizard Peninsula, and that generations of Norwegian immigrant Hansens had farmed before him, had inexplicably given way beneath the tractor. Looking down on either side of the knobby black front tire, he saw only darkness. He climbed back into the cab, started the engine and gunned it, only to have the front wheel dive even deeper.

"Son of a bitch."

Archie Hansen's verbal expressions of both disgust and surprise were limited. He yanked his mobile from the pocket of his dirt-encrusted navy blue coveralls and rang up his young neighbor, Bobby Tregareth. The two of them farmed adjacent fields just inland from Nare Head, on the soft, undulating hills above the pastoral reaches of the Helford River on Cornwall's English Channel coast.

A half hour later, Hansen had a chain hooked between the front axle of the tractor and Bobby's beat-up tan Land Rover Defender. Burning up the four-wheel-drive's clutch in low gear, Bobby managed to pop the tractor's wheel from its trap and pull it away. Archie grabbed a torch from the cab and, like a terrier after a fox gone to earth, tore away turf and stone until he managed to get both his head and shoulders and the light into the hole. What he saw, to his astonishment, was a rectangular stone-walled chamber. At the eastern end, two roughly five-foot granite pillars suggested an entrance tunnel, long since collapsed and filled with rubble. Directly opposite to the west, a six inch thick slab of granite the size of a small, misshapen door lay flat on the earthen floor, its surface studded with white quartz crystals that glittered like diamond chips as his torch beam swept over it.

"One of them ancient chambers, Bobby. Fetch a ladder; I'm going down an'll need a way back up."

"But Mr. Hansen, surely this is a matter for the archaeologists at the county council..."

"Don't be wet, Bobby; nothing comes to ditherers."

Bobby did it. He'd little choice; he leased much of his farmland from Archie Hansen and depended upon his good will.

After Bobby left, Hansen shoved the torch into a pocket, swung his legs into the ragged mouth of the hole, held himself suspended above the gap on wobbly arms for a moment, then dropped in, his arms extended above his head.

He fell farther and hit harder than he expected; the roof of the chamber was a good six feet high. Groaning, he rolled to his knees, stood, and looked around. The four walls of the chamber edged inward ever so slightly until they met three granite roofing slabs, roughly four feet wide, a foot thick, and five feet long. The tractor wheel had dropped through a weak spot on the edge of one of those slabs.

The day was clear and a shaft of light sliced into the musty chamber from the hole above like sun through a cloud. Hansen sat on the edge of the slab on the floor for some time, scanning the perfect walls, looking for anything of interest—not that he had a clue what "interest" might look like. It was like being inside the belly of a beast.

A restless, impatient man, as he studied the walls and waited for the ladder, he thumped the rubberized butt of his torch absently on his stone seat, as if keeping time with his pulse. It took a few moments before he noticed a tonal difference toward the center of the stone that didn't exist around its periphery. He stood up and tapped again. No question: hollow.

"You down there, Mr. Hansen?"

"You see me anywhere else, Bobby?"

"Right, right; I've got the ladder. You need help down there?"

Hansen thought for a bit, then yelled, "Send it down, I'm done here."

"What'd you see, Archie?" Bobby asked, his enthusiasm almost childlike as Hansen squeezed to the surface.

"Not a damned thing. Just another of them Iron Age holes. Bloody nuisance, they are, just like them big standing stones we got to plow around. Not to mention that Roman mosaic floor poor Johnny Sayer found in his field over Porthallow way. English Heritage were all over that and they'll be all over this, too, wanting to protect it for God only knows what reason, which means I lose one of my best fields."

"That's just not right, Mr. Hansen."

"Too true, Bobby, because it'll mean I'll need one of the fields you're leasing from me back again."

"Straight up? But I can't get by…"

"Hush now, lad; I know. I've a simple solution. We don't report this; we just carry on as per usual and no one's the wiser, yeah?" Hansen said, tapping a knowing forefinger to the right side of his nose.

"You won't report it?"

"Dime a dozen these underground chambers are hereabouts. What they don't know about they won't miss, am I right?"

"Sure. I guess. What about the hole?"

"Steel plate to cover it and then dirt so's it looks like everything else, only I don't plow near it again. Take me a couple of days and then—hey, presto!—it's just our little secret. Few weeks, it's grassed over. Invisible. Right, Bobby?" Archie looked hard at the young man.

"Right, right. Invisible."

LATER THAT AFTERNOON, Archie Hansen was back in the chamber, alone. He'd slipped webbed strapping around one corner of the stone slab and was cranking a come-along winch anchored with spikes he'd driven into the hard pan of the chamber floor. It was brutal, hot work, even for late March. The sweat from his forehead left small black craters in the dim dust. Several times he'd had to re-anchor the come-along as the slab inched away from its resting place in a slow, rasping arc. His back and arm muscles burned. He could have got Bobby to help, but he didn't want the company.

Having moved the slab some sixty degrees off center, Hansen shone the torch into the hole he knew would be there. It was roughly two feet square and the same deep. Nestled in its center was a lidded clay vessel. Belly down on the slab, he reached in and, lifting the lid, shone the light on its contents.

"Son of a bitch," he whispered.

ALSO BY WILL NORTH

Seasons' End (Contemporary Romance) Every summer, three families spend "the season" on an island in Puget Sound. But when local vet Colin Ryan finds Martha "Pete" Petersen's body in the road on the last day of the season, he uncovers a series of betrayals that will alter their histories forever.

Water, Stone, Heart (Contemporary Romance) Nicola and Andrew have each come to the tiny village of Boscastle to escape their troubled pasts. When they meet, they're bristly and sarcastic—and utterly attracted to each other. It takes a cataclysmic flash flood and a nine-year-old girl for Nicola and Andrew to see the truth about themselves and risk a second chance at love.

The Long Walk Home (Fiction) Forty-four year-old Fiona Edwards answers her door to a tall, middle-aged man shouldering a hulking backpack—unshaven, sweat-soaked and arrestingly handsome. What neither of them knows is that their lives are about to change forever.

MORE GREAT READS FROM BOOKTROPE

***Tulip Season* by Bharti Kirchner** (Mystery) Mitra searches for her best friend, a domestic-violence counselor, who has disappeared from her Seattle home. Following the trail, Mitra is lured to India and lands in a web of life-threatening intrigue where she can't be sure of Kareena's safety—or her own.

***Spellbound in His Arms* by Angel Sefer** (Mystery) Reporter Jackie Alexander and Detective Michael Apostolou are forced to work together to investigate the mysterious deaths of the heirs to the incredible fortune of Greek tycoon Andreas Demiris, but their suspicions and unanswered questions are devouring them, just like their rising passion for each other.

Discover more books and learn about our
new approach to publishing at **booktrope.com**.

CPSIA information can be obtained
at www.ICGtesting.com
Printed in the USA
FFOW03n1343240615
14577FF